Praise for Michael Mohammed Ahmad

'Ahmad's language is replete with lyricism, and a sense of wonder suffuses every page. It turns everyday experience into the stuff of poetry.'

— *Sydney Morning Herald*

'He has found a sharp and sensual tongue with which to speak and given us a new and welcome voice in contemporary Australian literature.'

— *Sydney Review of Books*

'Ahmad's piercing storytelling cuts away at the lace and trimmings of race relations in Australia today.'

— *The Lifted Brow*

'[*The Lebs* is] an open-eyed and highly charismatic novel broiling with fight, tenderness and ambition.'

— *Big Issue*

'The author never lets his superb command of idiom or his eye for the absurd overwhelm a deeply felt exploration of the hurt and damage that can come from encounters with the Australian Other. No one who reads *The Lebs* deserves to come out unscathed.'

— *The Saturday Paper*

THE LEBS

MICHAEL MOHAMMED AHMAD

hachette
AUSTRALIA

This is a work of fiction. All of the characters, organisations and events portrayed in this novel are either products of the author's mind or are used fictitiously.

 hachette
AUSTRALIA

Published in Australia and New Zealand in 2018
by Hachette Australia
(an imprint of Hachette Australia Pty Limited)
Level 17, 207 Kent Street, Sydney NSW 2000
www.hachette.com.au

Copyright © Michael Mohammed Ahmad 2018

A catalogue record for this book is available from the National Library of Australia

978 0 7336 3901 2 (pbk.)

Cover design by Design by Committee
Cover photograph courtesy of Big Stock Photo
Author photograph courtesy of Stelios Papadakis
Text design by Bookhouse, Sydney
Typeset in 12/17 pt Adobe Garamond Pro by Bookhouse, Sydney
Printed and bound in Australia by McPherson's Printing Group

MIX
Paper from
responsible sources
FSC® C001695

The paper this book is printed on is certified against the Forest Stewardship Council® Standards. McPherson's Printing Group holds FSC® chain of custody certification SA-COC-005379. FSC® promotes environmentally responsible, socially beneficial and economically viable management of the world's forests.

DRUG DEALERS
AND
DRIVE-BYS

THERE ARE NO BULLIES AT PUNCHBOWL BOYS. The school captain, Jamal, stands up and screams out at assembly like it's thug life. 'Bullying is for faggots and pussies. What kind of a sad fuck is bothered to pick on some other sad fuck?' Specks of tabouli blaze in his eyes. The teachers react by barricading the school, erecting nine-foot fences with barbed wire and cameras, and creating one way in, one way out, through the front office. They lose all their privacy but tell us it's a small price to pay for freedom. Students pour through the front door all morning, and the principal, Mr Whitechurch, who's White, and the deputy, Ms Aboud, who's Libyan, stand at the entry. 'Good morning, Bani,' they say to me at the same time, like two coppers. I step between them, along the blue carpet and past the reception desk, which has a bulletproof glass shield, and then through the door that leads into the school. It opens out from the front office, swings closed and locks.

There used to be seven hundred students at Punchbowl Boys, but when Mr Whitechurch was appointed he expelled three hundred and ninety-nine of them in one go. I was fifteen at the time but it starts over again like I'm staring at the western suburbs through my rear-view. Every day the remaining boys sprint along the corridor that joins to the front office, pretending they are driving a Subaru WRX. Their heads and spines are tipped back as though they are sitting in a bucket seat, their left hand is on their cock as though they're shifting a gearstick, and their right hand is out in front of them as though they're holding onto a steering wheel. While they move through the corridor they make engine and gear shifting sounds, 'Baaaaaa-baaa ba-baaaaaaaaaaa.' Then before they turn a corner they kick in the sound of the turbo, 'Bre-bre-bre-bre-bre-breew!' Mustafa Fatala moves so fast down the corridor that he crashes through a window. He tears open his hand and damages vital nerves, which means he can't write properly anymore, but that doesn't matter because he never receives a grade higher than thirty per cent anyway. He rambles on about how he's going to sue the school until one day Ms Aboud says to him, 'Yeah, tell the lawyer you were acting like a car.' Every Punchbowl Boy except me pisses himself laughing. I keep my pleasure to myself, grateful to see Fatala in pain because of the time I'd stepped past him in the corridor and he screamed 'Yaaaaaaaaa!' into my ear. I thought someone had put a bullet in my head; then I turned and saw him standing there staring at me with his jaw clenched and his eyes possessed by the *jinn*, a creature made of smokeless fire. Fatala seethed at me as air pushed in and out through the gaps in his teeth. Why he acts this way is a mystery between him and his maker. It brings me down – knowing that such a being exists and that we are only different to others within the walls of this school. In here Fatala is Black and I am White. I am at the centre of every teacher's affection because I can discuss Faulkner and Joyce and Dostoyevsky and Nabokov. The teachers look to me whenever they need to be reminded that it's the Boys of Punchbowl who are wrong, who are lesser beings. But then, when we're on the outside, Fatala and I are the same – we are sand niggers, rejected and hated and feared. Cops and transit officers target us and chicks and Skips avoid us. There's nothing I can do about it. Fatala and I look like the gang rapist Bilal Skaf, who is on the front page of every newspaper today.

The main corridor leads into the quadrangle at one end and the school hall at the other. All the way down the cracked vinyl tiles are the Maths rooms, six in total. My 2 Unit Maths room is between 3 Unit on the left and Intermediate on the right. I hate Maths like I hate being a Lebo – I am above it. I will be neither Isaac Newton nor Bilal Skaf, I will be a great novelist, like Tolstoy and Chekhov, and I will shape reality through my own words. I'm sitting in Maths writing a short story about a very young boy with enormous wings instead of learning equations when there is a loud screech outside that goes, 'Fucken black cunt!' All twenty boys in my class shoot up and tumble into the corridor like bodies through a windshield.

A Pacific Islander named Banjo is standing with his arms dangling by his sides, a kitchen knife in his right hand and a serrated pocketknife in his left hand. His jaw hangs open and his eyes are filled with the fizz of Coca-Cola. He looks like an ogre, towering over all the Lebs. His head is small and round and he's hunching, his size-seventeen Converses rake across the vinyl. Rajab stands in front of him; a short-arse Lebo with a wound shaped like the centre of a strawberry across his shaved head. Blood runs down his temple and cheek, dripping from his jaw onto his shoulder, his white school shirt blotching with red like a slashed lamb. Banjo isn't strong enough to penetrate Rajab's skull. That's the thing about Punchbowl Boys: we swing like men but we're still just boys – we're not as strong as the bones that hold us together, so the knives just ricochet against our flesh. Perhaps if we were smart enough to sharpen those knives, and smart enough to learn the most sensitive points in the head to swing those knives at, we'd kill each other. Perhaps stupidity is Allah's way of protecting us from ourselves.

The Lebs gather around Banjo like a pack of wolves, but nobody bothers to chase him when he bolts down the other end of the corridor, towards the school hall. We just stare at Rajab, who looks confused, his left cheek wincing, even

6

though he knows, like the rest of us, that all this happened because he stole Banjo's Nokia 3210.

Two students walk Rajab to the sick bay, which means the principal has had to unlock the front office, and everyone else is sent back into Maths. Mrs Stratton's dehydrated skin wrinkles as she scowls, 'Concentrate.' She turns her back to us and continues writing on the whiteboard, her arm reaching right up over her head because she's short and stumpy. She wears a thick woollen jumper that's so long it might as well be a dress, and her grey hair sways from side to side in a way that shows me it was blonde once – the envy of every dark-haired Wog she's ever taught. She writes numbers that mean nothing to anyone, the silence building inside the classroom until finally a student named Shaky spits out, 'Fucken Banjo, fucken pussy cunt!'

Mrs Stratton twists, her sharp nose and beady eyes snapping towards him. In her tight, nasal voice she says, 'Leave him alone. Banjo's just scared.' The teachers always take the side of the Fobs. Maybe they feel sorry for them because they're so heavily outnumbered by the Lebs, or because they're even poorer than us and stand out the front of the school in the morning sharing a two-litre bottle of Coke, or maybe it's because we call them Fobs, which stands for Fresh Off the Boat and makes no sense to White teachers because to them the Lebs are boat people too.

On the second level of the school building are the English classrooms, and the corridor is exactly the same as on the first level, with cracked vinyl tiles all the way down and light spilling in from windows that overlook the quadrangle. Every English room is the same, with unpainted brick walls and chalkboards that have been rubbed so many times they are covered in a permanent haze of white chalk. Mr Whitechurch pulls down the poster of Mecca hanging in our English room and says, 'If you can't respect other people's cultures, then the school doesn't have to respect yours.' This is because next door, in Ms Keller's room, the boys have burned two Aboriginal paintings that belonged to her grandfather. Mohammad Usuf says, 'Sir, that's racist, man – how do you know it wasn't one of the Fobs?' It seems like a fair point, and so all the boys except me start banging on the tables and chanting, 'Hoa, hoa, hoa,' and shouting, 'Rock job! Sir, you got rocked!' Mr Whitechurch waits for them to settle. Then his leathery skin sags at the corners of his mouth and he says, 'Referring to Pacific Islanders as Fobs is racist.' He walks out of our classroom with Mecca rolled up in his hand. He knows, as well as we know, that it wasn't the Fobs. What he doesn't know is that Mohammad Usuf never comes to school without his Zippo lighter. He bought it last year in Lebanon. It has the word *kafir* written across the lid in Arabic, which means 'infidel'.

The desks in our English class have metal legs and thin plywood tops. Using pens and knives, the Boys of Punchbowl leave their mark on the wood. 'Lebz Rule.' 'Fuck

Aussies.' 'Thug Life.' One of the engravings, which looks like a jagged wound, says, 'Jesus & 2Pac R Muzlim.'

All the chairs in English have a dick drawn on them in black permanent marker so that when you sit down it's like a cock just went up your arse. I always sit in the front row, usually the spot right up against the desk of my English teacher, Mrs Leila Haimi. She's twenty-eight and Lebanese and Muslim like the rest of us, but her skin is like milk. She's angry that she has lost the poster of Mecca but she cares about Aboriginal culture too, so the Boys of Punchbowl call her a traitor. They also call her Brad Fittler – because in her short skirts are thighs so chunky they're always pressing against each other. She'd be devastated if she knew they nicknamed her after a staunch football player, but the boys don't mean it as an insult; they love her thighs and the green and the red skirts that expose them, and every day after English they fantasise about being between them. She'd be devastated if she knew this as well. A Syrian student named Bara is *almost* an exception. He listens to the boys talk about Mrs Haimi's thighs and, as though they are talking about beauty and not about fucking, he says, 'Well, she has nice eyes.' Everyone laughs at him and replies, 'Faggot, what a faggot.'

'Wha-at!' Bara retorts, like he has a Big Mac in his mouth. 'Her eyes are blue.'

I know better. Mrs Haimi does have nice eyes but not because they are lighter than ours. The boys are staring at the black line between her hefty legs, and Bara might be looking at the surface of her eyes, but nobody except me has ever ventured into her pupils. Nobody but me listens when she says, 'Read James Joyce.' When she does, I find a short story called *The Dead* and I stay up all night reading about haunted love and the living dead and all morning memorising the final lines, and just as I am stepping past Mrs Haimi in the corridor I say, 'His soul swooned slowly as he heard the snow falling faintly through the universe and faintly falling, like the descent of their last end, upon all the living and the dead.' Mrs Haimi's gaze lights up, and it's like I'm looking into the centre of the universe. The next day in class she says, 'Read Gabriel García Márquez.' I find a short story called *A Very Old Man with Enormous Wings* and I stay up all night reading about the withered angel with dirty feathers and all morning memorising the last line, and just as I am stepping past Mrs Haimi in the doorway to her English room, just as we are breathing the same air, I say, 'She kept on watching until it was no longer possible for her to see him, because then he was no longer an annoyance in her life but an imaginary dot on the horizon of the sea.' Mrs Haimi's small black pupils begin to expand from her blue irises and now it is as though I am looking into the heart of the Archangel Jibrail. This time in class she says, 'Lear is a man more sinned against than sinning.' I have slipped into a realm that existed before there was any such thing as blue eyes, to a time when there was nothing but sand. I wish I could be alone with Mrs Leila Haimi. I will promise her to remain a boy, never to sin, a very young man with enormous wings so that one day she can hold me at her complete mercy and may drive me across the endless desert. Her reading voice is slow and soft and fluent and it assures me that I can be free when a loud squeal breaks in from the back of the classroom. 'Meees,' says Solomon, 'isn't it true that Shakespeare was a poof?' Every Punchbowl Boy but me considers this a serious question and waits silently for Mrs Haimi to answer. Her fair lips curl in my direction – enough to show me that I don't need to be alone with her to be alone with her. She says to Solomon, 'You're an idiot.'

Then Mrs Haimi hands out a questionnaire. The first question reads, 'The snail is a castle. What is the metaphor in this sentence?' It takes five minutes before Mohammed Khaled starts calling out, 'Meees! Meees! What's a meta-por?' Mrs Haimi looks my way again with the little smile and then calls out to the rest of the boys, 'Just skip the ones you don't know.'

'Meees!' the boys howl. 'Meees!'

'Skout ouh-laa!' Mrs Haimi replies in Arabic, which means 'shut up, you'. She sits, and straightaway I slide the questionnaire across my desk and onto hers. She looks down at it and quickly examines the answers. Then in her squeaky voice she whispers to me, 'It's good to be at a school with retards – you will stand on top.' The words are like a dagger between my lungs. This is the extent to which she sees my potential.

I was fifteen years old and longing for Leila Haimi like Majnun longed for Layla. Each time I turned a corridor at Punchbowl Boys, each time I stepped through a doorway, I did it with the anticipation and the hope that she would appear before me. Often she emerged amid a hundred Lebos like me and would not notice that I was even there; but then one day she called out to me and only me, as though all the other Punchbowl Boys around us were blind, deaf and dumb. 'Read *Lolita*,' she instructed. 'It's the most beautifully written book you will ever know.' I found an unopened copy in the school library, which had bright red lips on the cover and pure white pages inside. I read it over the three following nights, and then I ran with it for three years, believing that I understood it, that Mrs Leila Haimi had recommended the book to me in code. Perhaps she was Humbert Humbert and I was Lolita Haze, and she planned to one day take me around the country, far away from Punchbowl and Lebs and laws. Or perhaps I was Humbert Humbert and she was Lolita Haze, and her blue eyes and fair skin were destined to haunt me until the end of my days. And so I began to sympathise with Humbert Humbert, believing his love for Lolita was pure and innocent, like mine for Leila Haimi. His poetry became my poetry, and his flare for words became the only truth I would ever need. The next time I found Mrs Leila Haimi she was walking out of the library. Quickly I said to her, 'I am thinking of aurochs and angels, the secret of durable pigments, prophetic sonnets, the refuge of art. And this is the only immortality you and I may share, Mrs Leila Haimi.'

Suddenly she stopped, which was strange and exciting because usually she'd just smile at me as she kept walking. 'And . . .' she said, raising her thin eyebrows at me. 'What about the rest?'

'The rest . . . what do you mean? Those are the last lines.'

Then she smiled at me, like a schoolgirl in slacks, and carried on walking as my heart thumped.

Mrs Leila Haimi and I are caught between sex and skin, between war and peace. When she is alone in a classroom with her students she is an Arab like me, but when her English class comes together with the class of a White female teacher she is a woman like her. The head teacher of English is Ms Lion. She looks like a ninety-year-old prostitute, with dyed-blonde hair and monolithic sagging boobs and an arse like melted haloumi. Her cheeks are always bright pink and her eyes dressed in deep black mascara. She says she lives in Newtown. I never tell the Lebs but my family started off in Newtown too. My father and my grandmother owned a house on Copeland Street but they moved us out when I was ten because they said the area was full of pooftas and overpriced falafels.

'Miss, do you have any kids?' That's what the Boys of Punchbowl ask Ms Lion at least once a week. 'I have a dog,'

Ms Lion responds bluntly. This makes all the boys, including me, feel sick. In Islam we call dogs *najis*, which means 'ritually unclean'. Here is our proof that Aussies are scum – they love dogs more than they love people. It is revolting that Ms Lion compares her *najis* to a human child, lets it run around the house, sit on her couch, lie in her bed, sniff at her laundry.

Ms Lion brings her class together with Mrs Haimi's class to teach us an Australian play called *Blackrock*. She tells us that the text is based on true events: in 1989 a fourteen-year-old girl named Leigh Leigh was assaulted, raped and murdered at a birthday party in Stockton by a group of young men.

'What's this shit got to do with us?' asks Shaky. 'Those guys were Aussies.'

Ms Lion scrunches her mascara-filled eyes and her lips, and stares at him like he's some kind of animal. She must be thinking that Shaky is a self-hating traitor because his dad is Lebanese but his mum is Anglo like her. That's why Shaky's skin is fair and his eyes are green, the kind of green girls on the street notice. Whenever someone asks Shaky his background, he just says he's Leb like the rest of us but I've seen him take full advantage of his mixed heritage – he gets head jobs from Wog chicks that think he looks like Brad Pitt and he gets head jobs from Aussie chicks that think he looks like Enrique Iglesias.

Ms Lion gathers us in the school common room, an empty hall at the end of the English corridor. She breaks us up into groups of three to memorise scenes from the play. I stand in a circle with Shaky and Bassam and we read the first scene, which involves two Skips named Ricko and Jared. We put on the tightest nasal accent we can muster and read in unison, 'Piss off, Cherie – shut up, Tiffany.' Then we laugh like hyenas. Ms Lion will never admit it but the real reason she's making us read the play is because Lebos had pack-raped some Aussie girls last month and it's been all over the news. The problem is that the Punchbowl Boys aren't going to learn about misogyny and patriarchy from Australian literature, because even when Aussies are being sexist they sound like faggots to us. I read out Jared's line, 'Girls can't surf.' Bassam scoffs and says, 'Surfing is for pussies.' Then he steps in close and whispers to Shaky and me, 'Ay, boys, you think Bilal Skaf is guilty?' He looks around to make sure the teachers haven't heard him.

Mrs Haimi is standing with Hamza and Mohammed and Bader on the other side of the room. She's shorter than all three of them but whenever I see her standing on her own in the corridor or on the playground she looks like she could crush a teenage boy under her goddess hips and titanic chest. She is a woman who has completely grown into her body. Today she is wearing cargo pants that hug her huge thighs and butt in a way that makes me think about her husband. I'd hate to send my wife to Punchbowl every morning, knowing that the boys will be staring at that tight sweaty space between her legs for the next six hours. Mrs Leila Haimi got married two years ago, during my six-week break between Year 7 and Year 8. She was Ms Hussein back then and I was still hopeful that she would save herself for when I was a man or that she might even revert back to childhood so that we could love each other like Humbert and Annabel, a premature love marked by a fierceness that would destroy adult lives. Then she returned to school in the new year with a new name and a new walk. Shaky said, 'She goes on her honeymoon and comes back loose as a turkey.' Mrs Haimi's husband is a Lebo just like us, so he knows; he knows we can't be trusted. It's only me he shouldn't trust, though – I don't stare at his wife's thighs, I stare at her swirling curls of hair, searching for her bobby pins.

Mrs Haimi spots me watching her and first she jolts at the sight of a young man's unwavering gaze. Then she realises it is me and she smiles, her entire face squeezing together so that all I see is her mouth and teeth in the shape of a perfect cupid's bow. I feel a sense of shame pass between us – she knows that I know why we are really studying this play, and it's embarrassing for us both that a student who discussed *Lolita* with her last week has been subjected to this simplicity.

In every other section of the common room there is a group of Lebs rehearsing a scene from *Blackrock*. I bet they're all talking about how Jared and Ricko are faggots, how Bilal Skaf got a fifty-five-year jail sentence because he's a Lebo, and how those girls, in both stories, got what they deserved.

'Bros before hoes,' Shaky scoffs. Then he lowers his voice. 'I'm not saying Bilal was innocent, cuz, but Aussie bitches are always asking for it.'

Bassam stares at Shaky with a smirk. He doesn't have his glasses on, so his eyes look small and beady. 'No bitch will ever be able to pin shit on me, bro,' he says in a deep voice that sounds like it's full of pubic hair. From his pocket he pulls out one of the new mobile phones that has an FM radio and built-in recorder. We stare while he flicks through his applications and then presses a button. There is a muffle that breaks from the phone speaker followed by the voice of a girl who says, 'Is it recording? Okay. I agree to give Bassam and Ali and Mohammed and Ziggy head jobs.' In the background of the recording is the sound of cars driving by and the buzz of a broken streetlight. The girl's voice is gentle and soft, like the way I imagine Lolita might have sounded. 'Lowie,' hisses Shaky at the end of the message. That's what we call a woman who is so low she'll have sex with one of us. And it reminds me, *She was Lo. Lo. Lee. Ta.*

Only ten minutes after we've been broken up into groups, Ms Lion announces that she wants all the boys to come together again. The two classes of students gather in a pack on the tiled floor like they're on heat. I sit at the front and stare up at Ms Lion. Her legs look like the Twin

Towers and her head is cocked down at us in such a way that her neck has disappeared. To the side of the classroom stands Mrs Haimi, quietly watching. Ms Lion takes in a deep breath and I see the rims of her nostrils begin to tremble. 'I have been walking around listening,' she roars like a man. 'I have been listening to the filth coming from your mouths. "She was asking for it!" "She's a slut!" That girl was fourteen. When they found her she had severe genital damage and a crushed skull!' I am draped in a warm shower of spit as Ms Lion's words reverberate against the walls of the room.

All the boys stare straight at her with fire in their loins and skewers in their pupils. Usually when we're copping a lecture we just shut up and take it, but there is a ticking in the air right now like the clock from *60 Minutes* and every one of us can hear that girl who was sobbing at Liz Hayes on Sunday night, saying about us, 'They called me an Aussie pig but I'm proud of being Australian.' All at the same time the Boys of Punchbowl bark back at Ms Lion and I hear it like one long sentence: 'We don't get, we all get, racist, unfair, bullshit.' Then finally a kid named Ahmad, whom we all call Eggplant because of the way his head is shaped, rises to his knees and screams so loudly that it drowns out every other voice in the room. 'Aussies are the biggest sluts!' Forty heads swivel at him, as if we'd just picked up the scent of uncovered meat. Eggplant is already on his feet, already aware of his fate. His skin looks like it's made of woodchip in the dim fluorescent lighting of the common room and his eyes swirl into two black holes.

Ms Lion becomes a concrete statue, her pallid skin completely hardened. Her gaze sets on Ahmad as though she is a scorned goddess, imbued with the power to shrivel a boy's fertility at will. Her lips purse and she spits at the Leb in slow motion, 'Mis . . . Ter . . . White . . . Church . . . Now.'

Around the corner from the English rooms and the common room, directly on top of the school hall is the History and Geography unit. All the way down the corridor in that block sits one desk and one chair outside each classroom door, preset because the teachers have learned that at least once in every period a boy will be sent out for swearing or lighting a cigarette or because his phone went off. One day I am late to school and rushing to class when I see Bassam sitting outside by one of the doors, staring at the wall through his thick, round glasses. He's the only hard cunt at Punchbowl that wears spectacles. 'What happened?' I whisper at him before I enter the room.

'Remember the test where it said name the ancient city left in ruins by war and famine?'

'Yeah?'

'I wrote "Punchbowl".'

Inside the classroom three of the students have their heads out the window, howling at the girls walking past. 'Give us your number!' they scream. 'Head job for the boys!' Mr Flower straightaway snaps, 'Knock it off!' He has told us many times that he doesn't think single-sex schools should exist. 'You see,' he says, looking my way, 'you get this crap!' Then he turns around to write something on the board and Shaky screams out the window, 'Show us your flaps!'

Flower spins. 'Downstairs to Whitechurch, right now!'

Shaky stands with a grin and struts out of the classroom like he's Snoop Dogg. We hear him standing outside and talking to Bassam for five minutes, trying to show Mr Flower that he doesn't give a shit. 'Why the teachers beat down niggaz?' he hisses. We can't hear Bassam reply, so Shaky just keeps on going. 'This school's a maa-fucken prison, bro.' Finally Mr Flower sticks his head out the door and screams so loud that every student in every other class probably hears him too. 'I said, downstairs!'

'Later, Pete,' says Shaky, and then he moves off.

Mr Flower sneers as he walks back in. He looks like the Liberal politician Peter Costello and he hates it when we call him that because he tells us he's a communist. Mr Flower instructs the boys to copy what's on the board and then he says directly to me, as though there's no one else in the classroom, 'So, Bani, what do you think of the Taliban desecrating those Buddhist statues?'

I have already found a verse in the Qur'an that proves such actions are wrong, and I have rehearsed my answers in the hope that the teachers will distinguish me from the other boys. '*Lakum deenukum waliya deeni*,' I say. 'You have your religion and I have my religion.'

'Good boy,' Mr Flower responds, giving me a wink. He tries to teach the boys about Qin Shi Huang, the first emperor of China, but no one except me listens. He tries to teach the boys about Nicholas II, the last emperor of Russia, but no one except me listens. He even tries to teach the boys about Adolf Hitler. For a second he gets their attention, reading a detailed account about the concentration camp at Auschwitz. An Indonesian boy named Osama says, 'The Holocaust was a bullshit conspiracy so the Jews could steal Palestine.'

'Were it not for the Holocaust, you'd still *have* Palestine,' Mr Flower snaps, and then he punishes us for Osama's comment by deciding not to teach the Arab–Israeli conflict, fast-tracking to an American president named John Fitzgerald Kennedy. The boys say, 'Fuck that, bro,' and go back to not listening. They keep their heads out the window or down on the desks while Mr Flower rambles on about the magic bullet and the grassy knoll and Lee Harvey Oswald and Jack Ruby. Then by chance he tells us about an African-American civil rights leader named Malcolm X who said that the president's assassination was a case of 'the chickens coming home to roost'.

A Palestinian boy named Isa Musa stands up and says, 'Brother Malcolm was right, y'all. White people bring this shit on themselves.' Isa considers himself as Black as

Malcolm X, but just because your skin is black doesn't mean you're Black. Isa is the product of two Palestinian refugees.

The next day Mr Flower brings in two speeches for us to read: 'I Have a Dream' by Martin Luther King and 'The Ballot or the Bullet' by Malcolm X. 'Which do you prefer?' he asks. I say Martin. Everyone else says Malcolm. This is how Mr Flower teaches Isa and Bassam and Shaky and Osama and Eggplant about African-American history; this is how he teaches them language techniques in speech writing, metaphor and assonance and alliteration and repetition – skills that the English teachers could not have taught the Boys of Punchbowl no matter how many times they watched *Lawrence of Arabia*.

Mr Flower gets us to practise what we've learned by organising classroom debating competitions. I stand before the class, looking up and down from the boys to my black leather shoes and then back to the boys, and I say, 'Nonviolence is the way to peace.' Isa Musa rebuts the assertion with, 'Black people shouldn't have to make peace with anyone that doesn't speak a peaceful language.' I say, 'Integration.' Isa says, 'Separation.' I say, 'You only like Malcolm X because he was Muslim.' Isa says, 'Bani Adam is a house nigger. He thinks he's better than us.'

See, at Punchbowl Boys it is never enough to take the side of history, to read the work of great men and to fully understand why everyone in this country hates the Lebs so much – not because we are drug dealers and rapists, but because we are dumb cunts. In my debate with Isa Musa I reference a quote from Ghandi, 'Be the change you wish to see in the world.' I have to be the change I wish to see in Punchbowl. First I try wearing a black beret – it makes me feel like a writer. *I will bring poetry to Punchbowl Boys!* I tighten the beret around my head and tug it to the side. Not even a minute after I've stepped into the corridor Kadar Kareem from Year 12 has ripped it off my head and thrown it from a window. I tumble quickly down the stairs to collect it, blaming myself for testing him and expecting too much of him. Punchbowl Boys is not ready for poetry.

Over the next few days I observe the Lebs' outfits carefully, looking for what they might have in common, and I realise that they all wear pants that narrow at the ankle, their feet sticking out like a duck's, their black leather shoes bulging. *Okay, I will bring flares to Punchbowl Boys!* I start to wear my sister's navy-blue school pants that spread open at the feet and cover my shoes. Now I look like Gumby in comparison to the ducks, triangular and grounded and solid. Unlike a headpiece, pants are too much a part of a man for anyone to rip them off easily, so no one reacts. The problem is that there is only really one cut for men's pants, the duck cut, and so I have to keep borrowing my sister's flares – the ones that have a long crotch. Gumby wanders the corridors waiting to be called a faggot every day but the criticism never comes. Perhaps the boys haven't noticed, or perhaps they've accepted the truth – that I am unique among the lost-found Nation of Islam within this wilderness called Punchbowl Boys. Then one day I go too far in my attempt to dress differently and inspire change: I tuck my shirt in so that I look like John Travolta in *Saturday Night Fever*. I enter into roll call and straightaway this Leb named Bader, who is long like a cucumber and has worn the same black pants every day since Year 7 because his family are as poor as kebabs, locks his glare onto my silver belt buckle and screams out, 'Look at Bani Adam – he thinks he's fucken better than us!' Twenty other Lebos turn around and stare at me before the teacher arrives, and they all start to bark, 'Bani Adam is a traitor!' and 'Bani Adam is a *shum shoom*!' which means I'm a sniffer, as in I have my nose up the teacher's butt. 'Bani Adam thinks he's better than us!' they say over and over until finally I shout back, 'Shut the fuck up, shut the fuck up – I have something to say!' They all go quiet and wait for me to explain myself, redeem myself, pull my shirt out, rejoin the pack. I hold their anticipation for three seconds, and then, while they're all ablaze, I say out loud, 'I *do* think I'm better.'

On the other end of the second level is the school library. It's dim and deep and the bookshelves along the walls are virtually empty, like an incomplete jigsaw puzzle. The library is one of the only rooms in the school that's carpeted, along with the front office, and there are large square tables scattered around. The only time students other than me ever use the library is when a special guest comes to the school – like the Arab-American surgeon named Muhammad who was invited to talk to us about his career. The forty-five boys from my year, forty-one of whom are Muslim, sit around the tables and listen quietly as the surgeon stands out the front and speaks about how he became a cardiac specialist. First, he says, he completed his four-year undergraduate program at the University of Chicago, a year in chemistry, a year in physics, then two years in biological sciences. After his entry exam he went on to study for a further four years, two years in health sciences and two years training in clinical skills at the University of Chicago Medical Center. Then he completed an eight-year surgical residency, the first five dedicated to learning general surgery and then a further three years focusing on cardiovascular surgery. He tells us he has volunteered in Lebanon and Afghanistan and the Democratic Republic of the Congo. He tells us about his American wife, Elizabeth, and his two children, Don and Firas, whom he barely sees because of his work. His voice is high-pitched and has a vibration of Arabic, where the tongue flips, just above the curls in his Rs.

When we're given permission to ask questions, only one student puts up his hand, a boy named Mahmoud Mahmoud. This guy looks like Beavis from *Beavis and Butt-Head*, with buttery skin and a thick, curly afro. 'Is your wife

Aussie?' Mahmoud Mahmoud asks in a voice muffled by the thickness of his tongue and his crooked yellow teeth.

'No, she's American,' says Dr Muhammad.

'Yeah, but I mean, like, an Aussie; like, you know, Aussie, is she Aussie?'

Dr Muhammad is an unassuming man, only five-foot-six or so, like me. The hair on his arms is thin for an Arab and his hairline has receded into a perfect triangle. He has a typical Arab nose, long and sharp like a pharaoh's and it's twitching in confusion. He stares at Mahmoud Mahmoud, clearly baffled by the question, until finally he nods and says, 'Oh yeah, you mean she's Caucasian.'

Suddenly all the Lebs in the library spring up from the desks and start screaming, 'Cock-Asian, he's married to a Cock-Asian!'

On the way downstairs from the library Mahmoud Mahmoud says to me, 'That surgeon was the biggest fucken *kafir*, bro; he speaks for an hour about all his work and not once does he mention Allah.'

'Brush your teeth,' I reply.

Mr Whitechurch believes it's a good idea to bring in someone like Dr Muhammad to inspire us, to show us that we too can be doctors one day. Our principal thinks he's Michelle Pfeiffer and that we're the Hispanic and Black kids from *Dangerous Minds*. When he walks past our classrooms we holler at him, 'Gangsta's paradise!'

He snaps his head towards us like a lizard and says, 'Cut it out – there are no gangstas in my school.'

The second time Mr Whitechurch brings a visitor to the library it's a man with the nasal voice of a bush chick who introduces himself as Mr Guy Law. The visitor has shining fair skin and a small, bald head and he's wearing round curlside glasses and bland and shabby clothing that must be second-hand – like a White Ghandi. He tells us he is the director of an organisation called Bankstown Multicultural Arts, BMA for short, and he holds up a small magazine called *We Are Australian*. 'I'm inviting you fellas to write for a new one we're making called *Thug Life*.' I start to panic when the Lebs all ask Mr Guy Law questions about the magazine – like Mahmoud Mahmoud, who asks when will it come out, and Ali Ali, who asks do the writers get paid, and Daniel Taleb, who asks how many copies will be printed. Though I like the idea of having one of my stories published, what's the point if you're in there with a bunch of Lebos?

On the way down the stairs for recess I ask Mahmoud Mahmoud what kind of story he's going to write. He replies, 'Pffff, we're not gonna write shit, bro – that was the best, we got outta History.' Again I tell him he should brush his teeth.

I use the next double-period of Maths to write a short story about a woman with enormous black curls driving me down an endless desert road, and then I head back to the library at lunchtime to email the story to Mr Guy Law.

Three months later Mr Whitechurch hands me a package while I'm walking through the front office. I head straight up to the library and open it in front of the bookshelf where I found *Lolita*. Enclosed is a magazine with a street directory map of Bankstown on the cover and a post-it note attached to it which says in messy running writing, *Keep in touch – Guy*. On page seventy-two my story appears: *Confession of a Brown Virgin Boy by Bani Adam*. I check the first line of my story, my heart thumping: 'Leila, light of Punchbowl, fire of Bankstown. My innocence. My *rwh*.' I snap the magazine shut and slip it onto the shelves, between the books where the names of dead White men rest for eternity. I don't want to show anybody that I've been published. I want people to find out all on their own. Only then will I be famous enough to consider myself a *real* writer.

———

The third level of Punchbowl Boys has seven rooms from one end to the other. The first room is the Arts staffroom, and then next to it is Ms Capsi's Visual-Arts room and Mr Smith's Music room. All the boys love Mr Smith because he lets us watch pornos while we fist the drum kit and finger the keyboards. The only instrument that really matters to the Boys of Punchbowl is a Lebanese drum called the drumbaki. It's shaped like a bongo but even a table can be transformed into one. Every exam in every classroom one of the boys will get bored and randomly start banging on his desk. *Dom-dom-de-de-dom* the pounding goes, and all the boys begin to chant, '*Abu Salim, yoa yah, zebu taweel, yoa yah,*' which means, 'Father of Salim, oh yeah, his dick is long, oh yeah.' This will carry on for thirty seconds until the teacher screams at the boys to stop. Then everything drops dead again and our heads sink back onto our desks like nothing happened.

The Music room is where Punchbowl Boys High School breeds its own justice. Samson is the oldest and the toughest of all the Fobs. One day he goes from class to class rounding up the fifteen other Fobs in the school and marches them into the class. They smother Kadar Kareem and pound down on him like a band of gorillas. Samson kicks Kadar's fat nose sideways and breaks it in two places. He tears open the flesh on his left eyebrow too. They smash three of Kadar's ribs and fracture his left shoulder. They kick him in the dick over and over so that he looks like he's pissed blood in his pants. Mr Smith is in the staffroom at the time and all the Lebs just stand aside and watch like chimps while a porno plays in the background. Usually we stick up for our Muslim brother, but no one is upset for Kadar. He stares at you in the playground until you notice him, then he says, 'What you looking at, faggot?' He likes to bash Year 7s. He bashed Samson's little cousin this morning. The Fobs have had enough.

In the Music room Kadar Kareem's blood is soaking into the vinyl. While *eh, eh, eh* comes out of the television and the boys play with their circumcised knobs, I stand in the centre of the class with my feet apart and stare at the bloodstain on the floor between my flared jeans. In here the blood on the soles of my feet belongs to an entirely different species to the blood inside me, but to the outside world perhaps there is no difference between the blood of one Leb and another – perhaps every Punchbowl Boy, including me, will suffer a similar fate when the *kafir* declares war on us. No one else in the class seems to care; they are distracted by the woman groaning in a cotton-candy voice, saying, 'Yaah, stick that black cock inside me.'

Mr Abdullah is the head teacher of Arabic. His classrooms are on the same level as Music and Art. There are four Arabic classes running at the same time because there's so many Lebs at the school. Mr Abdullah walks into class an hour after taking Kadar Kareem down to the ambulance and stares at us as though we've committed treason – his beard sitting firmly around his jaw like it's been gelled. 'If you don't want to help one of your brothers, at least try to pull them off,' he says. 'They could have killed him.' He puts on an Arabic TV series called *Bab Al-Hara,* which the English subtitles translate to *The Neighbour's Gate.* It's a family comedy set in a small neighbourhood in Damascus. Mr Abdullah tells us that this is the way we'll learn to *speak* Arabic. A month later he starts putting on English movies such as *The Fast and the Furious* and *Gone in 60 Seconds* with Arabic subtitles. He tells us this is how we'll learn to *write* Arabic. Then he goes back to the staffroom to have Lebanese coffee with Mr Maleka, who has a hexagonal-shaped head, and Ms Ramadan, who has a rectangular-shaped head. Neither of these teachers speaks English, which makes me wonder how they got their teaching degrees, or if they even have teaching degrees, but I am not allowed to raise these concerns with the principal. If I get them fired the Lebs will shank me. That's supposed to be the best thing about Arabic at Punchbowl Boys: the teachers don't give a shit about the students and the students don't give a shit about the teachers. Maybe that's why nobody gives a shit about the Arabs.

Mr Abdullah wasn't always like this, though. In Year 7 he'd give spelling tests by reading out words from an Arabic alphabet book. Then one day he turned up with a little tape recorder. He'd recorded himself reading out the words so that all he had to do now was press play. The only students who ever passed these tests were the ones who had private Arabic tutors at home, like me, and those who had lived somewhere in Lebanon for a few years when they were kids, like Daniel Taleb, and those who had just migrated to Australia, like Ali Ali. The students who were only learning Arabic at Punchbowl Boys, which was about a quarter of them, got below thirty per cent in every exam. Mr Abdullah, Mr Maleka and Ms Ramadan had found a loophole. Those same students who failed Arabic classes failed every other class too, so it didn't look like the teachers had anything to do with the poor grades.

The Arabic staffroom is what it looks like in every Arab's home, including my own. There are four couches, each with a floral pattern in the fabric and a floral pattern in the timber frame. On each armrest is a white cotton doily that always looks new because Ms Ramadan takes them home every Friday and washes them. There are Arabic coffee cups and a coffee pot like Aladdin's lamp washed and waiting by the sink. On every wall hangs an Arabic tapestry. Above Mr Abdullah's desk is a beige tapestry with the Ninety-Nine Names of Allah stitched into the fabric. Above Mr Maleka's desk is a tapestry like the one my family owned when we lived in Alexandria: Bedouins in the desert draped in white robes and perched on their camels before an oasis. It is Ms Ramadan's tapestry that is the most striking to me – the name of the Prophet Muhammad woven in gold thread, and hanging from it on a gold-plated ring an evil eye made of glass. The eye is shaped like an apostrophe, the edges are dark blue, the iris is light blue and white, and the pupil is black like a speck of charcoal. I sense the eye staring at me each time I walk past the Arabic staffroom. In my culture, it's supposed to ward off curses that can be placed on you by an envious glare. My parents made me wear one around my neck in primary school, after I had exhibited the ability to read literature and write stories at a tenth-grade level. They worried that an overachieving Asian kid with overbearing parents would jinx me and I would wake up one morning dyslexic. Six months into my first year at Punchbowl Boys I stopped wearing the eye – no student in the school cared enough about their education to be jealous of my abilities. I was safe.

I try not to loiter before the evil eye in the Arabic staff-room. Mr Abdullah gets nervous when he sees me hanging out in front of his office. He thinks I'm an informant for the principals, for Mr Whitechurch and Ms Aboud. According to him, I have betrayed our people because I give the Anzac Day address and lead a minute's silence at school assembly each year. *Why doesn't he understand? I don't do the speeches for the principals – I do it for him. I want Muslims to embrace the values of this country. I want them to be grateful that the White people let us in.* Before Mr Abdullah slips in *The Fast and the Furious*, he says to me in front of the other students, 'The Anzacs killed Muslims in Turkey. Shame on you.' Then, in the same way that Mrs Haimi and Mr Flower look to me against the Boys of Punchbowl, Mr Abdullah looks to the Boys of Punchbowl against me, his stiff beard locking on each of them until they affirm their allegiance to him with a subtle nod. Mr Abdullah threatens that we'll have to do work if he hears us make noise from the staffroom and so the boys just sit quietly and watch the film. I know what they're all thinking, though. They're calling me a house nigger again. I feel no shame in such names. The only shame is that I look like them, I have black eyes and black curly hair and a fat nose; I am not born with the blond hair and the blue eyes and the small, sharp nose of the man inside the television, this man who uses the alias Brian Spilner.

The only time Mr Abdullah actually works is while all the other teachers at the school are taking a break, at lunchtime. He leads *salat al-zuhr* – the midday prayers. These are considered the most important of the five prayers in the Muslim day and they are conducted in the school hall.

Here inside the hall, the Punchbowl Boys conceal the diversity of Muslim denominations. There are two hundred and eighty-five Muslims in our school and all of them *say* they are Sunni. However, I know that at least fifteen of them are Shi'ites pretending to be Sunni because they carry Shi'ite names like Ali and Hassan and Hussein. I also know that ten of them are Alawites pretending to be Sunni because I'm an Alawite and I've run into the other nine at our people's weddings. I say, 'Ay, bro, you go to my school?' They reply, 'Yeah, so you're like me, cuz?' We laugh out loud, locking hands and stepping in for a shoulder hug, as if a DNA test has just confirmed we are long-lost brothers. The weddings we attend are filled with men drinking alcohol and non-hijab-wearing women in skimpy dresses. That's why we need to keep our identities secret – Sunnis don't consider us real Muslims and there's too many of them for us to take on if they attack us. Even if the Shi'ites – who are more devout than Alawites but follow a similar school of thought – had our backs, we'd be outnumbered nine to one. Secrecy is the only way to remain safe, especially while Sunnis and Shi'ites and Alawites are slaughtering each other in Lebanon and Syria and Iraq and Iran.

Finally, one day I think, *Why are we scared of these Wallah-Bros who fuck sluts every weekend?* I reveal my true self to them while we're waiting in the corridor for Mr Abdullah to arrive and let us into the hall. *'Anna Alawy!'* I shout out loud, which means, 'I'm Alawite!' It's the same way Bruce Wayne says, 'I'm Batman!' Mahmoud Mahmoud, who calls himself Sunni as a euphemism for Wahhabi, looks at me like he feels sorry for me, like I told him I have no genitals. His eyes turn grey and moist and his bronzed skin goes pale. Then Solomon Akawi, who considers himself an honorary sheik because his older brother is a sheik at Lakemba Mosque, says to me, 'Ay, you guys believe Ali is a prophet.' I say, 'No, we believe he's an Imam.' He says, 'Your women don't believe in the hijab.' I say, 'Just because they don't wear it doesn't mean they don't believe in it.' He says, 'You guys believe it's halal to drink alcohol.' I say, 'Do *you* drink?' He says, 'Yeah, but just for fun,' as though he is separate from his beliefs. 'Well, I don't,' I shoot back. Then his voice becomes hoarse and agitated. 'What do you guys believe, bro, what do you guys believe?' I say, *'Ashadu an la ilaha ill Allah, wa ashadu anna Muhammad an Rasul Allah,'* which means, 'I bear witness that there is no god but God and I bear witness that Muhammad is the Messenger of God.' It doesn't matter if you call yourself Sunni, Shi'ite, Alawite or even Jew; every Leb in the corridor knows that these words make me a Muslim, whether he likes it or not.

Five minutes later, Mr Abdullah is standing on the stage in the school hall – the same stage where I enforce a minute's silence on Anzac Day – and two hundred of us sacrifice our lunch to stare up at him from the hardwood floor. The bright fluorescent lights above the stage beam down on Mr Abdullah as though he is in heaven, and the deep red curtains on each side of the stage engulf him as though he were in hell. There is a small round hat called a *taqiya* nestling on his bald head and a baggy gown called a *thobe* hanging from his shoulders. 'In America, in New York, no woman is safe after dark, no woman is safe,' Mr Abdullah says, making eye contact with every boy except me. My presence is a splinter in his vision of a school run by the Taliban. The boys sit cross-legged and barefoot, their toes twitching and their heads nodding like lemmings. 'In France, during day time, woman have been raped in the street, and people just walk by, saying maybe they're enjoying themselves; the woman is being raped! Look, the nun, the nun, the nun, Roman Catholic Church, nobody gives them a second look. If Mary the Mother of Jesus came along, you won't give her a second look . . .' Then Mr Abdullah turns around and raises his arms, bracing us for the Call to Prayer. '*Allahu Akbar, Allahu Akbar,*' he chants. 'God is Great, God is Great.' The words wail in the direction of Mecca as we rise, standing firm and devout like soldiers awaiting their destiny, like we are Hamas and after this there is only *jannah* – only paradise.

In prayer we make six rows across the school hall and follow Mr Abdullah's lead. The boys stand with their hands pressed just below their chests. Alawites and Shi'ites are not supposed to pray this way – we pray with our hands by our sides – but the Shi'ites at Punchbowl, like the Indonesian named Osama Al-Hussein, conform; and the Alawites at the school don't even attend prayer; they're out on the oval playing footy with the Fobs. I'm the only one who stands in the hall with my hands by my side like a true soldier, eyes fixed on the spot where I will place my forehead when I kneel. I suddenly become aware of myself, like I am in a burka at a nude beach. The Boys of Punchbowl can feel my disobedience, my resistance, but they can't do anything about it. They too must concentrate on that spot where they will bow their heads in submission to God.

I keep my face directed to the floor. My flares have completely covered my bare feet. In each direction I sense the naked feet of the Sunnis. In front of me are the caramel feet of the boy who pities me, Mahmoud Mahmoud; to the left are the beer-stricken feet of the sheik, Solomon; and to my right, pressed deeply into the hardwood floor, the doughy white feet of the only Aussie student at Punchbowl Boys High School . . . A boy previously known as Matthew.

Back in Year 7, on Matthew's first day, he told us that his family have lived across the street from the school for the last eighty years and that they watched in terror as all the Skips moved out and all the Wogs moved in. 'My dad says he'll be here until every sand nigger is deported.' The Boys of Punchbowl take no offence at this comment – they show Matthew that in Punchbowl Prison, *he's* the sand nigger. For the next three years they gather around him down the corridors and in the common room, and they scream facts at him like they are one mouth: 'Every-president-except-jfk-is-a-mason-macca's-is-run-by-the-jews-illuminati-killed-pac-because-he-converted-to-islam-the-bible-said-there-is-gonna-be-a-prophet-after-jesus!' Then one day Matthew is in the hall, nervous and pale, ready for his first prayer, his first submission to Allah. We smile at him and pat him on the back. Once the prayer is over, every one of us goes to shake his hand in celebration of his conversion. Matthew is the only assessment task the Boys of Punchbowl have ever passed: they tell him to change his name to Bilal, after the Abyssinian slave, and he does it. They tell him he isn't a real Muslim unless he's been circumcised, and he does that too. By the end of Year 9, Bilal has memorised more verses from the Qur'an than any other Punchbowl Boy, and he recites them during prayer with an unshakable Anglo accent, which is nasal like a car horn. '*Saalaaaeeem alaeeekam,*' he says, 'Peace be upon ya.' *Bilal was one of us now and his father could suck on it!*

I feel Bilal's piety while he kneels beside me, as though there is a beam of light surrounding the small space he occupies. It's different for him. We are Muslim because we were born that way; he is Muslim because he believes.

The final stages of prayer begin with me and Bilal and the hundred-and-ninety-eight other boys and Mr Abdullah on our knees. Everyone except me says, 'Salam alaikum wa rahmat Allah' as they turn their head left and 'Salam alaikum wa rahmat Allah' as they turn their head right. I stare straight ahead, the way we Shi'ites and Alawites are supposed to, and once again I am aware of myself, like I am covered from head to toe and everyone around me is naked. All the boys to my left see my head poking forward, then they turn away and all the boys to my right see my head poking forward. They can't say anything. They just have to let me defy them with my profile, with my big nose and my bulging underbite. They want to ask me why I won't turn my head; they want to pummel me in the head, snapping my jaw in the correct direction. Everybody turns back to centre, to find himself where I already am, and then there is a release and the prayer is finished. Bilal turns and offers me his bleached hand. I take it in mine and shake. It is cold and thin and dry, like recycled paper. He gives me a warm smile through cracked lips and freckled cheeks as I pull away and then turn to shake Sheik Solomon's hand. 'Bani Adam?' Solomon says. 'You're still here?' *What a sad-case: acting like he was so focused on praying that he didn't notice the Alawite had been standing next to him this whole time.*

There are two ways out of the hall. One leads back into the main corridor, the other out into the quadrangle, which to me is Pompeii – a slab of tar with the school building casting an ashy shadow upon each student. Painted along the wall of the building is a band of flags. The Lebanese flag is in the centre; blood red surrounding a bright green cedar tree with points painted so fine it has become a serrated spear. To its left is Greece and to its right is Italy, their colours fading into cracked white paint like a sanded car. Erupting from the tarmac surface, right in front of the cedar tree, is a flagpole with the Australian flag mounted on top. The tips blow wild and tug at the Union Jack so that it glares over the entire school. No matter where the Boys of Punchbowl lurk it's always watching. Just before the bell goes to cue the end of lunch, I twist open a bottle of Coke and gaze up at it as I scull. Suddenly the enormous Fob, Samson, rears before me, shading everything I see like he's one of the alien ships from *Independence Day*. 'Gimme a sip, lad?' he says coolly. I hand the drink up to him and watch as he puts his lips and tongue around the rim and sucks so hard that the plastic implodes and the cola inside disappears in one gulp. The next time he asks me for a sip of my Coke, I give him a dollar fifty so he can buy his own. Now Samson is on the quadrangle searching for me every day. The Lebs say it's my own fault. Back in Year 7 Rajab Habib told me, 'Feeding a Fob is like feeding a cat.' Then he asked me if I could lend him a dollar.

Behind the quadrangle are six identical science class-rooms: each has a stage, chalkboard and overhead projector out in front and two rows of student lab desks that look like breakfast bars running to the end of the room. In Science Lab G.1, Mr Romero, who has a thin moustache, chubby red cheeks and thick, curly hair like an Israeli, tries to teach the Lebs biology. Romero is pudgy around the edges and his gut presses against the buttons of his white shirt. I sit there on my first day of class for the term, upright on a science stool with my pen and book in front of me, ready for the lesson. My childhood friend, Omar El-Assad, walks in, pisses himself laughing and says, 'Look at this gronk!' He grabs my exercise book and flings it out the classroom window. It hits the tarmac and lies dead in the shadows of the quadrangle. Next Omar starts to wrestle with Sheik Solomon. Omar and I live across the street from one another and we went to the same primary school. He was the leader in Year 6 because he was the toughest kid in the school, a spiky-haired Sunni with big round eyes like a brown Bart Simpson. Sheik Solomon isn't supposed to be tough, he's just big and religious the way I imagine Santa Claus is big and religious, but as much as Omar presses forward, his little head tucked inside Solomon's chest, he can't pin him. The wrestling match ends as Mr Romero enters the classroom and Omar's body is hanging out the window.

Like a bloated pufferfish, Romero yells, 'Settle down!' Isa Musa and Shaky and Osama exchange one-liners from Van

Damme movies. 'Because of my big legs and karate, I can do the splits no problem!' says Isa. 'I want Tong Po! Give me Tong Po!' says Osama. 'I'm going to take my boat and I'm gonna kick that son of a bitch Bison's ass so hard that the next Bison wannabe is going to feel it!' says Shaky. Rajab and Fatala and Bashir and Ali gather their stools around a science desk and play 400 with a deck of cards. They light cigarettes, puffing quickly and then holding them under the benchtop between their fingers, leaving a trail of cigarette ash around the desk like a charcoaled onion ring. Mr Romero screams, 'Fatala, put it out!' and Fatala ignores him. 'Bashir, pack those cards up,' and Bashir ignores him. 'Omar, get your head out of the air vent,' and Omar ignores him. Hussein, a Shi'ite boy with a high voice and arched back, and I are the only two students listening to Mr Romero, and he makes eye contact with us between shouting at the boys who are drumming on the science stools. 'Open to page—' he begins and then he snaps, 'Mohammed, Ahmad, stop it!'

More than half the lesson passes and Mr Romero has been able to state just two facts that have something to do with science and biology: blood flows through the arteries, and the strongest muscular organ in the human body is the heart. I've written them both down in my Maths book. Daniel Taleb starts to bang on his desk and shouts, 'I fisted your bitch, you fat motherfucker.' I'm sure Tupac said something like that to Biggie after he was capped in an elevator. Mr Romero looks away from me and turns to

Daniel. 'Young man, don't use that kind of language in my classroom.' Daniel gets off his stool and stands in the centre of the room, between the two rows of science desks, facing the front. His hair is so fine you can see the pale scalp beneath it and his nose is as long and thin as a vulture's beak. He gawks at the teacher and in a high-pitched voice that's been cracking since Year 8 he sings, 'I'm a straight rida, I'll fuck you till you love me.' Romero screams, 'Daniel, sit down!' and Daniel repeats, 'I'm a straight rida, I'll fuck you till you love me.' Romero shouts, 'Get out!' Daniel locks his fingers together so that they make a W and again he sings, 'I'm a straight rida, I'll fuck you till you love me.'

Daniel is about three-quarters of the way down the classroom now. To the left of him sits Isa Musa, who is laughing with his mouth open wide and his teeth completely exposed, like he's the Fresh Prince of Bel-Air. Daniel looks confused. His sharp left cheekbone elevates and he winces before grabbing the Palestinian around the collar and, swinging over the top, jabs at his head with a tight little fist. The first punch misses but the second and third land between Isa's fat nose and flabby cheek. Then, before anyone in the class can jump in, Daniel casually lets go of Isa and walks out of the classroom, while Romero is still screaming, 'Get out!'

Mr Romero turns to Isa Musa and is about to say something to him – something like, *Are you okay, son?* – but before he can, the Palestinian, who seems completely unfazed by Daniel's punches, screams out, 'Ay, boys look at this, Mr Romero wants to be my friend.' The boys all turn to the teacher from playing cards and drumming on tables and say collectively, 'Naaaaaaaar.'

I see despair dawn over Mr Romero's pudgy face; the way his cheeks sag shows me there is no point in science, no point in reason and logic. There simply must be a god – hopefully there is a god.

As Mr Romero turns around to write something on the chalkboard, Mustafa Fatala pulls a gigantic ball of paper out from his backpack and pegs it. The ball moves in slow motion, like a wrinkled planet, and lands flat against the flabby layers of skin on Romero's neck. 'Ow!' screams the teacher as he spins back around, and then a swarm of paper balls flies at him – from Shaky and Osama and Isa and Bashir and Ali and Omar and Rajab and Sheik Solomon and even high-voiced Hussein, and every other boy in the class. Every boy except me. Romero starts to shout, 'Stop it! Stop it!' while paper balls hit him in the head and belly and groin like a drive-by shooting. The paper balls fly from the boys' backpacks. Then the sound of paper tearing pierces the room as the boys rapidly make new balls from their exercise books and peg them as fast as they can, all screaming, 'Rom-maaa-row! Rom-maaa-row!' One of the paper balls bounces off Mr Romero's forehead and lands right in front of me, right on top of my exercise book, right over today's two notes. I look down and I see a clump of paper and the word 'artery' sticking out beneath it and I think, *Fuck it*. I pick up the ball and lock my gaze onto Mr Romero's head. His mouth is open, his arms are flailing and his belly is convulsing. He's too distracted by the usual troublemakers to consider looking my way. I peg the paper ball and watch it sail towards him, and I get him square in the eye, and I know that he doesn't know that it was me.

In the same block as the Science rooms are three Woodwork labs. Only the dumbest cunts enrol in carpentry and only the least literate teachers teach it, like Mr Ibrahim, who doesn't even know the English alphabet. Most days I find Mr Ibrahim up in the Arabic staffroom, hanging out with the other non-English-speaking Arab teachers. He says he's a carpenter just like Jesus. He's poetic like Jesus too. He leaves the boys for ten minutes and when he comes back the room has been trashed. From the corridor that joins the Science rooms to the Woodwork labs we hear him hollering like a Bedouin storyteller, 'This classroom is my plate and when you shit on my plate you shit on my food.' His voice is deep, all lungs and belly, and he has a fat tongue like Aladdin's genie.

Nothing ever comes out of the Woodwork labs except desk organisers and keyrings and boys who cut themselves on Stanley knives. About five minutes into recess I see Jihad walk out of the Science block with a pocketknife stuck in his thigh. Blood has soaked his entire pants leg and is leaving a trail across the quadrangle. All the boys gather around as he walks towards the front office with a grin on his olive-oil face. 'It's all good, boys. Accident, just accident.'

'What happened?' asks Osama, the Indonesian.

'Antony stabbed me.'

Antony Malouf is the only Lebanese Christian at our school. He's not related to that big-time drug dealer called Danny Malouf, but no one fucks with him because Antony's older brothers are dealers anyway. Antony asserts his dominion over us on the basketball courts, where he takes six steps without dribbling, throws the ball into the hoop and says, 'Fuck you, ye *spiks*!' That's what Lebanese Christians call Muslims in Punchbowl, *spiks*.

Sheik Solomon raises his arms over his head like a weight-lifter and spits back, 'Fuck you too, ye *khashby!*' That's what we call Lebanese Christians, *khashby,* which means wood – because they worship the cross, which to us is nothing but a piece of timber. Solomon is the only Muslim in our school brave enough to call Antony a *khashby* to his face. He's not afraid of dying for Islam; he believes *jannah* is waiting for him on the other side.

The basketball court becomes the closest landscape to an Arabian desert the Lebs of Punchbowl Boys have ever known, the hot air bouncing off the brick walls of the Science block, searing the tar until the ground becomes sandpaper. Antony the *khashby* and Sheik Solomon the *spik* agree to sort out their religious differences as warriors, standing before one another on the courts like Richard the Lionheart and Salahuddin. They collide and swing wildly at each other until the Boys of Punchbowl collectively decide it's enough and pull them apart. By the end of the fight Solomon has a black eye and a cut lip and Antony is unscathed – which is a relief. Had the fight tilted in Solomon's favour, we all know he'd be shot at the train station in the afternoon. That's the problem at Punchbowl Boys: even if you win, you lose.

The tension rises within these nine-foot fences and brick walls each day, after a Fob stabs a Leb or a *khashby* bleeds a *spik*, to the point where I become fully aware and fully sedated all at once, always on the lookout for a blade or bullet to penetrate my flesh but as ready for it as losing my virginity. Every Punchbowl Boy knows his limits within the school, every Punchbowl Boy knows how hard he is, and who to not fuck with, who to not even look at. I walk past drive-by drug-dealer gangstas like Usuf Harris in Year 12 – a guy who doesn't know shit about me – and he says out loud to all his hard-cunt Lebo mates, 'I fucked this guy's mum yesterday.' Even if I took him on and won, I'd get my head shanked at the station after school, so I keep walking without the slightest reaction, straight towards my next class. In this way my spirit is broken and reconstructed, elevated to a point so high that my effort turns to weakness. Reading means I care too much. Pulling out an exercise book means

I care too much. To stop walking means I care too much. There are no bullies at Punchbowl Boys. The school captain, Jamal, screams it out at assembly like it's thug life. 'What kind of a sad fuck is bothered to pick on some other sad fuck?' We are beyond this. We are the children of the desert.

We enter through the basketball courts and there it is, the oval, sprawling out before us like a prison yard. From this end there is nothing but a windowless brick wall with three cameras perched up top. They're too high to bring down with rocks and they can see to the far end of the fence. It is here, where binding oaths are made between lions and Lebs, that *The Iliad* makes sense to me. I slam Usuf Harris into the dirt but the drug dealer doesn't cap me; Sheik Solomon pins Antony but the *khashby* doesn't give him a black eye; and ten Lebos surround Banjo but the Fob doesn't pull out a kitchen knife. On this oval we are free to glare at one another, free to break each other's noses and shoulders and ribs and ankles; free to snap back each other's thumbs and toenails. 'Pass! Fucken pass!' the Boys of Punchbowl scream at me as we go at it again and again and again. There is no revenge on the oval; there is only a football.

We are fast and united because of that ball, but we are our fastest, we are most united, when we sprint across the oval not to score a try but to break out. We head for the corner of the fence, nothing to hide behind, just an open plain and three cameras staring at us from the school wall. We have ten seconds to cross before a teacher might catch us on the monitor in the front office and send for the police to find us. When I am bolting, beside Kadar Kareem, who ripped off my beret, and Samson, the Fob who nearly killed him, and Harris, the drug dealer, and Antony, the *khashby*, my heart pounds like iron on iron and the splints in my shins become shockwaves of fried chicken each time I hit the grass. I hurl towards the corner of the school oval where the barbed wires of Punchbowl Boys meet the clean fence of the train line. On that cross-section we scramble like rodents, up and over the railway fence and down onto the train tracks. For the rest of the afternoon I abandon any aspirations to greatness and Whiteness. I reign over the western suburbs as a sand nigger, hassling girls and picking fights with Skips and Nips and Curry-munchers. But tomorrow I will walk through the front office and once again Mr Whitechurch and Ms Aboud will be standing in the doorway. They will each have a smirk on their anaemic face, and as I casually step past they will say to me at the same time, like two coppers, 'Young man, what makes you think you are free?'

The Australian flag is perched so high that it can be seen from every corner of the school. We move from corridor to quadrangle, classroom to basketball court, oval to over-the-fence, ignoring its ever-present gaze. But today the Lebs march through the front office of Punchbowl Boys like on no other day, in a collective orgasm. Their heads are held high and they kick their legs out and swing their shoulders. They bare their crooked teeth as they strut behind me and in front of me, through the front door and along the blue carpet. Mr Whitechurch says the same thing as each boy steps past him: 'Wipe that grin off your face.' His voice is sharp like a throttled mule's as it pierces the ringing in my ears. I keep my head low and my eyes averted and my breath static. To me Mr Whitechurch says, 'Bani, it's okay.' He thinks I care about the planes that went into the towers. I don't say anything in response. I don't even nod my head; I just keep moving through like I have Post Traumatic Stress Disorder. My heart aches, heaving itself into my mouth, making it difficult to take breaths. I am overcome with images of Mrs Leila Haimi, sunrays pushing through her thick black curls and lighting up her bare white face. Before I turned on the television this morning I felt like I would be a boy forever and that I had forever for Mrs Leila Haimi to drive me away with her down that endless road; then I saw those towers coming down and suddenly I was becoming a man, and the world was ending and I could see the end of that road like a clifftop before me.

On the quadrangle fifty boys are drumming on garbage bins and dancing in circles, their feet springing from the floor like popping corn. They swing their hips and wave their hands. Even Riad from Year 12, who's supposed to be the school dux, is in the circle. Most days I only see him sitting in the library or moving from class to class. Sometimes I end up next to him during the midday prayers. His shoulders are so thick and round that he rises up beside me while breathing in and out like he's a hot air balloon. Today Riad's brick head and bloated shoulders rise above the boys and his arms are in the air, waving as though it's his wedding day. His buckteeth blaze and the boys around him sing, '*Airy bel-Yahūd, wa airy bel-Yahūd,*' which means, 'Fuck the Jews, and fuck the Jews.'

There are clusters of young men scattered throughout the quadrangle and spewing down towards the basketball courts. Their cracked voices spiral at me from every direction, 'Bush' and 'Allah' and this guy named 'Bin' something. In one corner is Rajab Habib. He stands facing Ali El-Masri and Mohammed Naymen, who are both a foot taller than he is. Rajab's head is shaved and dotted black with stubble except for the long white scar above his ear left by the Fob in the Maths corridor last year. Rajab's lips are twitching and his fingers and thumb are pursed out in the shape of a duck's beak, which he moves back and forth at the boys' heads. He's re-enacting the image he saw on the news this morning – an airplane gliding into a building. It's strange seeing Rajab care for something other than mobile phones and PlayStation games and picking up lowies. I had never considered that his life held any purpose beyond the kitchen knife that scarred him eleven months ago.

In another corner are boys from Year 12 standing around Usuf Harris, who's a half-Lebo half-Gypo like a silverback gorilla with an afro. Usuf is pointing to the sky and screaming, 'I prah-dick-ted it! I prah-dick-ted it!' Every day he walks around the school telling the boys to read a book called *Protocols of the Elders of Zion*. I wonder if that's where he came across his prophecy. 'I prah-dick-ted-it!' the ape yells again. He always talks this way, always dramatic and excited and fat-tongued, like the time he was arguing with the boys in our year about what was better, PlayStation or Nintendo 64. He held his arms out like he was squeezing a baboon's arse and yelled over all of us, 'Nintendo 64 is da most comfortable joystick I eva held in mah life!' I wonder if in his mind there's no difference between video games and war, where human life and human thought actually end after the trigger is pulled. I wonder if being inside the walls of this school for six years has completely worn away Usuf's ability to feel compassion for those among the dead and those who have to live on. He would probably make an excellent soldier, even better a suicide bomber, brainless and unquestioning, like it is just *Mortal Kombat* and everything is in reverse, life is death and death is life. I am the only Punchbowl Boy who believes suicide bombings are *haram*, forbidden in Islam. Every other boy stands with Mr Abdullah, who says in his sermon before the midday prayer, 'There's no other option for those of us that must stand before tanks with nothing but rocks.' All the boys nod but I keep my head frozen and think, *What a fuckwit.*

The air is dry and dusty today; it should still be cold but somehow the sun heats the bricks and the tarmac so that all of Punchbowl feels like a huge piece of cast iron. I stand at the far end of the quad, flanking the entrance to the basketball courts. As soon as Shaky spots me, he wraps his arms around my head and presses my forehead against his chest. I hear him from the inside, like a bass speaker: 'We gotta stick together, brother.' Shaky doesn't need to stick with us unless he chooses to. His father is from Lebanon but his mum is as Aussie as meat pie. Shaky knows full well that, unlike me, he can pass for a Skip, tall and hairless and fair-skinned. The Boys of Punchbowl say he could be on *Home and Away* because of those green eyes and that dirty brown hair. Inside the walls of Punchbowl Boys High School, Shaky demands we call him a Leb and he asks why the police have to beat down niggaz, but I wonder what he will say when the lowies ask him about his nasho at the beach tomorrow. I wonder what he'll say when the coppers ask him for ID at Cronulla train station.

Then Osama moseys on up towards us. He and Shaky hug and laugh together and shake hands for the next four minutes as though I'm not there. They are so different that it is like watching interracial gay porn. At least Shaky can say that he's half Leb. Osama tells every girl he meets that he's Lebanese but he's actually

Indonesian. His skin is brown like somewhere between the Fobs' and mine. He's going to put 'TERRORIST' on his Year 12 jersey next year. It doesn't matter what kind of third-world-looking person you are; Osama knows that his jersey will only have credibility if he's Lebanese, because Aussies are blaming Lebs for everything right now. Most days I feel like Osama, Shaky and I are the same breed of dog but today I become more conscious of our differences. This event will be blamed on the Lebs just like the gang rapes and drive-by shootings. But it is me, the only full-blooded Lebo among us, who feels any grief for the people who plummeted from the summit. Maybe I'm not the real Leb. Maybe Leb isn't something you're born with; maybe it's something you earn while you're in the gutter.

Osama starts to look back and forth between Shaky and me. His smile sits on thin lips and pronounced cheekbones as though he were a starving lizard. 'They're saying it was Bin Laden.'

At first it sounds like the Indonesian is actually talking about the child of an Arab, because 'Bin' means 'Son of' in Arabic. I picture a small boy with an innocent smile and big, brown eyes and bright olive skin. He's standing on the dome of a great mosque in the middle of a red desert with his hands by his side and his head towards the sun. He wears a white Palestinian scarf called a *kufiya* over his long hair and his body is draped in a white Saudi *thobe*. With a soft voice like a kitten he cries, *'Allahu Akbar!'* Then it hits me that Bin Laden is a name, just some Arab name. He must be a man, a grown man, dressed up in a long beard and a desert storm uniform and an assault rifle like the terrorists in *True Lies*.

'Who's Bin Laden?' I ask.

Osama doesn't answer me. Instead he nudges his head towards Shaky and says, 'This guy, bro.'

Once again I confirm their belief that I am a traitor. Every Punchbowl Boy except me must have known who Bin Laden was before he woke up this morning. Whatever this guy had done prior to today, he was the unmentioned hero in the heart of the Lebs, a revered figure they had heard about on foreign news channels and inside foreign newspapers and in the foreign languages of their parents. I, on the other hand, am like an Aussie. I only heard the name Bin Laden a minute ago. I only just started to give a shit.

———

Maths Period 1, Mrs Stratton has written four numbers on the board and I stare at them for ten minutes and still don't know what they add up to. I am sitting next to Bara Ahmed, who has his long nose directed at the teacher as though he's paying attention. I stare at his thin hand stretched across his exercise book and the pen in it, which is pressed on the top line of an empty page. He too can't seem to add up any numbers. The pen begins to rotate in small circles – a tornado of boredom – and it makes me wonder what's on Bara's mind. I know already that he's thinking about the terrorist attacks, but what I wonder is how he's relating to them. Bara tells the Boys of Punchbowl that he's Syrian as a way of distinguishing himself from the Lebs. He told me a joke once that went like this: *A Syrian walked into a pigpen and then he came running out. A Leb walked into a pigpen and then the pigs came running out.* I didn't really get what he meant because I don't know anything about Lebanese–Syrian politics, but my dad's brothers tell me Syrians are cocks because they come to Lebanon and take all our jobs. While my family hates Syrians, however, they adore Syria's leadership because the head of state is an Alawite like us. In reverse that's the one thing Bara hates about Syria. After Hafez Al-Assad died he said to me, 'Sorry, man, but it's bull his son took over.'

I watch as Bara doodles some maths across his page. First he writes the letter S and then he writes a plus sign. I look to the chalkboard to try to work out what he's copying but there is no algebra, no letters, no S's that Mrs Stratton has written – she's just produced a row of numbers. I look back to Bara's page. He's completed the equation and it now reads $S + 11 = \$$. Bara turns and gives me a wink. I wonder if he just thought that up himself or if someone else told it to him earlier this morning. It doesn't matter that Bara calls himself a Syrian – he's a Lebo whether he wants to be or not; girls call him a rapist just as they call me a rapist, and like every Leb except me the only book he's ever read is *Protocols of the Elders of Zion*.

The sound of chalk scratches across the board until finally no one can take it anymore and Bashir Gazelle, who bench-presses one hundred and thirty kilos, calls out, 'Miss, seriously . . .'

Mrs Stratton turns from the board. Her nostrils flare open, which is what happens when she's agitated, and why the boys call her a Jew – they say she has large nostrils because the air is free. They also call her a Jew because she doesn't believe in God. They think Jews and atheists are the same thing. 'What?' Mrs Stratton hisses. 'And this better be about maths.'

Bashir's hand massages the base of his head. The sides of his scalp are shaved right to the skin and the top is clipped at a number five. He looks like a circumcised penis. 'Do you think those suicide bombers are in heaven now?'

'Do you want to be sent to Mr Whitechurch?' Mrs Stratton spits back.

Bashir doesn't care about the threat. 'Come on, Miss, just tell us – you think those guys are in heaven or in hell?'

Mrs Stratton looks as though she's holding her tongue for a moment, and then she slowly replies, 'I have told you repeatedly that I do not believe in heaven *or* hell.'

Bashir's eyes sink as he takes in a deep sigh. I see his large Adam's apple judder from across the room. He keeps rubbing his hand through his hair and his fingers have spilled over his shaved sides as he says out loud, 'Maybe your ancestors came from apes but ours didn't.'

The teacher's lip drops open and she shakes her head at him, speechless. She looks like she just got dogged, like someone sucker-punched her and ran for it. Mrs Stratton tells us she's an atheist but no equation or formula can ever explain the nature of Punchbowl Boys – the power that comes not from being on top of the evolutionary chain but rather from being at the bottom. Around the room everyone is glaring at her, quietly and beady-eyed, waiting for her reaction; everyone except me. I'm looking at them, the olive-skinned Arabs with baby beards and thick, curly hair razored at the sides. Just yesterday I was above all this. Yesterday I looked into the future and saw myself telling stories about angels, young men with enormous wings. I saw myself rising out beyond the walls of Punchbowl – rising so high that I could no longer see the prison slab; in my mind the prison had ceased to exist. I try to concentrate on the argument that is flying back and forth between the teacher and the Lebs but their voices and their faces are slipping away from me. I am suffocating under my own breath. It's as though my mouth is filled with dust. How will I ever be more than a Leb while I'm surrounded by terrorists? I am no longer above this place. I am in the rubble, among the carcasses of suicide bombers.

English Period 2, and as the boys walk in, Mrs Haimi screams out in her squeaky voice, 'We're not discussing Bin Laden, we're discussing the Elizabethan Chain of Being!'

Once all twenty-two of us are seated, Bassam Hussein raises his hand. He pushes his finger up against the centre of his glasses and says, 'Meees, why you make us study Queen Elizabeth? What if I don't want to celebrate the queen's birthday? What if I want to celebrate the sheik's birthday?'

Mrs Haimi stares at him the same way I saw Mrs Stratton stare at Bashir, gobsmacked. 'What the hell are you talking about?' she squeals.

I'm sitting beside the Black Palestinian, Isa Musa, who's breathing as though he has Rice Bubbles up his nose. He starts calling out, 'What happened in 1948, huh, Miss? What happened in 1948?' His voice begins to crack before the entire class, from a boy's to a man's, evolving. Words force themselves out of his throat, and I can't figure out if they lend themselves to joy or to despair. I try to imagine how the Black Palestinian felt this morning when he saw the news and watched those towers melt before him. Maybe he chuckled. Maybe he wept. Maybe he found himself some-where between laughter and tears, somewhere between humanity and the dead, like that moment before a suicide bomber releases the detonator. I saw the towers come down at 6am while I was getting ready for school. The house was still and my parents and siblings had not yet woken. Our television rests beneath a tapestry that has the words 'Allah' and 'Muhammad' written in Arabic. I turned it on with the remote and pressed mute before the picture appeared, and then the images hit me as though it were a silent movie about the Bible. A second plane thrown into the building like when David slung a sharp rock at Goliath and it sank into his forehead. Under the footage in capital white letters it said, 'AMERICA UNDER ATTACK'. Like the television, I made no noise – just turned it off and crept out of the house. The air in Caitlin Street was calm and the clouded sun looked like an elegant blood clot. There was a haze all the way down The Boulevard, which crosses King Georges Road and leads to Wiley Park and Punchbowl. The few cars on the street moved slowly across the intersection. I decided not to catch the train; there was too much time ahead of me, so I walked between the railway fence and the road past Wiley Park Girls High School. The whole way I kept thinking how I should have written a story about today's events ages ago and given it to Mrs Haimi. I should have written it last year, straight after I read *The Satanic Verses*, a story about a young man with enormous wings from a great desert city where buildings rose into the heavens like a mirage. I should have written about how that city came under attack, how airplanes were ploughing into twin towers and how the angel soared between them, catching the falling man as he plummeted toward the ground and landing him safely on the sand dunes.

Mrs Haimi looks down in my direction and her blue eyes glow around my reflection in her pupils. Then her squeaky voice sweeps over the classroom as she says out loud, 'The Jews think that what they are doing is right.' I finally see her in a way that I have been avoiding. She's driving down that endless road, where the sky is pink and the great desert city looms and the sun is beaming through her thick, black hair and bouncing off her white face. Suddenly she flies through the windscreen of her four-wheel drive. She barrels into the air and bounces like a battered horse across the tarmac before I can catch her. I'm down on my knees. My school shirt has come off and I'm using it to soak up her blood and the sun is burning my back.

———

Throughout recess I stand quietly with Isa Musa in the centre of the quadrangle. There is a lull that runs across the concrete and along the brick walls of the school. Very few boys are playing football or basketball like they usually would; most are scattered in clusters, eating lunch and laughing among themselves. There's something about the expression on each boy's face today that reminds me of a knife, the way he looks at the teacher with a slicing glare and sharp curl of the lips. The Lebs know exactly how to offend Aussies; they don't need to answer the call to jihad, they simply need to smile. The only boy who seems normal and balanced at the moment is Isa Musa. He does not need to celebrate or mourn the deaths of innocent people; for him there is nothing *except* the deaths of innocent people. The Black Palestinian's neutral expression reveals to me that he cannot understand why anybody actually cares, why today's circumstances should be considered different from those of yesterday or the day before that or the days leading back to 1948.

Isa and I are standing quietly beside one another, looking out upon the boys, when from across the quadrangle strides Mahmoud Mahmoud, whose afro is ablaze like the burning bush of Moses. 'Yo, Bani!' he calls as he pulls up. 'Who's that Jew that rocks everyone?'

'What?'

'The Jew . . .' he says. 'The one that smashes 'em all.'

In my head I start going through all the Jews he might be talking about. Maybe it's just some celebrity, like Adam Sandler or Jerry Seinfeld or one he hadn't considered until now, like Woody Allen or Larry King. Maybe he's talking about an intellectual – Karl Marx, who wrote that everything is about money? Sigmund Freud, who wrote that everything is about sex? Mahmoud Mahmoud is so lost that he's probably talking about someone obvious and easy to remember, like Einstein. He could even be talking about that journalist who rocks everyone, John Pilger, or that president who rocked everyone, JFK. The Lebs at Punchbowl Boys think everyone who's famous and powerful and White is a Jew. They even claim that Adolf Hitler was a Jew, and not like when Mr Flower says Hitler had Jewish heritage but as in Hitler was an undercover Jew who faked the Holocaust so he could steal Palestine. Somehow it occurs to me that Mahmoud Mahmoud might actually be referring to a Jew who has something useful to say about today. 'You talking about Chomsky?' I ask.

Mahmoud's honey-brown eyes expand as though there were an actual burning bush beneath his skull. 'Chomky, yeah, that's him,' he replies. 'Chomky said it's all bullshit.' Even by Punchbowl standards Mahmoud Mahmoud is dumb. He has the same first name and the same last name, so all the boys say to him, 'Is your family that retarded they couldn't think of two names for ya?' Mahmoud considers this a joke and laughs it off but he comes from a long line of cousins marrying cousins. Sometimes when I'm sitting next to him in Commerce and I feel his long jaw protruding like there's a Frisbee lodged in his mouth and he's trying to fix himself on the teacher's notes and finds himself staring out the window by accident, I see a caveman just beneath his baked olive skin, a primitive creature trying its best to make sense of two sticks. Is he suggesting that Chomsky said that today's events didn't happen, or that it was an inside job?

When would Chomsky have said that? And how would a piece of shit like Mahmoud Mahmoud stumble upon it? I wonder what internet video or journal article or book some Leb read about Noam Chomsky which led him to go around telling all the other Lebs that today is some kind of cover-up. Mahmoud Mahmoud has less going on in his head than even Usuf Harris, who at least accumulates his days like video games. Mahmoud Mahmoud doesn't even remember his days. Yesterday all he spoke about was going to Macca's after school and tomorrow all he'll talk about is Hungry Jack's. He goes through his life like a philistine, one thought and one step at a time.

Before I respond, the Black Palestinian, who as far as I can guess knows nothing of Chomsky either, has the common sense to ask, 'What the hell are you talking about, bro?' He sounds just like Mrs Haimi for a moment. That is how much of an imbecile Mahmoud Mahmoud is – the gap between him and the other students is as great as the gap between the students and the teachers, the teachers and me.

Mahmoud Mahmoud steps in towards the two of us and even before he breathes out his words I can smell the arse on his dry teeth. 'Chomky said no Jews went into the World Trade Center today.'

'Man, I told you to brush your teeth,' I snap.

'I did,' he says, and he smiles wide open to show both Isa and me his row of jagged yellow seashells wedged in a rock.

Isa reaches out and sweeps his bear-like hand through Mahmoud's afro. With a sigh he says, 'Brush 'em again, dumb cunt.' Then the Black Palestinian and I groan in laughter while Mahmoud Mahmoud stares at us like Conan the Barbarian, skin glowing and cheeks swelling.

I laugh so hard that my face scrunches and my eyes close tight. I throw my head up to the sun and feel its warmth across my brow as tears form under my eyelids. Then I open my eyes and see the Australian flag. It is glaring over me, limp and calm and quiet in the warm air, halfway down the flagpole.

Isa is gasping for breath when I turn to him and point and say, 'Look.' His eyes follow the direction of my finger and then the Black Palestinian expands. His gorilla shoulders fold out, his colossal chest swells, his large jaw and Adam's apple poke into the air, and in this stance, I see Isa harden into a pillar of salt.

Mahmoud Mahmoud is watching me, still confused, and I am watching Isa, now confused too. Did I just make some kind of terrible mistake? Would anyone else have even noticed the flag at half-mast were it not for me? 'Ah, fucken bullshit, ay, bro,' I mumble at Isa, trying to sound casual. Isa doesn't respond. He keeps staring at that flag, static, subdued. 'Ah . . .' I groan, and I look to Mahmoud Mahmoud in the hope that he has noticed Isa's reaction too and that he might say something dumb again to break the tension. Mahmoud's crooked teeth are exposed once more as his jaw hangs open. He looks at me with the dull emptiness of hunger in his eyes, and he says, 'I'm gonna get a pie, brah.'

The bell goes and Mahmoud Mahmoud is hurtling towards the canteen and the Boys of Punchbowl move on to their classes with their heads down like baby elephants. Isa stands before that flag and I back away from him slowly. I only have one thought. *Arabs are dumb. Arabs are so fucken dumb.*

———————

Mr Flower tells us that there will be no History lesson today. All the boys from Year 11 have been instructed to go to the library. I am with the forty students from my grade in groups of five and six around each table. With me sits the Indonesian Osama and the half-caste Shaky and the hard cunt that wears glasses, Bassam, and the Black Palestinian, Isa. All four of them have the three top buttons of their shirts undone. This is the only evidence that reveals Osama is more Asian than Arab. His torso is smooth and shiny compared to the other three, who have chest hair long enough to plait. It might be a display of pride and masculinity that the boys have unbuttoned their shirts or maybe it's simply because the air is warming up as the buildings burn and we near summer. The Boys of Punchbowl are finally in their element. Day after day they are in a constant war with the teachers, a never-ending struggle to stop the textbook pages from turning so that they can jerk off over what's walking past outside. No teacher ever cared enough for Tupac or the Festival of the Sacrifice to indulge such nonsense but today even they need the pages to stop turning. It's only Isa Musa who says, 'Fuck this waste of time.' He seems to want classes to go on, even though all he does in History is doodle swastikas.

To the left of the library stand Mr Watson, a History teacher we call 'Nose Job' because he has excess meat blocking his left nostril, and Miss Wu, a Commerce teacher who has a masters in business, which doesn't mean anything to us because she can't speak English. On the other side of the room stand Mr Flower and Mrs Haimi. I try not to stare at Mrs Haimi. The boys can sense what I feel. They know I prefer to be close to a woman than to spend time with them. 'You're meant to put bros before hoes,' they say. 'Dog,' they say. They know exactly what I am. Even under the dim light that turns her bleached face into the swollen head of a cat, I would dog every bro that strode the corridors of Punchbowl Boys for another moment with that hoe.

Out the front of the library in a light blue shirt and with a chequered black tie clasped tightly around his neck stands our school principal, Mr Whitechurch. His thinning grey hair is brushed to one side and the cracks in his fair skin have disappeared beneath the fluorescent lights of the room. Maybe that's why White people invented fluorescent lights, because it hides the weaknesses in their flesh. He stands patiently out the front, waiting for each boy to look in his direction, which happens one person at a time over a period of five minutes, until finally the *khashby*, Antony, says out loud, 'Come on, boys, shut up!' I can only wonder what Lebanese Christians like Antony are thinking about today. Maybe they're glad the attack happened too – maybe their Arabness, and all the hatred that Arabness projects towards the West, overrides their Christianness. Or maybe the Lebanese Christians are with America today; maybe they are nothing but fed up with Muslims and the way we keep humiliating the Arabs. Either way Antony has been completely reserved this morning, concealing his thoughts as though they were the Dead Sea Scrolls. It's strange because Antony is gangsta enough to tell the boys how he really feels about the terrorist attacks without any consequences, but for some reason he's said nothing about it at all, and has used his authority only to keep us focused.

Everyone goes quiet and waits patiently for Mr Whitechurch, who clears his throat and says, 'Your teachers think that today's events have affected this group the most.' His voice is tight and shrill. I wonder if it's because that tie is blocking his windpipe. 'I wanted to give you all an opportunity to discuss it.'

As soon as Mr Whitechurch has made the offer, Isa Musa raises his hand. Mr Whitechurch looks at the Palestinian with smug recoil around his eyes like I've only seen on Salman Rushdie. He says, 'Isa, you can say something at the end – I'll be talking first.' Isa keeps his hand up in the air. He dips his head down across the desk like a bulldog and nestles his gaze on Mr Whitechurch. The principal hesitates for a moment – we can all see him weighing up the situation – and quickly he realises that Isa's hand isn't going down until he says what's on his mind. Then Mr Whitechurch does what any sensible principal would do – he just ignores the mongrel.

'Okay, so this morning we have heard that the United States of America was attacked. Three thousand people are dead. It's very probable that the perpetrators were Middle Eastern and Muslim, like yourselves, so I can see why you're all upset . . .' Whitechurch rambles on, and all the while Isa's arm is in the air. There is a bored expression on Isa's face, his bottom lip is pouting and his camel eyelashes are slumped over. He has his left hand stretched above his head and is holding onto the arm that's extended into the air to help it from straining. Everyone else just sits there silent and sombre, breathing steadily. To me the Boys of Punchbowl are a pack of wolves, their long snouts and piercing eyes on Mr Whitechurch like he's raw meat.

Mr Whitechurch goes on. 'The pictures of airplanes flying into buildings, fires burning and huge structures collapsing have filled us with disbelief. Boys, I only ask for your respect for all those who grieve, for the children whose worlds have been shattered, for all whose sense of safety and security has been threatened.' I feel the tension drawing itself around Isa's straining arm but all I can think right now is how I really should have written that story about the Twin Towers burning down and given it to Mrs Haimi last week. I look over at her in the hope that she can somehow feel my thoughts, but all she's doing is staring at Mr Whitechurch intently and nodding – in that way teachers do when they are trying to show us how *we* should behave. Maybe she *can* hear my thoughts, because suddenly I can hear hers. She is saying to me, 'Oh, Bani Adam, we are neither here nor there.' I turn back to Mr Whitechurch just as he announces, 'Okay, some questions.' Everybody in the room, teachers and students, wait for him to let Isa Musa speak but the principal looks around for someone else as though Isa were invisible. This goes on for ages, Isa with his arm perched so high that even the children in Gaza know it is raised, and Mr Whitechurch looking patiently around for someone else like the way George Bush stares into the distance.

Slowly, the hand of Bashir Gazelle rises. 'Go on,' says Mr Whitechurch. Bashir begins to massage the base of his circumcised penis-head as he says in a deep, croaky voice, 'You gotta admit, sir, America was asking for it.' Mr Whitechurch nods at him and replies calmly, 'I can see why someone like you would say such a stupid thing.'

Now three more hands have gone into the air, as well as the one that Isa has had up for the past forty-five minutes. Mr Whitechurch points to Hussein, whom everyone calls a fag because he has a high voice and sits with his back arched. 'I think the boys are just upset because they're feeling victimised,' Hussein explains. In a kneejerk reaction the boy sitting by his side, Omar, who lives across the street from me in Lakemba, says out loud, 'That is so fucken gay, bro.'

As soon as Omar's unbroken voice rings out across the library I'm reminded that the Boys of Punchbowl only pretend to be united as Arabs and Muslims. In the end it won't be America to bring us down; it will be our own people, fighting brother against brother, saying to one another *Your mum's a slut* and *Your dad's a poof.* When we were children, I could be best friends with Omar simply because we lived across the street from each other. Then, as soon as we arrived at Punchbowl Boys, we went our separate ways. Omar joined the IMs in the bottom class and I joined the 'smart' boys in the top class. But I think that my separation from Omar started even earlier than that. As Alawites living in Lakemba, my parents taught me to tread carefully among the dominant culture of Sunni kids. I avoided talking about the Imam Ali in front of them, and when I prayed I kept my hands just below my chest.

Back then Omar did not know the difference between Alawite, Shi'ite and Sunni. He didn't need to know. He was Sunni and this meant that he was normal, just like Aussies are normal, never needing to question their existence. Unfortunately, there was a Maronite kid that lived in our street named George. His parents had told him there were different kinds of Muslims, just like there were different kinds of Christians. One afternoon, in the lead up to our last days as primary school students, Omar and George and I were hanging out on my porch talking about *Super Street Fighter 2*, and then out of nowhere George asked my best friend a question. 'Hey, Omar, what kind of Muslim are you?'

I still remember Omar's face, his eyes rising up on George like two full moons and his tongue flopping from his mouth. 'What do you mean?' he responded.

'There are different kinds of Muslims,' George explained. Still to this day I don't know how that wood-worshipper discovered my sectarian background. 'Bani Adam is Alawite,' he said. 'What are you?' I stood in silence and watched this unfold, too overwhelmed to react. Omar looked at me confused. Then he turned back to George. 'I think I'm Alawite,' he mumbled. Of course Omar would think he was Alawite. We were best friends. We hung out together from 8am to 5pm every day. We played football together and watched *The Fresh Prince of Bel-Air* together and we prayed together, and in Ramadan we starved together. If I was an Alawite, why wouldn't that be normal and why would Omar be anything else? Now, finally, I had to tell him the truth. 'No, you're not, Omar. You're Sunni.'

'What's the difference?' he asked. I wanted to tell him there was no difference, that we were brothers and that would never change, but even as a child I knew it wasn't my place to speak such lies. 'I can't tell you,' I said. 'You need to go home and ask your dad.' I remember watching Omar slowly make his way across the street to his home. I don't know what his parents told him about me, but the person who walked into that house was not the same person who walked out.

The way Omar just shot down high-voiced Hussein makes me wonder if he secretly hates me as much as he hates the United States of America. He would usually be sent downstairs for punishment after a comment like the one he just threw at his classmate, but Mr Whitechurch is distracted by another arm in the air. Still ignoring Isa, the principal cues a boy we call Cabbage, because his hair grows in the shape of a cabbage, to speak. 'Sir, is there even any proof that Bin Laden did it? How do you know it wasn't the Jews?'

In the closest way possible that someone can actually take this question seriously, Mr Whitechurch inhales a deep, tired breath and replies, 'There will be a lot of conspiracy theories in the air right now. The best thing we can do is follow the information we are provided and not jump to our own prejudiced conclusions.'

Six questions later and there are no more hands up except for Isa Musa's. He still has his gaze fixed on the principal, though his face is drooping now in what appears to be complete indifference. Mr Whitechurch keeps looking around for someone else to raise his hand but we've all waited long enough. No one wants to say anything anymore, and we want to hear what the Black Palestinian has to say, so we sit quietly and wait for Mr Whitechurch to give his permission. There is a long and drawn-out delay before finally Mr Whitechurch sighs – he knew he'd have to give in eventually – and says, 'Very well, Isa Musa. What?'

Isa slowly lowers his gorilla arm and sits up straight. All forty Lebs and all four of our teachers turn and look at him, silent and still as death itself. It feels as though words from the realm of Michael Furey and *The Dead* are about to come out of Isa Musa. Then, just before he cracks the static air with his unwavering voice, a sense of despair washes over me, the kind of despair perhaps that drives us to martyrdom. Why would Isa Musa have anything special or meaningful to say? Has any boy ever said anything meaningful at Punchbowl? Why would Isa's statement be any cleverer than the things he's said before, or any cleverer than the statements made by the boys before him, who always get higher grades than he does?

Isa's chest is deflated. His shoulders are hunched and his entire face looks like it is sinking into the Red Sea. His fat lips slowly spread apart as he takes in a deep breath and says in a croaky voice, 'I've been at this school since 1998—' Before he can continue, every student in the room laughs. 'Naaaaar!' they all say, as in, *Who's this poof? He thinks he's Malcolm X; he's been sitting there the whole time actually preparing a speech.* It's shameful the way Punchbowl Boys bring each other down even when we're on the same side. Isa Musa ignores the laughter, as though guided by the will of Allah, his voice springing from his ribs and erupting above the Lebs. He starts again, more clearly this time: 'I've been at this school since 1998 and throughout that time a million Arabs like us have been murdered by America and Israel and you never cared, then this morning some Americans die and you put the flag at half-mast.'

There is not even a breath between when Isa Musa stops and the Boys of Punchbowl explode, with all forty of them in unison screaming, 'Yaaaaaaaaa!' and banging their hands on the tables so that it sounds like an army is making its way into the school. Osama the Indonesian and Shaky the half-caste have their mouths pulling forward like they're fully Leb and they are screaming in Arabic at Mr Whitechurch, *'Kol khara!'* which means, 'Eat shit!' From across the room Ali El-Masri and Bashir Gazelle are on their feet singing, *'Airy bil Yahūd! Airy bil Yahūd!'* Even Antony, the Lebanese Christian, the wood-worshipper, the *khashby*, has his hands around his mouth in the shape of a megaphone directed towards Mr Whitechurch. I think he's saying 'Fuck you!' but maybe not; maybe he too is screaming, 'Fuck the Jews!' High-voiced Hussein is waving his hands in the air as though he were at an Arab wedding, and Omar, who just called him a faggot, is ululating like a woman, *'Le-li-li-li-li-li-li.'* Then up on his feet Mohammed

Solomon, Sheik of Punchbowl Boys, calls, '*Takbeer!*' which means, 'Shout out loud!' and all the Muslims reply, '*Allahu Akbar!*' which means, 'God is Great!' Once again '*Takbeer!*' and '*Allahu Akbar!*'

The teachers say nothing, including Mrs Leila Haimi, whose skin is withering in the fluorescent light, her soot-black lashes matted, her blue eyes turning grey and vacant. I see myself walking over to her, right now in the midst of this muck and mire, and delivering the same last words to her that Humbert had delivered to Lolita. 'Mrs Leila Haimi,' I will say, 'this may be neither here nor there but I have to say it. Life is very short. From here to your car, which I know so well, there is a stretch of twenty, twenty-five paces. It is a very short walk. Make those twenty-five steps. Now. Right now. Come just as you are. And we shall live happily ever after.' Then I see that endless desert road we would travel, and her corpse bathed in blood, only this time I am not there to soak it up. I am here, neither child nor man, neither man nor angel, just a Punchbowl Boy. And she is shaking her head at us. Mr Whitechurch tries to raise his voice over the Lebs, saying, 'There were Australians that died in there today; there were Australians!'

It is only me who listens, who knows the truth – that there is no difference between Punchbowl and Palestine, that it would be better if we just disappeared off the map. It is too late for the other boys. They have entered that realm where no White person can go, their souls swooning slowly as they hear suicide bombers exploding faintly through the universe, like the descent of their last end, upon all the living and the dead. 'Shout out loud: God is Great! Shout out loud: God is Great!'

GANG
RAPE

THERE ARE NO SLUTS ON THE BANKSTOWN LINE. Just as the train is about to leave Punchbowl station, Osama the Indonesian presses his foot against one door and I press my foot against the other, holding them open as the carriage begins to tug. Hot wind blows in our faces as the train jolts past the endless fencing between the train line and the white terraces on the other side of The Boulevard. We cross over the open stormwater tunnel and then, where the houses of Punchbowl end, Wiley Park Girls High School emerges. The building is low and the front gates are open in a way that we Punchbowl Boys see only as a mirage in our school. The carriage clanks along the tracks and I begin to hear the barks and howls of pit bulls and rottweilers from the rescue shelter that adjoins Wiley Park Girls. Osama and I take in the deepest breaths we can at the same time, like we are bracing ourselves for a missile strike, and as we pass the centre of the school building we both scream, 'Dog pound!'

I was seventeen when all this happened but it starts over again like I'm staring at the western suburbs through my rear-view. On the platform of Wiley Park station sits a girl in a school uniform. Her breasts pop from her tight white shirt like she's hiding a two-litre Coke bottle in there. I say, 'Ay, give us your number.' She looks up at me and she bares her buckteeth and dry white gums and without hesitating she replies, 'Zero, four, one, five . . .' Her dark-brown eyes are on me but between each number they twitch towards Osama.

Nada and I speak on the phone later that night and agree to meet at the park on Friday. She promises to bring a friend for Osama but she comes alone and so Osama finds himself waiting in the park amphitheatre while she and I take a walk. My hand is small and sweaty in hers and I don't really know how to lock them together the way couples do in movies. 'Stop fingering my finger,' she says with a snigger, airing the hard flesh of her gums at me.

'So, can I be your boyfriend?' I ask.

She doesn't answer, just continues smiling, looking straight ahead towards the pond where Osama and I peg rocks at the ducks on Saturday mornings. I don't know why ducks come here; the water is black from old bikes and punctured car tyres. 'I killed one last week,' I say to her. Still she doesn't respond. I look her up and down side on. She's dressed in her school uniform – tight black pants that wrinkle against her thighs and butt and a white school shirt that gets tight around her stomach and her massive breasts.

When we get back Osama is standing in the corner of the amphitheatre, which is an outdoor concrete slab shaped like a crescent moon, with his blue shirt unbuttoned halfway down. He's wearing loose dirty denim jeans and flip-flops. 'I like your friend's style,' Nada says to me. It's the first thing she's said in the past ten minutes. The sound of her voice is a turn-off. It's deep, like a cross-dresser's. She's staring at the centre of Osama's chest, which is hairless and bony and gleaming with drops of sweat. I know why she's attracted to him; it's because Osama, in contrast to the Lebs at Punchbowl Boys, the real Lebs, looks like a little boy, hairless and smooth on the face and body like a typical Nip. That's what little girls like: cute little boys. I, on the other hand, already look like a man, with the permanent shadow of a beard and a chest full of hair. This is a difficult place to be caught in as a teenager, too much like a man to appeal to girls and too much like a boy to appeal to women.

'Ay, what took yas?' Osama says as we approach. He thinks it's my fault that Nada didn't bring a friend for him. I don't say anything. We've only been gone fifteen minutes. I turn to Nada, who has let go of my hand and is still staring. 'Sorry, we were just talking,' she says, her voice easing up so that she actually sounds like a young girl now.

'Bani, listen,' Osama says at me. 'I wonna talk to Nada about her friend, okay.'

I think there is something perverse about this request but if I say no Osama will tell the boys tomorrow I'm a dog, that I'm always putting hoes before bros, and it's not worth copping that for Nada, who doesn't even seem to like me. I feel the two of them wandering off while I sit on the amphitheatre stairs and stare at the concrete stage and concrete walls arching before me like raw potato wedges. It is here that I come to think again about Mrs Leila Haimi. She left Punchbowl Boys last year to take on a head teacher's position in Seven Hills. I can't bear it, the thought that Aussies who are covered in freckles and still have their foreskins will be checking her out all year. On her last day at Punchbowl I whispered to her that I would change schools, that I would follow her, and she said, like it was the first time she had ever said it, 'Stay here, Bani Adam. It's good to be at a school with retards – you will stand on top.' I had never seen white skin in the desert before, but I saw it then on her glowing cheeks, like she was born from the Well of Zamzam. Every day since I have searched for her like but I only find girls such as Nada, who bore me with their naivety and predictability. I pursue them anyway. If one of them will let me be her boyfriend, we might fall in love and I'll forget about Mrs Leila Haimi forever and put an end to my agony.

For twenty minutes I sit there trying to remember Mrs Leila Haimi's eyes, which were light blue like a jellyfish, until suddenly I realise that Osama and Nada have been gone for twice as long as they promised. I walk around the park looking for them, crossing over the dirty hilltop where

Lebs barbecue chicken with their families, around the far end of the pond where the Viet kids collect tadpoles, through the slides and swings where Fobs smoke bongs at night. My girlfriend and my best friend are nowhere. I am biding my time, avoiding the place I know I will find them.

The public toilets in the centre of Wiley Park are what I imagine the toilets in an American prison look like. They're built from bright orange bricks and sit low with a flat roof. The women's toilet faces the swings and the men's toilet faces the pond. Light bounces from the orange bricks on the outside but once I step into the men's doorway it goes dark and damp. There are hinges where the gate used to be and it smells like pickled piss. Beyond are the faint moans of a teenage boy with a high-voice. The floor is smooth concrete with deep-set marks on it like rings on the stump of a tree, and overhead a fluorescent light hums as though it's a spastic angel. I step past an old aluminium sink that no longer has taps and stand between a row of cubicles on one side and a row of stainless-steel urinals on the other. The first two cubicles are open but the door to the one that meets the wall at the end of the row is closed. Down the bottom, in the space between the door and the floor, I see the soles of a pair of black leather boots. They're worn of all their traction, heels up against the inside of the door and bent where they hit the concrete.

I step towards the second cubicle and slowly lower myself onto the toilet lid. Then I listen. I expect to hear a loud sucking sound and groans like in porno movies but instead there's the light swirl of saliva and 'eh' from Osama every three seconds. Then he says, 'Your teeth, man!'

'Sorry,' Nada mumbles in a husky whisper. 'It's my first time.' Then a slurping sound as the fluorescent light buzzes from above. Osama giggles and says, 'He-h, I think I need tissues.' I can see in my mind the grin at the corner of his thin lips under his pronounced cheekbones. At the sound of public toilet paper chafing against what I imagine to be his little brown cock, I stand up and creep out.

Osama and I live at different ends of the same street. As we make our way home I say, 'So, what'd you and Nada talk about?'

He smirks. 'She said she likes me, bro. Don't worry, I told her to like you instead.'

I delete Nada's number and start over. Next I meet Alinta outside Parramatta train station. She's wearing a short white skirt and ugg boots. She's skinny and flat-chested and has a big forehead. I say to her, 'Your feet are cute,' and she smiles at me like a five-year-old, her smooth and shiny face bulging at the cheeks. As soon as we're in the under-eighteens club I dance with her. The room is dark, with laser lights zapping across the faces and walls. Teenage girls are moaning 'Weeeww!' and teenage boys are howling 'Yaaa!' in every direction. Most of the boys are Lebos and they're all walking around with dropped shoulders and dropped faces like trolls. I know that face of theirs, the same expression I keep slapped on me, trying to play it chill, not wanting to give away too much, not wanting to come off desperate. Worse, not wanting to come off like the Aussies around here, smiling with metal-mouthed teeth and chatting with the girls as though they might actually meet their wife tonight. The music screams from the speakers – Christina Aguilera, whom the boys loved two years ago because they thought she was a virgin like Britney Spears, and whom they love now because she's come back in mud and a G-string like Lil' Kim, only she's White. The virgin-skank sings about how she wants to get dirty, sweat dripping over her body, while I smell the real sweat of teenyboppers mixed with sugary perfumes and farts and pizza breath all around me. There's so many girls and there's so little space that I might accidently rub another guy's girlfriend, so I dance up against Alinta like a crab, stepping side to side with my arms crossed against my chest. Every few seconds I feel a hand flick against my back and my butt and I'm hoping it was a girl's but I can't be sure, so I tell myself that none of it counts. I keep my eyes on Alinta and we bob up and down and every other head in the room bobs the same way so that from above we probably look like ants in an orgy.

'Gonna go look for lowies,' Osama the Indonesian and Shaky the half-Aussie say out loud at the same time. They're hoping to find girls who might be interested in dancing as an excuse to dry-hump them. I'm staring down at my white Air Maxes, trying not to step on Alinta's fluffy boots. Sisqo blares from the speakers – he wants to see a tha-a-a-ong – and Alinta winces at me between braces; one tooth is completely sideways. She steps up close so that her groin presses against my crotch and begins to sway. If there were a gentler song playing I could see myself pressing my brow against her large forehead and trying to connect with her but instead the music just screams, 'Booty. Booty. Booty.' I try to coordinate my movements with Alinta's but I move in at the same time as she moves in and my pelvis pounds against hers. She ignores it and comes in again and I'm hit with a whiff of perfume from the bones of her iron-board chest. I recognise the smell – Britney Spears Fantasy, like my sister Yocheved wears, which is nothing but condensed fairy floss – and it makes me dizzy. My pelvis pounds against Alinta's again as I try to catch the rhythm, try to dance sexy with her. A small smile flickers along her mouth between the blink of the disco lights; flashes of glee in her grey eyes as she moves in and out, as though she's trying not to laugh at me. I collide with her again and again until I'm bathing in her warm breath and body.

Suddenly a brown hand reaches out in front of me and takes Alinta by the arm. I don't even have a chance to realise what's happening before Osama and Alinta are up against each other. 'Just one second,' Osama mouths at me, beneath the music. He puffs his big round cheeks and raises his eyebrows. There's a sincerity in his black eyes that makes me feel as though I have no hair on my nuts, like he's doing this for Alinta's sake.

Osama sways against her, moving in and out like he's wanking. He has his left thigh stretched out across her hip and he's thrusting his pelvis back and forth. Alinta slides against the inside of his dirty denim jeans. She has her head tilted back and her eyes closed like a heathen. It makes my heart drop – that feeling of jealousy because I'm not the one pleasing her.

I squeeze through red and blue and green lights bouncing off bleached faces, searching between the short skirts and dirty denim jeans for a lowie low enough for me. Each girl I look at either has her eyes locked onto some other Lebo or stares back at me with indifference. I don't think girls like my face, not in the way they are drawn to Osama's baby cheeks and Shaky's green eyes and fair skin.

Shaky is standing under the white fluorescent lighting of the men's toilets. He steps from the doorway, solid and tall and evenly chiselled like Michelangelo's David in boot-cut jeans and a tight black T-shirt. 'Osama dogged me,' I shout over the music, looking up at him. 'That girl was mine, man.'

Shaky's Roman nostrils twitch as he steps in close and says, 'Don't be a bitch, bro.'

We wander through the congested hall. The darkness thickens as the music grinds into the air. Shaky sees this place only as it is: tight and sweaty and loud. Girls make little invitations to him with their eyes and eyebrows slumped like melted cheese. Why do girls become vague and silent and dumb when they are around a guy they're attracted to? They move out of Shaky's way and their short Lebo boyfriends with gelled hair thrust out their chests and give him death stares. '*Shraameit* everywhere, bro,' Shaky screams out, which in Australian-English means, 'There are sluts everywhere, mate.' I would jump in for Shaky if some Lebo took a shot at him, if only to avoid being called a dog at school, but unlike him and all the other hairy-eyed Lebos here, I see this place for more than it is – I see it for what it could be. I know there is a force of nature past the miniskirts and G-strings and push-up bras, that all girls have the capacity to become Mrs Leila Haimi. Sometimes Mrs Leila Haimi let me see the girl in her. A couple of times she had walked past me in the corridor of the English block taking little steps with her legs pressed against each other. Then she winced as our eyes met, her lower lip wobbling before she mumbled, 'I have to pee.' I had no idea why she was telling me, but the words seemed to come out of her mouth so innocently, like a child who says she needs the potty, and it reminded me that she was only human, perfectly imperfect.

Shaky looks down at the girls and I look up at them as though we are Aristotle and Plato at the centre of Raphael's School of Athens; to Shaky it is the physical world that matters, the anatomy of each woman he sees, and to me it is the world of faith, the promise that beyond the skin and blood and bones, there is a soul. We circle until finally we've made a full lap around the hall and are back in front of Osama. He and Alinta have stopped dry-humping and are now just standing there, glaring at each other like their parents have caught them at it. Before anyone speaks Alinta slides quickly into the crowd. Osama turns to us. His lips are tugging to the right like he's been slapped in slow motion.

'What's up?' Shaky asks.

Osama mouths something but I don't hear it because Barbie is whining from the bass speakers of the club: she's blonde and single and wrapped in plastic. Shaky and I both step in close and Osama says it again. 'I came.'

I look down at his crotch, and just where Alinta had been rubbing against the inside of his thigh is a thick wet stain. 'Sick cunt!' screams out Shaky. He takes Osama's hand and they shake. Then they step in towards each other for a little shoulder hug. I try to hold back my disgust as I stare at them, twisted like two desert cobras having sex. I don't think Osama is a sick cunt; I think he's a dirty cunt. I'm supposed to be a bitch, but why isn't Shaky calling him a dog? Osama grass-cut me, not the other way around.

The strobe lights shoot across the faces again and I find myself tasered by visions of Alinta. I see her under the fluorescent beams of the female toilets, pink rays bouncing from her pale forehead and purple braces as she washes Osama's cum from her skirt and feels sorry for herself. I feel sorry for her too. There is no way I could have shown her that all I wanted to do was press my forehead against hers.

――――――――

Immediately after Mrs Leila Haimi left Punchbowl Boys, I received a note from the duty boy to go upstairs and meet with the school psychologist. I didn't even know we had a psychologist. Which Leb or Fob would ever be gay enough to talk about his feelings? This silver-haired woman named Adrienne with tanned skin and a calm voice answered my question. She said, 'A boy who sorts out his problems by stabbing another boy in the head needs someone to listen to him, don't you agree, Bani?'

'But I've never stabbed anybody,' I retorted, racking my brain for what I might have done to end up in that dim little office.

'Ms Haimi recommended I talk to you,' Adrienne replied softly, her voice like a harp. I couldn't help but notice she called her 'Ms' instead of 'Mrs'. Maybe she was a feminist. 'When did this infatuation begin, Bani?'

I wouldn't tell her this, but if she was using the word infatuation as an understatement for love, then I knew the second it began – February 1st 1998 at 10:14am. My first high school English teacher, Mrs Haimi asked each of the new boys in Year 7 to introduce themselves and say what they wanted to be when they grew up. Most of them said a builder or a mechanic or a plumber, and some said they were going to work at their dad's fruit shop, and some even said 'a drug dealer', and one said 'a backstabber'. Then my turn came and my eyes met Mrs Haimi's, and it was love at first sight, at last sight, at ever-and-ever sight. I said to her, gently, 'I don't want to be a writer, I'm already a writer.' I think she was charmed by my cockiness because she smiled, lips spreading like the earth had torn open and sucked me in, and I was falling into her forever. Then a copper-skinned boy in the class who said his name was Firaz screamed out, 'Who the fuck's this gronk? He thinks he's better than us!' and just like that Mrs Leila Haimi's smile was gone. The Lebs had stolen it from me.

Adrienne tolerated my refusal to answer her question for two seconds before she tried another question. 'How about we start again, and you tell me how you're doing, Bani?'

Oh Allah and Mrs Leila Haimi – why had you both waited so long to show me what compassion looked like? Over the barbed wire of Punchbowl Boys, I had completely lost faith that anybody cared for me enough to ask this question, and then suddenly my heart was splitting like the Red Sea and I opened myself completely to this stranger they had sent me. 'I see Leila Haimi in my dreams hanging off a cliff,' I whispered to Adrienne. 'I'm trying to pull her up but I'm not strong enough and her blue eyes are open wide and staring into my soul.'

Adrienne smiled. I think she had never met a Leb who spoke like me before. Then she said, 'If you're looking for Ms

Haimi, perhaps you will find her in a person your age when you're ready for a relationship.' I noticed she said 'person' instead of 'girl'. Maybe she thought I was gay.

————————

I continue my search for Mrs Leila Haimi along the phone lines and the postcodes of Western Sydney. I meet a girl named Zara on a chat site called mIRC. She gives me her number. Her voice is grainy and dry. I ask where's her favourite place to hang out. She says, 'My bum hole.' I ask what's her favourite love song. She says, 'Only a poof asks questions like that.' Then she cracks open a can of soda. To me the fizz is what it sounds like when people are burning in hell. I ask another question and I don't even hear the words come out of my mouth because of her gulping. Then instead of answering me she burps into the phone. I ask again, 'What do you look like?' She says, 'I'm size eighteen – you got a problem with that?' I get what's happening here – she's being awful to me before I can be awful to her because she's fat. I delete her number but I'm not sure if it's because she's cruel or because I'm superficial about a girl's weight.

I find out with Casey. I meet her on mIRC too. She gives me her number. Her voice is soft like her throat is coated with honey. I ask her where's her favourite place to hang out and she says, 'The clifftops at Watsons Bay.' I ask her what's her favourite love song and she says, '"Endless Love" by Mariah Carey.' I ask her what she looks like and she hears me the first time. She says, 'I'm size eighteen. I hope you don't have a problem with that.' I delete her number. It's not that I'm into looks; I just can't go out with a fat chick. I'm too skinny. The boys would call us Kit Kat and Kit Kat Chunky. I find myself thinking with a sense of bravado: *I can't let a heifer go through such a thing.* Any girlfriend of mine will have to start off skinny like me, so that no one judges us, then I'll be the one to fatten her up. I see myself opening those small bread rolls from KFC and making her a burger from my 2 Piece Feed. First I'll strip some skin and breast. I'll lay it all down on the base of the roll. Next I'll line up some chips. I'll pour gravy and watch it seep into the crevices. Then I'll put the burger to her mouth and her lips will press down on my fingers and exchange the residue of salt for her saliva on my fingernails as she bites. And she'll know; she'll know what it means to be loved.

I finally find her, the girl for my fingernails, in front of the women's toilets at the Royal Easter Show. Osama and I are looking for a place to rest and we pass a row of clown heads and a carny who's yelling, 'One dollar a toss, one dollar a toss.' There's three Lebos walking in our direction, all dressed in tracksuit pants and Everlast singlets, and just as they approach one says, 'Fuck that, bro, I can have a toss at home for free.'

I spot the girl a moment later while we're sitting on a park bench and I'm wondering how those Lebos didn't see her first. She stands in a short denim skirt with her thighs apart and her bum against a brick wall and the dull expression of waiting on her face. Her bare stomach bulges around a silver belly ring with a dangling ornament that looks like a slug, a top layer of fat pressing down on the bottom layer so that her belly button is closed shut behind the piercing, the rolls of flesh creating a straight line across her stomach. I like the colour of her stomach: white like breast milk is white, white like Mrs Leila Haimi is white. It's the kind of white that I want to stroke with my fingers just to see how the colours of our skin contrast. The girl's chest is hidden from my apish eyes by a hot-pink sports bra, and behind it must be juvenile breasts no different from Lolita's. Two bones pop from the top of her décolletage – divided by a groove in the skin at the bottom of her throat. Between these bones and just beneath the groove is a small piece of metal with red at the bottom, red at the top and a green cedar tree in the centre of a white backdrop – a pendant necklace of the Lebanese flag. It makes no sense, because from looking at her face, I would swear on my grandmother's grave this girl is an Aussie – not an Aussie like me, an Aussie like Pauline Hanson. I try to look into her eyes but she keeps them set out into the distance, in the direction of the farm animals. She has the perked nose of a piglet and her hair glows orange in the sun. Beyond her, emerging like an ancient octopus, is the ferris wheel and the screams of children and teenagers and the whooshes and swooshes of the rides sending them through the air. The girl is pretending she hasn't noticed Osama and me noticing her.

We are watching and she is waiting and her friend finally steps out of the women's toilet, a short and chubby girl with long blonde hair. Osama turns to me with a sneer on his lips so sharp and thin that right now he looks Chinese, not Leb. 'All right, which one do you want?' he asks. The smell of barbecued sausages and onions drifts over the park and it takes me back to my childhood in Alexandria. For ten years I associated sausage sizzles with Aussies and Aboriginals, who ate pork. Then we moved to Lakemba and the Muslims introduced me to halal and beef sausages and vegetable oil. This broadened my imagination in ways that no Aussie could ever understand. All of a sudden I could desire a sausage. I wonder which of these girls is more likely to imagine new possibilities too. I wonder which would give up pork for me. I turn to Osama and say, as sincerely as possible, 'I can't hook up with a girl who uses a public toilet for that long, bro.' It brings up too many questions: what was she doing in there, and if she was doing what I think she was doing, what facilities are available in a theme-park toilet, where people are constantly vomiting up and shitting out fairy floss and hot dogs, to practise good hygiene afterwards? *Al-nadaafy min al-imaan*, I think; cleanliness is equal to holiness.

Osama looks at me as though I have a disease, his round face rearing, and then he turns to the girls and says out loud, 'Ay, ladies, come heyaah!'

The girls have already begun to walk away, but they stop and twist towards us. 'You come here,' says the girl with the Lebanese flag around her neck. I hear her voice for the first time but I know it from a thousand and one days in the western suburbs. It's the voice of an Aussie who knows Lebs; a voice both feminine and masculine, gentle and coarse.

When I'm standing right before her, sizing up our height and weight, which seem about the same, I finally get a good look at her face. The freckles are sprinkled on her like a dot painting. I see a short line of ancestors deteriorating in the sun on that face. I get a good look at her belly ring too, which as it turns out is not a slug but a grey butterfly. It dangles from the top of the piercing down over the crease in her belly. She isn't fat, just plump around her stomach. Her thighs are plump too, wide and tanned, and she stands before Osama and me in that short denim skirt with her legs apart, the way a boxer stands to keep his balance. The girl presses her hand against her chest and massages the pendant of the Lebanese flag between her small, delicate fingers.

'What's your name?' I ask her.

'Banika,' she answers, letting go of the pendant.

Meanwhile, her blonde friend stares at Osama as though Banika and I aren't even there, lips pouting. She's standing with her back upright, perking her broad chest at the Indonesian, one button undone – a small shadow where she is trying to show off what little cleavage she has. I hate the way girls my age try so hard to have big breasts, instead of waiting patiently for them to come about of their own accord. I remember Mrs Leila Haimi's burden, an inch of cleavage within the V-neck of a red shirt on the first day of March 2002. I stared at the line only once, by accident, as I entered her classroom and she stood at the door waiting for all the boys to be seated. For the rest of the lesson I kept my head down, pretending to take notes, while she spoke gently about a Black king named Othello, allowing her voice to vibrate inside my head until my entire body was throbbing. The boys were more attentive than usual, Osama saying, 'Iago was a fucken dog cunt, bro,' and Solomon and Bashir and Bassam agreeing, 'Yeah, Iago fucken dog cunt,' and Isa Musa the Black Palestinian saying, 'Iago was a fucken racist cunt, man.' Nobody seemed to care about Desdemona. Then at recess, while the boys stood in a circle on the quadrangle passing around hot chips, they talked about how hectic Mrs Haimi's titties were, how they were better than Angelina Jolie's. My heart was caving in as I listened. No Punchbowl Boy would ever understand that I loved Mrs Leila Haimi not because of her tits, but because our gazes met when Othello's words came out of her mouth. 'She had eyes and chose me.' After that I could not wear my heart upon my sleeve, for dogs to peck at; I was what I was.

Banika's friend has thick eyebrows, and they start to twitch. 'What nasho are ya?' she asks Osama.

'Lebo,' he answers. Then he shoots me a quick look and winks like he's James Bond. He doesn't want me to tell the girls he's Indonesian. Sometimes I think it's because Osama is around Arabs so much, and Arabs all call themselves Lebs so much, that he actually thinks he's a Leb. Then he carries on about how great Indonesians are, how most of them are descended from the Prophet Muhammad, and he snickers about how stupid Lebs are, how we must be descended from apes, and I think he tells girls he's Leb because he doesn't want to taint the Indonesian name. Every girl Osama meets knows the deal when she hears the word 'Leb'. If she wants to fuck, she hears 'Leb' and lets him push her head down to his crotch. If she wants a boyfriend, she hears 'Leb' and gives him a fake number. It works out well for both of them.

'Wonna go for a walk?' Banika's friend asks Osama. Her gape upon him is making me feel sick. She doesn't even know his name yet. I know that it will be impossible for me to ever speak of love while Osama calls himself a Lebo; he makes it look like all the Lebs are players who only want head jobs and one-night stands. He and the blonde take hands and wander back in the direction of the clown heads. 'Come on, I'll win ya a prize,' Osama says as he puts his arm over her shoulder.

I remain standing still in front of Banika, examining the girl who looks more Aussie than beetroot but wears a Lebanese flag above her décolletage, and I ask, 'Are you Lebo?'

'Nah, half-Aussie, half-Serb,' she says, 'but I don't speak Serb.'

'Why do you have a Lebanese necklace?'

She doesn't look me in the eye, her glare searing past me when she responds, 'This might sound a bit weird, but I plan on marrying a Leb.'

My first instinct is to assume she has a Lebo boyfriend, and then there's this unnerving part of me that thinks she just loves Lebs like the way Nicole Brown Simpson just loved Black guys. 'Ah . . . a particular Leb or just any Leb?'

'Just any Leb,' she says, followed by a pause that begins to mount between us until finally she adds, 'Look, I've only ever dated Lebs and they're the only guys I like, okay.'

'Yeah, that's okay,' I say. *'I'm Leb.'* I suddenly feel sorry for her. She's comfortable with Lebs, she trusts Lebs, she has only ever been with Lebs, because Lebs chase after her all the time. If only she knew that Osama – and every other Leb except for me – wants to get close to her not because he has any intention of marrying her but because he thinks she'll put out. Maybe that's why the Lebs who passed her before Osama and I came along kept walking – they realised that a White girl who is desperate to marry a Leb might put a hole in the condom, and the only reason they'd be using a condom, the only reason they'd even be having sex with her outside of marriage, is that they have no intention of marrying her.

I mosey in the direction that Osama and Banika's friend have wandered off. Banika walks beside me, with her legs spread open like she's about to squat and her hand in front of her crotch tugging her denim skirt down.

'Why are you walking like that?' I ask.

'My thighs are sunburnt,' she says.

I wonder what kind of a girl opens her thighs wide enough for the sun to cook the chafing space between them. I remember Mrs Leila Haimi's thighs, beneath her coloured skirts. They were always fair and they always matched the colour of her face. She didn't spend time in the sun; she spent time in the snow. Once she came to school with a bandage around her wrist and I ran to her and asked what had happened. 'Skiing,' she said faintly.

'Kharjik,' I replied, which means, 'Sucked in.' It was just a joke, of course. In actual fact it gutted me that I could not be there to catch her from falling. Where was her husband? Why hadn't he caught her? Why hadn't God created her fifteen years later or me fifteen years earlier?

———

On Friday, a week after the Easter school holidays, while half the boys play football on the oval and the other half pray in the hall, I slither into the dark side of the school library. Right up at the back where the books have thinned and the shelves are dusty and the fluorescent lights have run dry, Osama the Indonesian, Isa the Palestinian, Mahmoud Mahmoud and I sit facing each other. Day after day we are here in our black leather shoes and navy pants and white school shirts, collars cocked, sleeves rolled and the top two buttons undone. Osama's honey-cut face is a mere outline in the dull light while he laughs and says, 'You know who's the funniest cunt? George Costanza.'

Mahmoud Mahmoud's hand is dipped into his dark-brown afro and he's scratching his head like a caveman. 'Nutt,' he says, 'they're all Jews on that show, bro.' Then, picking up from an earlier conversation, he adds, 'You know your hand burns in hell for seventy years for every second you wank.'

'Then *you're* going to hell forever, bro!' Osama scoffs, and the three of us laugh in Mahmoud's face.

'Wahhabi crap,' Isa spits. He tilts back so that his black skin and black beard merge with the shadows. Isa was Sunni until Osama finally came out as a Shi'ite and began hounding him about the Prophet's cousin and son-in-law, Imam Ali. 'He was the first-born Muslim! He was born inside the Kaaba! He was raised inside the Prophet's house! He was wed to the Prophet's most loved daughter, Fatima!' Osama says. Then he points at Mahmoud Mahmoud and roars, 'You say you love the Prophet but you murder Ali and poison his grandson Hassan and chop up his grandson Hussein at Karbala!'

I listen closely and wait for a moment to interject. In the lull following Osama's words, the cries from the oval echo up into the library. 'Fuck. Fucken. Gronk. Shit.' It sounds like Shaky but then again it might have come from Bara the Syrian or Antony the Lebanese Christian. It's hard to tell, because when the boys are playing football they all start to sound the same. There's no way it could be Sheik Solomon, though, because he never misses the afternoon prayers.

'You think you're gonna have sex in heaven, boys?' I ask. All three snap towards me like bronzed raptors.

'What da fuck?' Mahmoud Mahmoud gasps.

'I don't think you can,' I say.

Mahmoud's bottom jaw dangles open. 'You can do *anything* in heaven,' he grumbles.

I'm about to shoot straight back but I feel the vibration of a text message go off in my pants and it jars me for a moment before I say, 'Yeah, you can do anything in heaven, but if you're good enough for heaven you wouldn't be focused on sex.'

These are the kinds of questions and answers I contemplated as a Punchbowl Boy. The more I read, from Plato to the Old Testament to the New Testament to the Qur'an to *The Origin of Species*, the more complicated the world around me became, so I began to revile the third-grade Islam they were teaching us in Scripture, things like *Your eyes burn eight weeks in hell for every second you undress a girl in your mind* and *You get one virgin in heaven for every slut you turn down on earth.*

'If there's no sex in heaven, then what's the point?' asks Osama, but he asks it rhetorically, with a smug little curl on his upper lip as if to insinuate that I have no common sense. Over the top of him Mahmoud Mahmoud starts to shout, 'You can! You can!' These Punchbowl Boys: take away their heaven and you take away their faith. 'I reckon you can,' Osama says reassuringly, a smile easing through the darkness as he looks to Mahmoud Mahmoud.

Isa Musa says, 'My heaven is just hanging with old men, bagging out Israel.' This is where I lose interest. I take out my phone and press the centre key. I own a Nokia 8850, which has a titanium casing and a blue screen. Once I've activated the phone it lights up the back of the library like Luke Skywalker's lightsaber. The boys' brown faces are illuminated by a text message from Banika that says, *hey babe lol*. Osama is in the middle of a new discussion topic, something about how he finds short chicks sexier than tall chicks, when he stops and snaps, 'Please don't tell me that's that lowie from the Easter Show.' He stares at me like a toddler sitting by a night lamp, with unblemished skin and teddy bear cheeks and long black eyelashes flapping as he blinks into the blue light. He thinks I should have done with Banika what he did with her friend Melissa: get a head job on the ghost train and then say my parents will never accept her. Had I gone for Melissa, it could have been Banika sucking Osama's cock – that's why he calls her a lowie, because he doesn't know the difference between one Aussie and another.

I can feel all three of the boys ogling me, judging me as I concentrate on my phone screen. I try to make it clear that I don't care by not reacting to their glares until finally they get back on with their discussion about shorties. I text

Banika, *Give me your school address – I have a surprise for you.* Since we met I've been thinking of ways I can get her to fall in love with me. My plan is to photocopy my favourite pieces of writing and bind them with a silver belly ring, and post them to her school. She'll open the packages I send in front of her girlfriends and they will all be jealous and tell her how lucky she is to have a guy as romantic as me. Shakespeare will show Banika that love may be compared to a summer's day. Kahlil Gibran will show her that when love beckons, she should follow, and when love speaks, she should believe. Nabokov will show her how all at once we can be madly, clumsily, shamelessly, agonisingly in love with each other. Bani Adam will show her that there are no Lebs like me.

'What's this girl's name?' Mahmoud Mahmoud asks. He's staring at the carpet but he's talking to me. I don't want to answer. These guys will mock her, and they'll mock me for dating her. Then again, if I refuse to tell them they'll say I'm acting like a bitch, defensive and insecure and caring way too much about some lowie. 'Banika,' I mumble.

'Banika?' Isa scoffs. 'Tell her *bedi-neeka.*' Then he and Osama and Mahmoud Mahmoud all laugh. *Bedi-neeka* is Arabic for 'I want to root her'. I keep my face intact – it's not funny.

'Bro, I heard this girl's a stinky bitch,' Mahmoud Mahmoud says to me, and again, all three of the boys start laughing. This time, however, I find myself laughing along with them.

It's hard for me now to admit that at times the sexist atti-
tudes of the Punchbowl Boys appealed to me. It was such an
arbitrary comment, to have heard Banika was a stinky bitch.
Heard from whom? And why, of all the things Mahmoud
could have heard, would he have heard that she smelt? Smelt
like what? He must have been joking – he knew full well
that I'd rather date what the Lebs called an 'ugly bitch' than
what they called a 'stinky bitch'. The thought of a bad smell
always made me want to flush a toilet.

'Give me your phone,' says Mahmoud Mahmoud as the
laughter dies down. 'I'll show ya something.' Again I hesitate;
what the hell does he want my phone for? I hate how people
ask for things like this without telling you why, a deliberate
power game to fuck with my head. He's waiting with his
hand out and a Smurf-like smile on his face, and I can feel
Osama and Isa watching to see what I do. They will jump
on me for being too precious, for caring too much about
my belongings, so I just hand it to him. I try not to care as
Mahmoud fiddles with the buttons, try instead to listen to
Osama and Isa's discussion but I don't hear anything they
say. I need to work out what Mahmoud Mahmoud is doing
with my phone. I can sense his fingers moving across the
keypad. *Is he sending a text, adjusting the settings, adding a
number?* I count fifteen seconds that feel like five minutes
before he finally hands the phone back to me with a casual
glance. Then he pulls out his own phone and plays with

the buttons. Osama and Isa have stopped talking and are staring at Mahmoud Mahmoud curiously now.

I look back at the blue screen of my phone and I am about to go through and try to work out what Mahmoud has done when I get another text message from Banika. This one says, *fuck u cunt*. My heart sinks. Mahmoud Mahmoud has ruined this for me. He's texted her from my phone, texted her something dirty and offensive. Now Banika thinks I'm another typical Lebo and probably wants nothing to do with me. I turn to Mahmoud with my eyes wide open. 'What did you do?' The phone drops from my hand and I rise up in the darkness. Mahmoud starts to laugh, like this is still a joke. My fists clench. He's cackling so hard he starts to choke. I see an opportunity to take a shot at him, right now, right inside his blubbering mouth, right against his grimy teeth. I step in and am about to throw a wild jab when he starts to mutter, 'Et wasn her, bra, et wasn her.' I freeze, staring into his honey-brown eyes, which are laminated amid the shadows. 'I swapped her number with mine,' he finally gets out.

I feel my face twitching as I try to make sense of what he has done, that he's changed his name on my phone to 'Banika' and then sent me a text message from his own phone. The thumping in my chest subsides and I am suddenly at ease. I sit back down like jack-shit happened, not angry about the joke, just relieved that nothing has changed between Banika and me. Then as I bend down to pick up my phone I notice Osama staring at me with what I know is complete repugnance. 'This guy, bro,' he mumbles, looking towards the fluorescent lights down the other end of the library. He turns to Mahmoud Mahmoud. 'You shouldn't have told him.'

I see the glee in Mahmoud's eyes twist into the flaccid expression of guilt, like maybe he didn't think this through entirely. 'Why not?' he grumbles.

'Because that's the *real* Bani Adam,' Osama says. Then he stands and sighs and glowers down at me. 'I'm gonna take a shit, see yas in class.'

He makes his way towards the library exit. I wonder what he thinks about while he's shitting. Does he try to block the stench from his mind or does he enjoy it like everything else that comes out of him? I wonder why he spends so much of his time trying to break me. What is so wrong with me? The *real* me? What is so great about him? The *real* him? The one who gets secret head jobs in the park toilet? Osama pretends to be invulnerable but I've seen the other side, the real side. We were on a train last year and he had his foot on the edge of the seat in front of him. This fat White transit officer with a square head stepped into the carriage, looked down at him and asked, 'Where's your ID?' Then the officer examined Osama's student card for a second and said, with a stony face, 'You know you're gonna get a fine for having your foot on that seat, right?' He wrote out a hundred-dollar ticket while Osama pleaded with him. 'Officer, please, I didn't even have my foot on the seat . . . My parents don't work, we have no money, man.' The officer didn't flinch, just handed my friend the fine and said, 'If you want to contest it, there's information on the website.' It was the first and only time I'd ever really felt sorry for Osama. He got that ticket because he was a Leb. I knew the pain.

Once Osama has disappeared from the library, Mahmoud Mahmoud and Isa Musa return to arguing, shouting back and forth words like 'Wahhabi' and 'Shi'a' and 'Abu Bakr' and 'Imam Ali', but I don't pick up much else. I sit in silence, rearranging the names in my phone to their correct numbers, when suddenly it rings. Banika's name flashes from the blue screen. I want to answer but I don't want the boys to call me a dog again. They grimace at me, waiting for me to reject the call so they can repeat the same arguments they've made to each other. The phone rings another three times and Isa's ape-shape jaw grinds until finally he snaps, 'All right, just answer it, bro!'

I get up and walk to the centre of the library. 'Banika?'

'Nah, cuz, it's Linda,' someone on the other end responds. She sounds like a Lebo, a deep, chaffing voice as though her mouth is full of hamburger.

'Where's Banika?'

'She's next to me,' says the girl and then her voice drops out. I hear a group of teenage girls murmuring in the background. There's laughter and a faint drumming, like it might be raining, and a few high-pitched groans and then the girl on the phone says to me, 'So, are you a terrorist?'

'Fuck, what!' I don't mean to sound hostile but I'm completely caught off guard. Then I lower my voice and say, 'Sorry, what did you call me?' I don't want to damage my chances with Banika by insulting her friend.

'There was a bomb threat at our school,' the girl says.

'Yeah, so what if there was a bomb threat?'

Her voice suddenly eases. 'Yeah, so you just asked Banika for our school address, right?' She's gone from sounding like a *habib* to a *habibty* – from a lad to a lover girl. Maybe she likes the idea that I made a bomb threat. Maybe she likes hard cunts and she thinks I'm one, a serious gangsta or at least a wannabe gangsta. I don't consider myself either serious gangsta or wannabe gangsta. I consider myself a serious poet. I'd even settle for wannabe poet. 'Put Banika on the phone right now!' I shout, and then there is a muffled grunt and the drawn-out hiss of poor phone reception.

'Hello?' Banika finally answers.

As soon as I hear my girlfriend's voice I say, 'You need new friends.'

'Sorry,' she whines, stretching out the 'ee' sound. Then she tells me about what she had for lunch – a meat pie and a Red Fanta – and what she's wearing – a blue checked school skirt and a white short-sleeved T-shirt. I wish I could see her right now, standing with me on a mountaintop in our school uniforms because we'd skipped class, holding hands and hugging and pressing our foreheads together like two children in bursts of love with the ocean and the sky and the sun sprawling around us.

I move along the cracked vinyl tiles of the school corridor towards History class. Mahmoud Mahmoud and Isa Musa walk alongside me but neither of them speaks. I can tell there's something on the Black Palestinian's mind. He has been sneering since I got off the phone and every time I look to him his cheeks drop and he gives me a grunt. He grunted the same way last week at an old White woman. She walked past as we stomped towards the train station and he burped loudly. The old woman didn't say anything at first, just kept walking until she reached the corner of the street, then she turned and screamed back at him, 'Fuck you, you fucken darky!'

Finally, while the Boys of Punchbowl gather outside their classrooms, Isa Musa stops in the middle of the corridor and hisses at me, 'Chicks are the only thing that stuff you up, man.' He sounds devastated, like he just got called a nigger. How can he possibly think that it's *my* attitude towards chicks that is stuffed up? I'm not the one who treats girls like pieces of uncovered meat. Maybe that's the problem; maybe I don't treat girls like meat.

'Fuck you all, grass-cutter cunts!' I shout. 'You all know Osama got a head job off Nada and none of you told me.' I say it loud enough for every Leb in the corridor to hear but none of them reacts. No one turns around to watch, no one starts calling Isa Musa a hypocrite, or a fucken darky. They have better things to do, like draw dicks on the wall while they wait to be let into the classrooms. I anticipate Isa Musa's response. I expect him to look shocked and rock-jobbed and embarrassed – caught out as the real backstabber because he didn't know that I knew the truth about Osama Al-Hussein.

'Nah-ah, this gronk!' Isa laughs. 'How do you know that?' Then he and Mahmoud Mahmoud are grinning at me, not angry anymore, but nor are they remorseful like I had imagined they would be. Their reaction makes me so limp. I can't win – when I'm dogging them they say I'm stuffed, but when they're dogging me they laugh it off. 'I just wonna know why yous didn't tell me?' I say. I try to sound angry and masculine but instead the words come out of me like I'm a squealing warthog.

The Black Palestinian raises his eyebrows, then takes in a deep sigh, as though what he has to tell me is common sense. 'Simple,' he says. 'You look after her, and Osama gets head jobs whenever he wants.'

All throughout History class, and still to this day, I have asked myself how the Lebs spoke to me of Muslim brotherhood while they betrayed me like the Babylonians.

———

At seventeen I played out each of my days like a chivalrous poet. When the sun descends from the centre of the sky and I tilt my beret to the left I know that my skin will glow golden like my ancestors' and that Banika will see something unique. I keep my head slanted and my eyes out over the clifftop, remembering the very old man with enormous wings who disappeared on the horizon. I can feel my heart beating loudly and I count the blows as I take slow breaths in and slower breaths out. Banika sits between my legs with her chubby bum pressed flat on the rock and the back of her head resting against my chest. She's in a checked miniskirt and her thighs are tight and burned like fried chicken. The flared denim at the bottom of my feet is pancaked across the rock. 'Why do you wear those?' asks Banika, and I tell her, 'Because they keep my shoes clean.'

I peer along the left side of her neck and her shoulder. To me her skin is beautiful, like recycled paper, white with tiny brown freckles as though recomposed and made new again. 'Did you like Kahlil Gibran?' I ask. 'The poems I sent you?'

'Yeah, they were cute,' Banika replies.

'Did you read them?' I ask.

'No, but my friend did.'

She says it so casually, as though her friend can earn my affection on her behalf. Then again, maybe I've earned Banika's affection on her friend's behalf. That's what I wanted, wasn't it – for her friends to be jealous? Isn't that what a girl wants – to be the envy of every other girl?

Banika starts to readjust, wriggling her bum and pressing further up against my crotch and chest so that my head falls onto her shoulder and all of a sudden I'm staring down through her singlet – down at her left breast and bright pink nipple. Before I can process this sight, Banika pulls forward and turns to face me. Her light-red eyebrows rise and she says, 'So, you gonna get onto me already?' She gives me a smile that glows like something sexy and innocent at the same time, with all her teeth exposed and her piglet nose twitching.

'Yeah, okay,' I say and sit up on my knees, my heart starting to pound again, and I fall so far into her dim blue eyes that all I see is their black centres, and now they are no different from mine. Beyond those eyes is a cliff and beyond that cliff is the ocean and above that ocean is the blood-draped afternoon sky of Watsons Bay. She starts to pull in towards me and her wrinkled lips pout as they get closer to mine, and for a moment I think that this is it, this will be my first kiss. Then it hits me like a needle in the eye of a camel – the longer I can make Banika wait, the more she will love me. *Oh, how long I waited for a sign from Mrs Leila Haimi, and every day I found myself rising higher and higher above the walls and cameras and barbed-wire fences of Punchbowl Boys High School.* I tip my jaw up and press my lips against Banika's forehead, holding onto the kiss while I wrap my hands through her thin red hair and around her neck. I press my forehead against hers and, drawing inspiration from the Arab poet Kahlil Gibran, I say, 'Love grinds you to whiteness.' Banika's left cheekbone, which I see from the corner of my eye and which is tight and high and shines like a polished pebble, recoils. I close my eyes and try to breathe in her breath. She smells of milk and honey and old cigarettes. I count my heartbeats and I try to find hers and then I whisper into her right ear, 'Let there be spaces in your togetherness, and let the winds of heaven dance between us.' Banika pulls back from me and replies, 'Hey, shit, isn't this the place where people kill themselves?'

Three days after my date with Banika I turn left from Bankstown train station for the first time and walk through the Old Town Plaza instead of turning right towards the shopping centre and the cinema. I walk across the footpath of stone tiles, past a garden in the centre of the plaza that has a small tree growing from a patch of grass. There are hijabs with strollers and *sha-ab riz*, rice people, wheeling boxes of fruit. Hundreds of kids who are coloured and spread like Skittles disperse from the school buses in front of the Arab Bank, heading straight for the other side of the station. At the end of the plaza is a row of shops, a Commonwealth Bank and a Vinnies and a store called Modest Girl that sells outfits for Muslim women. Then, between a chemist and a two-dollar shop, is an unassuming glass door that looks like it leads up to a brothel.

Beyond the glass door is a series of yellow stairs that creak after each step, and then I am on an orange carpet that must have been made from rabbit fur. There is a door to the right that says 'Bankstown Theatre Company' and a door to the left that says 'Bankstown Multicultural Arts'. Between these two organisations is a long corridor that leads to another door, which says 'Rehearsal Studio', and beside it is a black arrow pointing right that says in capitals underneath, 'TOILETS'.

Behind the door to Bankstown Multicultural Arts works a man named Mr Guy Law, who visited Punchbowl Boys two years earlier and invited us to write for a new magazine called *Thug Life*. He is an Aussie with a long nose like a Muslim, and two years ago I could tell by the way he spoke and the way his skin glowed that he wasn't poor, even though he was dressed in bland, baggy clothing. I remember thinking that this is the type of man who doesn't divide the world into sluts and virgins; a man like the Aussies on *Home and Away* and *Neighbours* – morally superior to the Lebs.

I knock on Mr Guy Law's door, expecting to see him appear before me, but instead a skinny Lebo in a pink shirt opens it. The Leb doesn't say anything at first, just looks me up and down, and then smiles, revealing a series of fine spaces between each of his off-white teeth in his big head.

'Um, I'm here to see Mr Guy Law,' my voice cracks. I suddenly realise that I'm nervous. In fact, I've been nervous since I started to make my way up the stairs.

'Mr Guy Law?' the Lebo scoffs. 'Well, ooh-la-di-dah, Mr French Man.'

First I raise my eyebrows at him, unsure of what he's talking about, and then suddenly it occurs to me that he probably only ever addresses Mr Guy Law as 'Guy'. 'It's respect,' I explain, 'like "Mr Elijah Muhammad".'

'Okay, Malcolm X,' the Lebo responds, smirking. 'Mr Guy Law is wandering the orient with his chopsticks and self-hating Vietna-wife.' I've never heard a Leb speak like this before. I can't tell if he's serious or making fun of me. There's another moment of silence that lingers between us until he starts to realise my bewilderment. 'Guy is on holidays. I can help you.'

The Lebo lets me in and tells me to take a seat. Then he slips through an open door in the other corner of the room. Based on the length of the stairs, I'm guessing this is the entrance to a long and narrow office. I sit on the couch closest to me, the one that looks like it's made of dust. I can't tell if it is pink turning brown or if it is brown turning pink, and I sink right into the old cushion. There are other options but my nerves prevent me from being fussy. I face a blue sofa and a striped lounge. Mr Guy Law must have found these couches at a tip or out on the street or maybe they were in his house before his kids demanded new furniture. The walls in the room are painted light pink from at least twenty years ago and there are scratches and blemishes in the fibro lining from corner to corner. There are also posters and laser-jet printouts sticky-taped to the walls in no particular order or fashion. I find myself staring at one sheet of paper that has the name 'Cormac McCarthy' up top and an extract underneath, the first line stating, 'Nobody wants to be here and nobody wants to leave.' I'm pretty sure that these are words from *The Road*, though I'd only started reading that book because I thought it would impress Mrs Leila Haimi; when she found out she said to stop immediately and read *The Autobiography of Malcolm X* instead, which I did without question. I learned that Malcolm had red hair because his mother was fair-skinned, and his mother was fair-skinned because a White man had raped his grandmother. I wondered if this was Mrs Haimi's way of telling me that she was only fair-skinned on the outside, that inside, she was actually an Arab just like me.

The McCarthy extract is slapped sideways on the wall. I don't understand what kind of person cares enough about literature to pin it to a wall but does not care that the words are crooked. This person, who I later learned was none other than Mr Guy Law himself, seemed to live between the Lebs, who did not want literature to be here, and me, who did not want literature to leave. Mr Guy Law both valued literature and took it for granted.

Beneath the McCarthy extract is a bookshelf made from woodchip with piles of magazines and VHS and cassette tapes inside. No one else I know has VHS and cassette tapes anymore. I even notice some books on the shelf but their dust covers are missing and they're made from those old woven hardcover boards that have no text on them.

I adjust myself in the sofa and the orange floor creaks beneath my feet. The carpet is discoloured and chaffed into patches of loose and faded fabric, like citrus fairy floss; it looks as though it's hardly ever vacuumed and has never been steam-cleaned. I don't think the Aussies who run this building would consider it to be dirty or messy, though – they probably consider it to be a place of freedom. This was a fundamental difference to me between Aussies and Arabs back when I was a teenager: Aussies were obsessed with freedom whereas Arabs would rather be slaves to a clean house than free to live in a dirty one. My mother instilled the act of cleanliness in me as far back as I remember. She became obsessed with cleaning the bathroom in a desperate attempt to stay ahead of the two dozen relatives living in our house in Alexandria, including my father, grandmother, five siblings, three uncles, two aunts and seven cousins. My mother would barge into the bathroom while I was sitting on the toilet. 'Pooooooh,' she would gasp as I began to scream at her to get out.

'*Kib mai, kib mai*,' she would say, 'Throw water, throw water.' Then she would flush the toilet while I was still on the seat and the cold water would splash my arse. I would have to wipe myself in front of her as she scrubbed the toilet floor and the bathtub and the basin and the toilet before the next person came in. Later, when I asked my father why Mum was so crazy about cleaning the house, he frowned at me and said in his deep, reverberating voice, '*Al-nadaafy min al-imaan,*' which, in my limited capacity to translate Arabic, meant 'Clean is holy.'

The Lebo in the pink shirt steps out from Mr Guy Law's office and sits on the blue sofa in front of me. He crosses one leg over the other, like a woman. I'm not used to people looking at me this way, with their eyes set on mine as though every movement I make has a meaning, like the way the school psychologist once looked at me. The Lebo's eyes are dark brown and he has bushy black eyebrows and straight black hair. His skin is as fair as Banika's, only without the freckles and pasty little dents. 'So, what is your name?' I ask. I try not to crush my words together; I don't want him to work out I go to Punchbowl Boys.

'Bucky,' he answers.

'I've never met a Lebo named Bucky.'

'I'm not Leb,' he says. 'I'm Greek.'

'I'm not Leb either,' I say. 'I mean, not like the other Lebs.'

Bucky goes back to holding his gaze on me, completely static, and then his huge lips fold out and he starts to laugh. 'What the hell are you talking about?' he scoffs. 'Everything about you is Leb.'

It's like being punched in the face. 'No, I'm not,' I say. 'Look at me – do I say *shu cuz* or anything like that?'

Bucky doesn't respond. Instead he returns to his intense, unflinching gaze. I feel like he's operating on me. Thank God I catch sight of a poster just behind his head that reads 'CONDOMAN'. Beneath the heading is a Black guy in red spandex and on his mouth is a speech bubble that says, 'Don't Be Shame Be Game. Wear Condoms!' I keep my eyes on Condoman until Bucky finally decides to go on. 'Anyway, you know, my real name isn't Bucky,' he says. 'When I was born my mum was exhausted. They asked what name to put on my birth certificate. She said Lambraki. The nurses said to her, "That's Bucky in Australia."' I have no idea how to respond, so I give a little nod like I know what he's talking about. I'm actually still thinking about Condoman. I wonder why he's Black.

'What's your name?' Bucky asks.

'Bani Adam.'

Bucky's thick eyebrows narrow in on me. I can see him going over my name in his head. 'Bani Adam? Bani Adam? Oh, I remember you, you wrote about that older woman you wanted to pork.'

What? Fucken gross! I didn't want to pork anyone – Muslims don't eat pork. 'I think you read the wrong story,' I say bluntly.

'*Read* the wrong story?' he responds, his left eye twitching. 'Sister, I'm the one who published the story. We Wogs do all the work but you're here to give Mr Guy Law the credit, aren't you?'

I get the feeling that Bucky doesn't like his boss and it's making me uncomfortable. Were it not for Mr Guy Law, I would never have heard about the magazine called *Thug*

Life. I bet if it weren't for Mr Guy Law, this guy wouldn't have a job either; he'd be just another Wog outta work. I wonder why Wogs aren't grateful when Aussies help us out. 'I'm here because I need some advice,' I say. 'Do you think Banika sounds like *bedi-neeka*?'

This time Bucky raises his eyebrows instead of lowering them. He seems curious enough for me to go on. I tell him about my girlfriend, about her silver belly ring and her pink sports bras and her checked miniskirts. I tell him about how my friends call her a lowie and tell me to use her for head jobs. I already know what people in youth centres and arts organisations are supposed to say about this stuff because I've seen it on *Beverly Hills 90210*; they're supposed to say, 'That's sexist.' I'm here because I need to hear it – need to be told that I am better than the Boys of Punchbowl and that there is nothing wrong with dating and loving a girl like Banika.

Bucky listens with intensity, as though he were Freud and I were Hamlet. 'Oh, Bani Adam,' he says. 'You're every pop song from the late nineties.' I don't even know what that means. Then he says, 'Look, Bani, I had a boyfriend who was basically a dumb Aussie slut masking himself as a fash hipster, and I thought I could change him, and in the end he dragged me to his level. I saw this *Oprah* episode once where Oprah said that we find people to have relationships with because the part of them we find attractive simultaneously brings out an issue in ourselves that we feel uncomfortable with.' He stops talking and now he stares at me with those thick eyebrows slumping again, waiting for a response, and I sit looking back at him, completely cowed, too mesmerised to look away. His intent when he looks into my eyes strikes a fear in me that is entirely new – I could betray all I know about myself. Bucky is a man and I'm not supposed to be attracted to men. Up until then I had longed to meet a homosexual, to become friends with a homosexual, but only ever to prove to myself that I was more open-minded than all the boys at Punchbowl and all the Muslims on earth. I never thought that I could love a homosexual, or that a homosexual could love me. My search for Mrs Leila Haimi had ended, then and there, and in her place I found myself looking for Bucky, who seemed to know something I did not.

Bucky is still staring at me, waiting patiently for my response to his advice, of which I have absorbed very little. I would like, as a response, to encapsulate all my thoughts in a single question but my mind and my toes go numb. I slowly open my mouth, hoping the right words will come out of their own accord, and I say, 'Are you gay, bro?'

He smiles at me in yet another sincere way, how you might smile at a cub, your eyes wincing and your lips pouting. Finally, I've met a real gay person. Not a poof in black leather tights with his butt-cheeks hanging out, just some guy who casually calls his ex a 'he' instead of a 'she'. I try to sound confident in front of him but what I say next comes out like a cough. 'Can I ask you some questions about being gay?'

Bucky's smile disappears from his fat lips. He uncrosses his legs and tips in towards me, like he's going to slap me or maybe like he's going to kiss me. 'Of course you can,' he says. 'I find your ignorance endearing.'

Saturdays become dogging-it days so I can be with Banika. First I take her to the movies on George Street to watch *A Walk to Remember* and then we cross the road to McDonald's. I know I won't run into any Punchbowl Boys there, only stuck-up Aussies who don't eat Big Macs but buy cappuccinos at the McCafé, and tightarse Asians who buy Happy Meals and thirty-cent cones. Before I bite into my Quarter Pounder I ask Banika what she thought of the movie. She says, 'Landon was a bit of a fag.' I know she's just saying that because she doesn't believe any Leb will ever treat her like Landon treated Jamie, who's played by Mandy Moore. He learns to dance for her and builds her a telescope and he marries her before she dies of leukaemia. He says that his love for her is like the wind – 'I can't see it, but I feel it.'

I pick the burger up in both hands and take my first bite. The bun and the tomato sauce are sweet and the mustard and the pickles and the onions are salty. My mouth is full when I say to Banika, 'This is the shit, babe.' She doesn't respond, just sips from her Diet Coke and locks her eyes up at the lights as though she wants to make it clear to me that she's bored. I wish she understood the power of McDonald's. My dad always says that my mum's food is better, but he was the one who exposed me to the pleasures inside the golden arches. I was six and we still lived in Alexandria. My father owned two stalls at the Grand Bizarre, a trash-and-treasure market in Prestons, and he kept all his stock in a deep concrete warehouse on Mitchell Street, three blocks from our house on Copeland Street. The warehouse was dim and dusty like an ancient Egyptian tomb; it reminded me of the Cave of Wonders where Aladdin found the enchanted lamp, but instead of mounds of gold there were mounds of old shoes and mouldy backpacks and cast-iron stoves. On Friday afternoons my dad would take my brother Bilal and me to the warehouse to load his van for the weekend. This took about three hours and Bilal always remembered to ask what we would get if we did the work. 'I'll take you to Macca's,' my dad would say, 'but only if you sweat.' The problem was that no matter how hard and fast I worked I did not perspire, and it made matters worse that Bilal looked as though he'd been wandering in the desert. Whenever my dad turned his back Bilal would come over and swipe his fingers across my forehead to see if I'd begun to sweat. 'Amid a-uu-nak,' he'd say, which meant, 'Close your eyes.' He would step back about a metre and spit on my face. I'd quickly smear the saliva across my forehead. Then our father would come back and smear his fingers across my forehead too. 'Yes . . .' he reassured me, 'just.'

Banika keeps sipping at her Coke until the straw starts to suck and scrape at the bottom of her cup. Finally her eyes return to me and she says, 'My first boyfriend was a guy named Mohammed Ahmad.' She pulls out her wallet and hands me a student ID, which shows a kid who looks like he could be my twin brother, except he has one eye bigger than the other. His hair is black and curly and razored at the sides. His nose is fat and crooked and red along the edges of his nostrils like he has a cold, and he has bumfluff growing above his top lip.

I sink into my chair while Banika rambles on about this guy. I don't hear a word she says – I just ask myself what is going on in her head, what kind of a gronk does she take me for, when I realise she's asking me a question. 'Know what I mean, jellybean, know what I mean?'

'Why do you have his picture in your wallet?' I ask.

'Oh, um . . . yeah, we're still friends.'

I don't understand how someone with a mouth full of sugar syrup can sound like a dry lemon. There's no way that Mohammed Ahmad is still her friend. There's no way Mohammed Ahmad was ever her friend. I hate it when Aussies tell me they're still friends with their exes, especially when those exes are Lebs. Either Banika's a two-timing liar or she's too dumb to work out this guy is just keeping her on the side for head jobs. Banika wants to marry a Leb, but why doesn't she *know* Lebs by now? Mrs Leila Haimi knew Lebs. I could see by the way her soft little nose twitched and the corners of her lips curved that my advances always flattered her but she never let me get too close. On her final day she didn't hug me goodbye or even shake my hand. I knew why, because I was thinking, *Don't touch me; I'll die if you touch me.* Mrs Leila Haimi just winked at me and whispered, 'A year from now you will have left me where the weeds decay.' Then suddenly I remembered reciting the ending of *Lolita* to her; tears forming around my eyes, I said, 'And what about the rest, Mrs Leila Haimi?'

'Oh, yes,' she said. 'Well, the rest is rust and stardust.' I knew then, as clearly as I know I am to die, that I loved Mrs Leila Haimi more than anything I had ever seen or imagined on earth, or hoped for anywhere else.

I consider taking another bite of my Quarter Pounder but I look down at it sitting there like a lump of mucus and suddenly it occurs to me that I need to be classier than George Street Macca's.

After lunch I take Banika to the top of Centrepoint Tower and we wander around in circles while she rejects phone calls. She steps up against the glass, and her chin fattens as she gazes below. 'Everybody is like a bug,' she says.

I don't climb buildings to look down and say that people are ants and cars are cockroaches and that the monorail is a centipede. I look across Sydney to find the places I come from.

It starts with a yellow-brick house in Alexandria, where my grandmother, my *tayta*, raised her eight children and forty-five grandchildren. The sky is clear and blue but there is a haze that sprawls across the west like a dust storm. Beyond Alexandria I know the Lebs are lurking in the streets of Punchbowl. I bring Banika to places they will never come. From here I can hide and see everything and everyone at the same time. Is that not the power of God – to see all and to be unseen?

We return to Town Hall the following Saturday. Banika's hand is sweaty and warm in mine and I like the way our fingers clamp so naturally together now that we text every couple of hours and talk every night. Our texts are meaningless and the same each day: *miss you babe, miss u 2 babe, I can't wait to see you babe, cant wait 2 c u 2 babe*. Our phone conversations are more specific, though often it is like we are each talking to someone else, each responding to what we *wish* the other had said. Last night after I finished reading *The Old Man and the Sea* I called Banika and said to her, 'If I ever go out to sea I will remember to bring a rock.' Banika gasped loudly and shouted excitedly, '"Rock with Me" is totally my favourite song right now, I love Ashanti!' Then I said, 'Do you know that the Ashanti warriors helped liberate Ghana?' She replied, 'Ashanti is beautiful, don't you think?' And I said, 'Yeah, I think the Ashanti are Muslim.' And she said, 'No, I think she's Christian.'

It is during these conversations that I consider hanging up on Banika, deleting her number and simply pretending she never existed. But then she says to me, 'Hey, if we ever got married, I'd wear a hijab for you,' and I regain my hope. I wouldn't expect her to wear the hijab – my mother and sisters don't even wear the hijab – but if she cares enough to be veiled for me and I care enough that I would not wish such a burden upon her, then perhaps we can lock hands until they begin to sweat as only two lovers would dare.

We cross the road on the intersection between George Street and Bathurst Street, towards the only KFC in Sydney that has Hot and Spicy all year round. My dad still complains that I eat too much takeaway food and every day he reminds me that Mum's food is better, but it's different here. The KFC building is three storeys high and made from stone, not plastic. Its bricks are red, as though they're a hundred years old, and all the windows have arches in them like the arches in my ancestry. I know my mum and dad would approve of me eating here, even though they wouldn't approve of me being with a girl named Banika.

'I have to be at Hurstville by three,' Banika says. 'I'm meeting Melissa.'

I place two hot chips dipped in gravy up against her bottom lip and I want her to slide them into her mouth gently so that I feel her warm saliva on my fingers, but instead she snatches them from me with her little teeth like a chihuahua. She chews with her mouth open and says, 'I'm not saying those guys were innocent, but those girls were the biggest sluts.' The hot chips and gravy clump into a ball of brown mash on her tongue. She swallows and adds, 'Know what I mean, jellybean?'

'You mean you hang out with too many Lebos,' I say to her.

She doesn't respond, just swallows the chips and licks the salt from her bottom lip. She sticks her empty tongue out at me. I wonder if this is her way of saying she wants to put it in my mouth. I find tongue poking to be a vulgar gesture – it makes me think of people eating pig meat and drinking alcohol and smoking cigarettes and lapping up Osama's ejaculation. I can't keep out the thought of Banika with her head over Osama's crotch. Had Osama chosen her and had I chosen her friend, would it simply have turned out that Banika would have given Osama a blow job on the ghost train and I would be sitting here with Melissa still contemplating our first kiss?

'Why are you sticking your tongue at me?' I ask quickly.

'I'm gonna get a tongue ring,' she says.

'What? Why?'

She gives me a smug little smile and raises her eyebrows like she's saying, *Think about it, boy.* Since that Black Spice Girl got a tongue ring there's a head-jobber born every second. The Boys of Punchbowl go out looking for them, these Aussie girls with holes and sterling silver in their mouths. They say, 'Nice tongue ring,' but what they really mean is, 'Do you give head?' Maybe Banika wants a tongue ring simply because she thinks it's sexy, or maybe because she thinks metal will taste good inside her mouth, or maybe because she doesn't think at all, she just acts on impulse and desire. But regardless of her reasons, Lebs will think she got it because she sucks and blows – and she *knows* that's what they will think.

'Imagine it,' Osama said the first time he heard about Scary Spice, his legs open and his hands and fingers spread above his crotch as though he had a girl's head in them. 'A moist little piece of metal on your knob while she licks off your cum.' We were in Year 10 at the time and sitting at the back of the Arabic room, a bootleg of *Basic Instinct* with Arabic subtitles playing on the television while Mr Abdullah drank coffee in the staffroom. 'What's so good about head jobs?' I asked, being the only boy among Osama, Shaky, Mahmoud Mahmoud and Isa Musa who had never had one. 'Wouldn't you just prefer to stick it in her pussy where it belongs?' All four of them looked at me as though I had just slapped my cock in their faces. 'Are you fucking kidding, bro?' spat Shaky. 'You can't root before you're married, you'll go to hell forever!'

It breaks my heart, the thought that a girl as innocent and sweet as Banika believes she needs to pierce her tongue. She is better than that; I know she is better; beneath her freckled skin Leila Haimi is waiting for me. 'Oh Banika,' I say, 'you are my girl, as Vee was Poe's and Bea was Dante's and Lolita was Humbert's, and what little girl would not like to whirl a silver ring inside her mouth?'

While we head for the train station and sit in front of the yellow line, I talk to her about my upcoming exams, for which no classroom at Punchbowl Boys has prepared me. I tell her what I'm planning to do after Year 12, which is to write books, though I haven't really thought about how to get them published. I'll work that out later, or it'll work itself out; Mr Guy Law will appear like Jesus one day and offer me a lucrative book deal. I tell Banika that I'll dedicate my first book to her. 'Would you like that?' I ask.

'Sure,' she says but it sounds sarcastic. Perhaps she shrugs off my offers because she doesn't believe they will ever happen. Maybe she thinks I'm going to turn out like every other Lebo, a builder or a plumber or a mechanic or a manager at my dad's shop or a drug dealer or a backstabber.

'Melissa was really upset that your friend never called her,' she says.

'He was using her for head,' I reply.

Quickly Banika rolls her eyes, as though she doesn't want me to catch her doing it, but I do. Why does it annoy people so much to be told the truth? What does she want me to say? That Osama misses her friend? That his parents simply wouldn't have accepted her?

'I need to call Melissa,' Banika says. 'But fuck, shit, I'm out of credit.' She stands up, her thin fingers caressing the pendant of the Lebanese flag around her neck. Silver diamantes on her white tank top spell 'HANDFUL' across her chest, shimmering against the thick air and dim lighting. Platform 16 is empty of people but it's crowded with the echoes of trains pulling in and out on the various levels.

'Here, use my phone,' I say.

'No, I'll just find a payphone.'

'What, why?' I can't tell if she's serious or if she's simply embarrassed to ask me. 'Just use my phone. I'm your boyfriend, for god's sake.'

My blue screen lights up in Banika's hand as she wanders down the platform and slips under the escalators. The shadow of her wide hips in skin-tight jeans and her narrow shoulders looms across the platform tiles in the shape of a pear, disappearing onto the train tracks so that her neck and head are missing. I sit and wait on an old bench, looking out over the tracks. In front of me is a billboard that has a blonde girl with tanned skin and blue eyes staring at me over a man's bare shoulder. The billboard says, *You could have an STI without knowing it.* These billboards are all over Sydney at the moment. 'What a slut,' the Lebs laugh whenever she stares at us from the platforms of the Bankstown Line.

Banika strays back over and hands me the phone. She remains standing so that her butterfly belly ring and bloated white stomach rest before my nose. Her skin smells like raw sugar, like the memory of sugar. Faint blue eyes narrow down over me and her piglet nostrils flare. I think it's her way of thanking me.

'All good?' I ask softly.

'Yeah, all good,' she replies.

While we sit on the empty train, I initiate our first kiss. I keep my mouth and my eyes closed and I peck at her quickly, and then again. She sighs like she wants more every time I pull back.

'Do you love me?' I ask.

'Yes, I do.'

'Why?' I ask.

'Because you're not like other Lebs.'

She takes my hand in hers and rests it in her lap and we watch as the train pulls us back towards the west, moving past Erskineville and St Peters. Just before we sweep into Sydenham, Banika's eyes shoot open, like she's just realised she's made a horrible mistake. 'Hey, is your phone on private number?' she asks.

'Yes.'

Then Banika gets off the train without any worries. I sit in the lower level of the carriage staring up at her white sneakers on the platform. As soon as the train starts to tug me on to Lakemba and her feet have swept by I take the 8850 from my pocket and go to the last dialled number. I'm praying that the voice on the other end will be Melissa's, and the reason Banika wants my phone to be on private number is because she doesn't trust her head-jobber friends. My heart thuds as the phone rings. Once. *Thud*. Twice. *Thud*.

'Hallow,' answers a voice straight out of Punchbowl, like he's got a mouth full of Double Quarter Pounder with Cheese. My heart stops drumming and sinks into my bladder. I knew, I knew, I already knew, but it's different when I hear his voice. 'Yeah, who's this?' I say, trying to sound like a man, and more than a man, like a Lebo.

'Cassem,' the guy on the other end of the phone says, and then immediately realises he shouldn't have told me his name and he barks, 'Whoa, wait wait wait, who the fuck is thi—'

I've hung up before he finishes his question and I ride on towards Lakemba, telling myself it's all good, it's all good, you already knew, you already knew . . .

———

The next morning my father, while on his way to the fish market, drives me to Campsie library. There must have been a car accident further down Canterbury Road because we have been stuck in traffic and moving slowly since we got on from Willeroo Street, which is in front of the halal Red Rooster. After five minutes of us sitting silently in his van, a 1989 Toyota HiAce that has no radio, my father, staring straight ahead, finally says to me, 'Bani, what's wrong?' I'm surprised by the ease in which he addresses me. I expect him to be more assertive, to speak as he usually does, in a deep and commanding voice that negotiates with no one. His entire face looks carved out of stone like The Thing in

The Fantastic Four. His arms look like stone too, muscles and veins rippling as he tightens his hands over the steering wheel.

'Nothing,' I whisper, staring ahead also, at the number plate of a Nissan Skyline that spells HECTIC. Then my father turns to me with a tired smile and says, 'You're not in love, are ya?' I'm so shocked that straightaway I say, 'No, no, no.' Why would he ask? He wouldn't allow me to be in love, especially with an Aussie like Banika. I'm supposed to wait until I'm at least twenty-one and then I'll have to marry a Muslim Alawite like me. Why can't he just think I'm worried about my HSC exams? Is it so obvious that I have a lowie on my mind? I mean, why does Banika even go out with me? What does she want from me? Why doesn't she dump me? Or why won't she just love me? Me. Just me. I start to wonder how I'm going to explain any of this to my father when suddenly he looks beyond me, his frown bending into a grin, and says, 'Haaahaaa!' He has spotted a woman standing in front of a car yard. She's wearing baggy beige pants and a bright red jumper. Her hair is long and blonde, but not like the women on television; it's dry and dirty like I only ever saw on the lesbians and hippies when we lived in Alexandria. The woman has her fingers through the diamond wires of the car yard's chain-link fence, and standing peacefully before her on the other side is a guard dog, a large rottweiler with shoulders like boulders. I watch her massage the dog's chin, her fingers moving sluggishly back and forth, back and forth, back and forth, back and forth. I see the dog's face sedated and seduced, receiving with no will to resist, as though he is at the mercy of a slow and oily hand job. *'Saahibtou,'* my father says, this time in his deep voice. 'She's befriended him.' Then he goes back to laughing, like a small boy, his goatee flickering and arm muscles flexing as he releases the gearstick and the van starts to move.

'What's funny?' I ask. He is staring straight ahead again, his Arabian nose sticking out above the steering wheel like a wooden spear.

'Woman,' he says. 'Woman is funny.'

At Campsie library old Asians and young Asians are quietly in control. I prefer them to the Lebs because they don't make any noise and I can concentrate. I'm supposed to be revising the Weimar Republic and Nazi Germany for next month's HSC trial examinations. Usually I'll write down each key point I extract from my *Excel* study guide in dot form and then memorise it, but today there's only one note written on the page: *Rust and stardust*. Nothing I read sinks in, and I keep writing: *Rust and stardust. Rust and stardust. Rust and stardust.* Until finally I write, *Hitler had one testicle*, but I might have got that from *Lolita* as well and there's no evidence it's even true.

Only shitbox trains run through Lakemba, jolting and staggering and rattling along the tracks as though they might derail at any second. Osama and I stand at the platform waiting for Shaky to arrive. It's nine-thirty in the morning and the station is clear. All the gronks have made it to school now, the Lebanese Christians who got off at Lakemba heading to Holy Spirit College and the Lebanese Muslims who got on at Lakemba heading to Belmore Boys and Punchbowl Boys and Wiley Park Girls. Osama checks his phone and says to me, 'Shaky's on the train but hey, listen, he only has Samantha.'

This doesn't mean anything to me, but Osama won't skip school unless there's a girl waiting on the other side of the fence for him. 'Oh, shit. Are you spewing?'

'Nah,' Osama says. 'We'll share her.'

Neither Osama nor I have seen Samantha yet. Shaky met her on the chat site called mIRC. He picks up under the name Sexy-Shake. He talks to a girl for half an hour, sends her his picture and then they exchange numbers and meet up a few days later. I'm on mIRC every night too at the moment but I never give out my number. I still feel committed to Banika and I am testing how far I can bend for her. My name on mIRC is Leb-Prince. The girls love it. They write, *can i b ur princess?* I write back, *Sorry, I've got a girlfriend but we can be friends.* They usually log off ten minutes later. I'm pretty certain they log back on under a different name but there's no way I can know for sure.

Shaky isn't on the first train that comes past Lakemba, so Osama and I just have to stand there like dickheads and watch it go by. Two of its doors land right in front of us. They slide apart and a girl in a pink miniskirt and high heels steps out over the gap. She has an orange tan and short blonde hair and is wearing round sunglasses. She cocks her head in our direction but doesn't make eye contact, just looks straight ahead as if Osama and I are not there. When she approaches we step apart and she brushes in between us. I get a whiff of her perfume, which smells like Fanta. Just as she steps away Osama swings his arm and head back towards her and says, 'Ay, come ee'ah.' She keeps walking without even a flinch. Then Osama says to me, 'Fucken slut, bro.'

I laugh but it feels forced and desperate, like I'm hiccupping. I don't even know what makes that girl a slut. Isn't Osama the slut? He's the one who always gives his dick away to strangers – he wanted to give it to that girl just a second ago. How does rejecting us make her a slut? Isn't that supposed to be the opposite of what the Lebs call a slut?

I look to the far end of the platform and see another person get off the train. He steps out in front of the signpost that says 'LAKEMBA' and turns towards us. As he wanders under the train timetable, I realise that it's Bucky, the homosexual from BMA. Bucky is my closet friend – I visit him twice a month at the BMA and update him on all the sexist and homophobic comments the Lebs made that fortnight. He always responds the same way: 'You're a self-hating Wog,' but at least he listens. I feel safe hanging out with Bucky inside the confines of that creaky arts building; however, I would never be seen with him on the streets of Bankstown. I'd be killed if I were caught with a faggot. I told Bucky about this during my last visit: 'Do you know how many of my hard-cunt Lebo friends meet gays in the park to beat them up?' He replied, 'Do you know how many of your hard-cunt Lebo friends I meet at the park to suck their cocks?' I hate how gays claim everyone is gay.

As Bucky walks towards us it hits me that this could be trouble. He will want to talk, and Osama will discover that I'm friends with a poofta. He'll tell everyone at Punchbowl Boys and then I'll be called a poofta too. Bucky spots me standing with Osama. He doesn't change his pace, just keeps walking. He looks like a Leb but he calls himself a Wog. He has a five o'clock shadow coming on and he's wearing tight jeans and a green short-sleeved shirt. One time he told me that in his world he's hot stuff, that White men love Greek cock. 'But aren't Greeks White?' I asked.

I keep silent as he approaches. My heart begins to pound. *What's this fag gonna say?* I play it out in my mind. He will walk up to Osama and introduce himself: *'Greetings, I'm Bani Adam's homosexual friend Lambraki. I love brown dick and I don't believe in God.'* Osama will respond by throwing him onto the train tracks. Then tomorrow after school I'll get thrown onto the tracks too. Even if Bucky doesn't say anything I'm busted; Osama will be able to tell he's a faggot just by the way he's walking.

Bucky steps past and I take in a deep breath. He says, 'Hey, Bani.' I look at him and say, 'Aa-umm ay . . .' I try to think of the least gay thing I can say next but Bucky hasn't stopped to hear it, he just keeps on walking towards the stairs of the station. Then I see Osama staring at me like I'm a freak. 'Who was that faggot?' he says.

The next train pulls in eleven minutes later and Shaky sticks his head out of the third carriage, yelling, '*Shu oh-laa!*' His head almost hits the top of the train door. His hair is spiked and he has shaved the bumfluff that grows down the side of his face and above his top lip.

Osama and I run over to the carriage and sit by the doors. In front of us is a girl that has to be Samantha. We latch onto her like vultures. 'What nasho are ya?' I ask straightaway.

'Assyrian,' she says in a lazy voice. She takes Shaky's hand and sits up, perking her boobs at us from a white V-neck singlet. I try not to look at her cleavage and focus instead on the fine dark hairs above her upper lip. She has a long nose, just like us, and long black eyelashes. I already feel sorry for her. *If only you were smarter,* I think. I stare at her like this for almost a minute and she stares straight back and I know that she feels sorry for me too. She's thinking, *You poor thing, shorter and skinnier than all your friends, you got that big crooked nose and pimples and bumfluff – the only girl you're gonna get is the kind that sucks off your mates.* I'm staring at her as though I want to lick her brown skin and she's saying in her mind, *Not in a million years, you ugly cunt.* I wish she knew that I don't want to lick her brown skin; that I have a girlfriend named Banika, that I love my girlfriend and that she loves me – then maybe Samantha would trust me.

Osama says, 'So, do you like Shaky?'

Samantha brushes back her long brown hair and her black eyes light up. 'Yeah, I do.' Of course she does. Every girl likes Shaky. The Leb girls like him because he looks Aussie. The Aussie girls like him because he looks Leb. Shaky has an Aussie mum with blue eyes and a Lebanese dad with black eyes. His eyes have come out green. Girls examine them on the street in front of seven other Punchbowl Boys and say, 'You, I want you.' Osama and Isa and Mahmoud Mahmoud and Mohammed and Muhammad and Mohamed scoff, 'What a horny slut!' I just wish that the girls weren't as dumb as we are.

Osama smirks at Samantha in a way that makes me feel sick, like he knows her better than she knows herself. He thinks he comes from a line of Semitic prophets; that he's related to Abraham and Ismael and Moses and Jesus and Muhammad and Muhammad's nephew Imam Ali and Imam Ali's son, Imam Hussain. That's why he smirks, because he truly believes he's better than everyone else. Osama grew up on my street in Lakemba, where 'Lebz Rule' was spray-painted on every fence. I remember when we were children playing hide-and-seek on Caitlin Street with the other boys from primary school – his small round face and big round eyes would peer at me from behind parked cars and front-yard fences. He gained leverage over us at fourteen, when puberty sprang and we all became interested in girls. Those of us with actual Arab ancestry lost our baby faces – our button noses, our smooth olive skin, our choir voices. Osama's true origins, perhaps China or Mongolia, ensured that he would remain the only Leb with a gentle voice, hairless brown skin and a nose proportionate to his face. He was the only one who appealed to girls younger than we were, girls who until they were women were afraid of real men but drawn to the dangerous reputation of Lebs. Arrogance spews out of Osama, brought on by both his sense of divine ancestry and his deceitfully innocent face. Yet I remain his friend, perhaps in a desperate search for the sweet boy I knew at ten who went by the name 'Sunny' and hid behind the cars; or perhaps because I secretly envy the confident and physically attractive boy he has become; or because I haven't fully understood yet that friendships can end, and that we are not destined to be friends into adulthood simply because we were friends as children.

Samantha's thin black eyebrows narrow in on Osama as he prepares his next smile. 'Well, if you like Shaky, show us,' he says. He tells her to copy everything he does, and then he puts his hand on my leg. Samantha lets go of Shaky's hand and places it on his kneecap, her brown fingers gently caressing the fabric of his white tracksuit pants. I'm jealous,

I wish there was a girl stroking my kneecaps, but instead I feel the scratch of Osama's fingernails clawing up my thigh and I watch Samantha follow with her hand up Shaky's. Then, just as Osama approaches my groin, I spot Shaky's dick go hard inside his pants and shoot down like a police baton. Samantha raises her eyebrows at me and grabs onto the erect penis and I straightaway grab Osama's hand and say, 'Get off me, ya faggot!' Then the four of us bleed ourselves laughing as we slide past Canterbury station.

Osama talks to Samantha about sex between Hurlstone Park and Erskineville. He asks what's her bra size and does she wear G-strings and how big exactly is a big dick according to her. She answers casually and comfortably, her face deadpan, as though she were simply being asked about her favourite lollies. She gives the impression that she's very experienced, not only that she has had many sexual encounters, but also that she understands how to turn the boys on. She must know that talking so indifferently about sex and sexual objects will excite us. This was a girl who up until then I had known only in literature, openly sexual and salacious and aware of her power over boys and men.

Finally Osama asks, 'So, do you root?'

My phone starts to vibrate in my pocket but I want to hear Samantha's answer, so I ignore it. She's massaging her left arm with her right hand and sitting with one thigh crossed over the other. Her face drops like I've only ever seen once before, like death when I saw it slapped on my grandmother. Samantha's brown pupils begin to expand until they become black holes, and she stares straight at me as she says, 'Yeah, I was raped.'

My phone stops vibrating. At first there is nothing but the sound of the train slicing along the tracks, then for the first time in my life I hear the deep voice of Tupac calling to me from beyond the grave: *They got you staring at the western suburbs through your rear-view, my little sand nigga. Go on, Bani, scream to God – He can hear you.*

I lock onto Osama and Shaky, and they lock onto me, and onto one another, a triangle of thorns. I hear the thoughts transmitting through their gaze, telling me that this isn't the girl from the plays we learn at school; this is the girl from the news, the girl who sends us to prison. I can tell that Shaky is asking himself whether Samantha's comment makes her harder or easier to get on to, and Osama is asking himself whether Samantha's comment makes her easier or harder to share. I'm thinking we need to get the hell out of here. Why would a girl who was raped go out with three Lebos she doesn't know? And why would she tell them she was raped? Does she want to scare us, or impress us with her ability to speak the unspoken so casually? What does she want from us? Bucky the homosexual comes to mind and I wonder what he would do, or at least what he would tell me *I* should do. I listen to the train against the tracks and to Osama's loud breathing and I hear the words over and over in my head. *I was raped. I was raped. I was raped.* Suddenly Shaky springs up, his head and chest cocked like he's Kyle Sandilands at 2Day FM. 'So, Samantha, is that the only experience you've had?' Then it goes silent and awkward again until Osama finally says, 'I think we need to cut this segment.'

———————

From the dark tunnels at St James erupts the overwhelming light of Circular Quay. The Harbour Bridge is looming over us like the bow, and the sails of the Opera House like the arrows of God. Emily Dickinson is saying to me that this is all us Lebs will ever know of heaven and all we will ever need of hell, as my phone vibrates for the fourth time. I separate from the boys and move into the lower carriage of the train with the 8850 to my ear. The carriage is empty and smells of piss. 'What's up, Banika?'

She makes some breathy grunts and says, 'I miss you soooo much.'

'What's happened?' I ask. One of those sand monkeys has done something to her for sure – maybe the guy she met up with the other day, Cassem, or maybe her ex-boyfriend, the guy she keeps a picture of in her wallet, Mohammed Ahmad.

'Nothing,' she responds. 'I just wonna see you.'

She speaks more sweetly than I've ever heard her speak before – like how I always thought a girlfriend is supposed to sound. And though I find it annoying and fake, I'm also flattered. Maybe this means she actually sees herself as my girlfriend. I stare up at a drawing of a red penis on the ceiling of the train. I am in paradise. A paradise whose skies are the colour of hell flames, but still a paradise. 'I can't this week,' I say. 'Gotta keep studying for trials.' This is of no value to Banika. I can't even get her to care about prophets and old men with enormous wings. She says she's dropping out next year to become a hairdresser. At least then she can pay for her own Zinger burgers.

Banika starts to sob. 'Baby, but I just miss you so much. Please jig school, yeah, baby?'

No one has ever called me baby before. I like how desperate it sounds. 'Okay, I'll come to you tomorrow,' I say.

Next stop, Town Hall.

Osama, Shaky, Samantha and I stand at the lights across from the George Street KFC. The orange bricks and arched windows are calling to me like reverberations in a Hamada but I know I won't be going in there today. Shaky takes his girls to Hungry Jack's.

When the lights change and cars squirm up against each other and a hundred people start to move over the crossing, Osama and Shaky step forward. Samantha is standing still and I turn to find her staring at my feet – where the flared denim spreads over my Air Maxes like the base of a cedar tree. She realises that I've caught her looking and casually starts to walk behind the boys, who have gone straight past the only Hot and Spicy KFC in Sydney. Samantha and I follow slowly, slipping between White professionals and Chinese tourists and Indian curry-munchers, and I can sense her fixation on the back of Shaky's head. I know she's aroused by his tall, solid stature, by his dirty blond hair and broad shoulders and tight waist. I quickly point to the KFC and say, 'You should ask Shaky to bring you here.' A skinny Chinese guy moves through us and then when we're reunited Samantha is smiling at me like a smartarse and says, 'Hot and Spicy, yeah.'

We're standing inside George Street Cinema and I'm too shocked by Samantha's remark to play any part in deciding what to watch. How did she know about the KFC? It sucks that she's with Shaky. I hate how girls pretend they don't care about looks. If she were smarter we could go to KFC together.

Osama, Shaky and Samantha stand a few metres in front of me discussing which film they should watch. I see them point and examine times and titles. They make me purchase a ticket to the original *American Pie* movie, which has been re-released in cinemas to promote the upcoming release of *American Pie 3*. I've already seen the original *American Pie* once before, back when I was in Year 9. It wasn't at the cinema, though; it was during Arabic class while Mr Abdullah sat in the staffroom drinking non-alcoholic beer he special-ordered from Saudi Arabia. The sound of the movie was muffled and the picture was blurry and shaking and you could see the black tops of two peoples' heads at the bottom corner of the screen. Bader Morris got the copy from Lebanon. The boys howled like dogs and screamed 'Yaa aeeer', which means 'Oh, my dick', when Nadia flopped out her tits. I didn't, though. Nadia looked different from all the other girls in *American Pie* – her skin was dark olive and her eyes were dark brown and her nose looked like it had been imported from Egypt. I would swear she was a Leb were it not for the fact that Lebs don't take off their clothes in movies. I tried my best to concentrate on the story but there was so much groaning from the boys the whole way through that I only absorbed the film in snippets. I remember white faces and a sock on a cock. I remember a pact that the boys made to lose their virginity by the end of the year and I remember an intellectually disabled girl say that one time, at band camp, she stuck a flute up her pussy. I'd prefer to watch *X-Men 2* or *The Matrix Reloaded* and I'm starting to think that Samantha feels the same way. The problem is that Osama and Shaky aren't likely to get head jobs in films with superheroes and chosen ones.

We sit along the last row of seats, and because it's the middle of the day there's hardly anyone else in the cinema. There are a couple of heads down the front that move like they must be teenagers, and then one big head on its own in the middle. In the far right corner are two heads that probably belong to a couple in their eighties because their hair is short and grey. I sit next to Osama. Osama sits next to Samantha. Samantha sits next to Shaky. On the screen are trailers promoting adamantium claws and a bullet-time brawl, and then the lights go out. The film starts with a teenage boy who has the heavy nose and dark eyes of a Lebo and the fair skin of an Aussie masturbating while watching a scrambled porno channel. Then his mother and father walk into the bedroom and catch him with a sock over his erect penis. 'This guy's a *Yahūdi*, bro,' Osama says out loud.

I turn to shush Osama and instead I find myself looking past him at Samantha and Shaky. They've started making out. I see the back of Samantha's head like a shadow bouncing off the movie light and Shaky's dark-white face slipping from side to side as he slides against her. Osama gives me a little nudge with his leg. 'Keep your eyes on the screen, bro.' I turn and watch the film. Four boys are standing outside a cafe and the *Yahūdi* asks, 'What does third base feel like?' The jock smiles like a horse with a hard-on and holds out two fingers. 'Like warm apple pie,' he answers, bobbing his head.

I feel Osama's body move away from me. He's slid up to Samantha and is whispering something into her ear. Shaky doesn't seem to give a shit, just staring ahead watching the movie now. I hear Osama's whispers only as coarse breaths into Samantha's ear lobes. She starts to giggle as she stares ahead too. Her teeth are straight and white and they light up when her lips spread. I turn back to the screen. The *Yahūdi* is lying on a kitchen bench with his pants down.

His fetta-arse clenches as he thrusts his dick into an apple pie his mother baked. '*Tfeeeee!*' gasps Osama, which means 'gross' in Arabic.

The man with grey hair in the corner of the cinema turns up towards us, revealing an oval-shaped face. He wears large square glasses and has a nose like a piece of cauliflower. 'Keep it down up there!' he shouts. His voice is deep and arrogant like Bob Carr's, who recently said, 'Obey the law in Australia or ship out of Australia,' referring to us.

In a tight nasal accent Shaky yells back, 'Fuck off, mate.' Then the cinema goes dead silent and *American Pie* unravels. Onscreen, Stifler, who has the familiar energy of Punchbowl, drinks a cup of cum-spiked beer and runs for the toilet bowl. An Asian guy obsesses over a picture of Stifler's mum and screams, 'MILF! MILF! MILF! MILF!' Kevin walks down the stairs saying, 'Enough of this blow-job bullshit, I gotta get laid already.' His girlfriend Vicky hears him and storms out of the party.

Once again Nadia flops out her tits. I see her now as I could not have seen her in the Arabic classroom: clear and colossal, her breasts hanging down the screen like two ancient domes. A web camera has been set up so that the boys from her school can perve while she stares at her tanned and topless figure in the mirror, and it feels as though it's my female self in the reflection, as though I'm peeping on my sister. Nadia lies on the bed and then slides her olive fingers down her white panties and she starts to massage her groin. The boys on the screen are howling in front of their computers but the boys in the cinema are just watching quietly this time. Osama's eyes are glued to the screen. *'Yaa aeeer,'* he mumbles. 'Fingerin' herself, bro.' I bet on a cab ride home that he's as hard as a rock right now. I wonder how Samantha feels being between two erect Lebos. I don't think Brad Pitt with his dick flopped out on the screen would have the same effect on her that Nadia is supposed to have on us, but maybe I'm wrong. Maybe Samantha understands.

The *Yahūdi* lies on his bed before Nadia. She pulls down her white undies and says, 'Shaved is the expression?' She's supposed to be a foreign exchange student from Eastern Europe but her English reminds me more of the relatives who visit us from Syria. Her fingers stroke at the *Yahūdi's* thigh until he gasps and drops open his mouth and his eyes roll back and he's cumming in his shorts, and then Shaky and Samantha stand up. They move down towards the green exit light at the bottom of the cinema.

'What's going on?' I ask Osama.

'Nothing,' he says. 'They'll be back soon.'

Shaky and Samantha take each other's hand as they open the exit door. Light spews into the cinema and then they slip out, the door claps shut and the cinema goes dark again. As soon as they've disappeared Osama whispers into my ear, 'You think it'll be okay if I get onto her after Shaky?'

'No,' I say, staring straight ahead. In the movie Vicky is asking her friend if sex hurts. I think that even if Samantha lets Osama get onto her it's still not all right. She told us she was raped. We've seen the story. Samantha ends up on *60 Minutes* and we end up with fifty-five years. I wonder if painful sex has anything to do with the size of the guy's dick. I bet Vicky's boyfriend Kevin has a pin dick.

About three minutes after Shaky and Samantha left I feel a shadow quietly float into the cinema from the top of the stairs. Samantha slips in beside Osama again and smiles at us the way in-laws smile on their daughter's wedding day – as new members of the family.

'Hey, where's Shaky?' I ask.

Samantha points up at the entrance to the cinema but she doesn't say anything. In that exact moment my phone vibrates twice in my pocket. I read the text message that says, *bro come up*.

'I'll be back,' I say, leaving Osama and Samantha together. I run out with my phone in my hand. In the lobby of the cinema Shaky is standing like a hyena on its hind legs.

'What happened?' I ask.

'I fucked 'ah, bro!' he hisses at me. 'I came in 'ah. I came in 'ah.'

Before I can say another word Shaky spins around and bolts out of the cinema lobby. *Oh Allah, what has happened? Did Shaky really just lose his virginity? He's the one who said you burn in hell forever if you have sex before you're married. Where is he going? Why is he leaving?* I'm about to chase him when my phone rings. Shaky is running and the phone is buzzing and Shaky is disappearing and Banika's name is flashing. I hesitate for so long the phone stops ringing and I've missed the call. Then, a moment later, while I'm still standing there in the dark wondering what to do, the phone rings again and this time I answer. 'What's up?'

'Yeah, look,' Banika says casually, 'earlier today my mum was kissing my neck and I got this thing that looks like a hickey, so yeah, just wanted to let you know in case you notice it tomorrow.'

I take the phone from my ear and hold it out in front of me. I try to imagine what Banika looks like right now. I see her red hair and pale face and her freckles, her pendant of the Lebanese flag resting on her chest, her white tank tops and white stomach and silver belly ring, her white miniskirts and her white Nikes. I hear her on the other end of the phone squawking, 'Hello, hello, are you still there?' I want to repeat the only intelligent thing I've ever said to her, *You spend too much time with Lebs*, but instead my thumb slides across the keypad and I hang up. My thighs go numb and my knees start to buckle as I limp in the dim light of the lobby. Is it possible Banika's telling the truth? I mean, how long does it take to give someone a hickey, anyway? Her mum would have had to be sucking on her neck for a good five minutes, right? That's even weirder than if she'd cheated on me. Maybe a hickey just takes a few seconds to form on the skin of a very white girl. Maybe it's just an Aussie thing. A White thing! A Jerry Springer thing! Or am I just the dumbest cunt in Bankstown? I know what Osama is going to say; he's going to say he told me so. *Why, Banika? Why am I not enough for you?*

I wander back inside the cinema, which now feels like a tomb. I sit next to Osama. I wish I could squeeze in between him and Samantha so I can talk to her, but there's no way Osama is going to let that happen. He's already leaning in on her. 'Ay, bro,' I whisper to him and he ignores me. I kick his leg.

'What?' he hisses, twisting his torso so that his head faces me but his groin faces Samantha. Osama breathes loudly as he waits for me to speak but there's no way to tell him what's happened without Samantha hearing it too. I let out a deep sigh and look to the movie at the same time that Osama rolls his eyes back onto Samantha. On the screen Vicky tells Kevin she wants to hear the words; Kevin pauses so that his face looks sincere, and then in a contrived tone of voice he says, 'I love you.'

I pull out my phone and type: *Shaky ran away.* I give Osama another kick and this time when he turns I have the message shining blue in his eyes. His round face and thin shoulders suddenly compress. Again we find ourselves staring at each other, breathing loudly without words. Suddenly Samantha puts her head forward and says with a little smile, 'What's going on?' She asks so innocently, so unaware. She peers at me, waiting for an explanation, and Osama is sitting there as hard as his cock and I know that I'm the one who has to tell her. I say to myself, *Rust and stardust*, and then I say to Samantha, 'Shaky went home.'

I expect her to explode into screams of *What the fuck!* but instead, as light reflects off the cinema screen, her mouth shrivels like foreskin. She pulls back from Osama and stares at the film. I search for something to say, maybe some advice Bucky gave me back at the BMA, or maybe a quote from a poem on love by Kahlil Gibran. On the screen, Kevin is lying on top of Vicky. 'Go slow,' she whispers, and then her mouth is open like a clown's. She's gaping up at Kevin with her eyes half-closed and her cheeks are darkened by the shadow of his head. 'You okay?' he asks as he begins to thrust into her.

Osama whispers into my ear, 'What should we do?'

I ignore him and say to Samantha, 'Are you okay?'

She keeps her eyes on the screen and mumbles, 'Whatever.'

Osama takes in a deep breath and then he says to her, 'Hey, would you mind if I got onto you?'

Samantha just keeps staring at the screen. Again she says, 'Whatever.'

I have waited long enough. I grab Osama by the shoulder and pull him back. 'I think we should go, man.' Osama nods at me, as though his dick has finally lost its lead. 'Hey, Samantha,' I say. 'We're gonna leave, yeah.' She refuses to look at me, just keeps her big brown eyes on *American Pie*. 'Okay, I think we're gonna go,' I say one more time.

Osama and I find Shaky on Platform 22 at Central station. He's standing on the yellow line in front of a Coca-Cola vending machine, and I examine him closely. I want to know if losing your virginity transforms you, if it really does mean you lose your innocence. Just half an hour ago I saw him running for his life – his nuts empty of their cum and his head full of regret and sin. Now he looks calm and relaxed, standing casually with his arms dangling loosely from his broad shoulders, with the cool deadpan expression of a Backstreet Boy nestled on his buttered face. His gaze is on me, and yet it seems distant, like he's looking inside me, into a version of himself that he once was.

The first thing Shaky does when we reach him is pull out his phone and read back the last text message he received. 'How could you use me like that? Fuck you.' Then he brings together two fingers and puts them in my face, and he says to me, 'Warm apple pie, cuz.'

———————

We sneak back into school at 1pm to mark our names off the roll. On the corner of Kelly Street, where the oval meets the train line, the barbed wire of the school fence has been cut and all the boys use this as an entry and exit point for jigging. Last week boys from our year, Ali and Jihad and Bassam and Abdul, were standing along this fence, trembling the wires and telling Ten News that our school was a prison. 'Jail, bro, jail,' they said. It's easy to get over the fence without being caught. We're disguised behind the students playing football and there are no teachers or surveillance cameras that can see us on the far end of the oval. Shaky scurries up first. He's tall and solid and gets to the top in two upward steps. Osama is waiting for him to jump down as he says to me, 'Bro, would you root Stifler's mum?'

Before I can even think to answer he has gripped onto the fence and is climbing. I try not to look up at his baby-arse while I consider the question. Stifler's mum is monstrous to me; I imagine suffocating beneath her enormous breasts. I'm not surprised that she is the mother every boy would like to fuck. I am the only Punchbowl Boy who has heard of a man named Freud. I already know we all secretly want to fuck our own mother. Maybe that's why I longed for Mrs Leila Haimi, because she was the mother that I would like to fuck. Once I sat beside her when she was on playground duty, staring out at the boys on the oval playing touch football while I stared down at the pink flowers on her skin-tight trousers. She hummed the tune to 'Drops of Jupiter' by Train and my entire body throbbed as I resisted lowering my head onto her god-like thighs to lie in her lap forever. Oh, to have her sing to me while she rolled her naked fingers through my curls.

I step up to the fence. The tips of my Nikes slide into the gaps. The thin metal wire digs straight lines into my palms and fingers. When I get to the top I squat and hold on to the cross-bar. All at once I pounce off and my shins sting on impact with the dry dirt. *Tell me, Mrs Leila Haimi, do you miss me while you are looking for yourself out there in The Hills?*

I follow Osama and Shaky through the bushes against the school fence and onto the oval. There are only twenty-five boys in Year 12 – because fifteen dropped out in Year 10 – and all of them are out there today playing football. I watch five of the boys pile on top of Bassam, the Alawite who usually wears glasses. They're trying to bring him down, two at his legs, two up on his shoulders and one with his head up his arse. It looks as though Bassam is running under water, the boys holding him back as he pushes forward on his large thighs until he finally goes down. I think of what Bucky would say if he saw this right now. *Nothing gay about twenty guys sticking their heads up each other's butts.*

We approach a boy named Abdul, who is standing by the sidelines. He is tiny and transparent and looks as break-able as a china doll but no one messes with him because his older brother is a dealer. Once, while we both waited along the yellow line for a train at Punchbowl, he walked up to me without a greeting and said, 'Cuz, why is it that when an Aussie rapes a girl he gets seven years but when a Leb rapes a girl he gets fifty years?'

'Yeah, why?' I asked.

'The Jews, cuz.' Then he put his index finger to his temple. 'Think about it . . .'

There's a purple welt throbbing under Abdul's left eye. It looks like he's been kicked in the head. As he spots us walking towards him his right eye spreads open in a way that tells me to keep my mouth shut about it. His gaze sits directly on me, like he's been waiting all day for me to arrive. A numbing feeling runs through my body all over again, up my thighs and loins and stomach and into my chest, sucking the air from my lungs. *Oh Allah, what now?*

Abdul pulls out his phone and holds it up, smiling through sharp little teeth under his fat crooked nose. At first I see what he sticks in my face only as capital letters – B and A and N and I and K and A. I blink and look at the letters again, trying to make sense of what he is showing me. This time I see a word: BANIKA.

'Who's that?' I say, trying to keep calm.

'You know who it is,' he replies, stepping in so close that his breath hits me like a wall of tar and shit. 'She told me she's your girlfriend.'

I try to smile. 'That's not my girlfriend.'

'Eh-he-he-he,' Osama and Shaky both snigger at the same time. 'We told ya, bro, we fucken told ya!'

Abdul hits the dial button on his phone and lets it ring on loudspeaker. His flaccid lips stretch like bubblegum when Banika answers. 'Hey, lowie, what ya doin?' he says in a slick voice.

Banika giggles. 'Nothing,' she says.

'You fingering yourself?'

Banika giggles again. 'No, just lying in my undies with my feet in the air.' Then Abdul hangs up and the bruise under his eye bulges as he tries to wink at me. His skin looks like it's made of sandpaper. I am overcome with visions of Banika rubbing against him until her white flesh has been chafed away. The boys across the oval scream, 'Pass, fucken pass!' Shaky's teeth are bared and saliva thickens around his gums, and Osama has that smug little smile hanging off one corner of his thin lips. He is waiting for the real Bani Adam to appear, but that guy won't show his face on this oval ever again; that guy has been dumped where the weeds decay. Bani Adam takes Abdul's hand, shakes it and says, 'We'll share her.'

WAR ON TERROR

THERE ARE NO QUESTIONS ABOUT TUPAC IN THE HSC. The Punchbowl Boys lose interest half an hour into each exam, stand up and walk out of the school hall. The night after our final examination we celebrate, cruising down the street in a two-door 1990 Celica with pop-up lights. Osama drives, since the car belongs to his cousin and he's just received his P-plates. Isa Musa always gets the passenger seat, because he is too fat to fit anywhere else, and Mahmoud Mahmoud and I are wedged in the back seats.

'No weed, boys,' I say. 'I can't smoke weed.' Smoking *anything* is completely unacceptable to my father, who had started on cigarettes in Lebanon when he was six and quit when he was thirty-six because the doctor told him he'd be dead by forty.

'It's all good, we've got some vodka for this guy,' Osama replies, his head rearing over the steering wheel. He knows that Alawites are not so strict about alcohol, that I would get into serious trouble from my father if I come home stoned but probably not if I come home drunk. Osama knows a lot of things: he's taught me how to roll joints and Drum cigarettes, how to make a bong and how to lick-sip-suck tequila.

We pull over outside the park at Wiley Park. The boys stay in the car and watch me stroll down to a bench with a bottle of vodka. I drink as fast and as hard as I can while they get high in the car. Just the smell of the alcohol makes me dizzy, like being punched inside out, but I have to ignore it; I want to get drunk. I have discovered, over a series of evenings, that getting drunk is the easiest way to be a Punchbowl Boy – to laugh off the last time I heard Banika's sugary voice. I didn't break up with her; I just deleted her number and pretended she never happened. Whenever her number appeared on my phone I ignored it, and whenever a private number appeared I ignored that too, on the chance that it might have been her. I never ran into her, though one time I saw a girl with red hair in a pink tank top at Parra who might have been Banika and I quickly turned into a McDonald's before we passed each other.

I put the rim of the vodka bottle to my mouth again and continue to scull. My lips go numb three-quarters of the way down into the drink. I close my eyes, go for it again. Now I can taste it, pungent and bitter like ear wax. I'm still not drunk. Marijuana fumes escape from the car windows. 'Look at this guy!' Osama screams out. 'Fucken Alawy!' His call rattles me like a left hook to the chin. Is he impressed that my people can consume alcohol in such a way? Is he disgusted? The Celica headlights fling open like giant squid eyes and I catch Osama sneering at me from behind the steering wheel. Isa Musa gazes at me from the passenger seat, eighteen but looks thirty, big fat lips erect. Mahmoud Mahmoud's afro-head is tucked away in the tight rear seats. 'Come on,' he howls, sticking his mug between Osama and Isa. Mahmoud's grumbling voice reminds me of last week: the two of us picked up an Italian chick at Bankstown Square who wanted my number instead of his. 'That's bullshit!' Mahmoud scowled at me in front of her, 'But you're an ugly cunt, your nose is bent.'

I walk over to the car, disappointed. 'I'm not drunk yet.' Isa, stepping out of the two-door hatch and pulling his seat forward, hisses, '*Yullah.*' I climb in beside Mahmoud Mahmoud. Everything shrinks back here, the two rear seats, the side windows, the ceiling a centimetre from our heads, the back dash. The subwoofer is pressed against my head; Isa's seat skidding back until it pushes against my knees. Squashed in the back seat of that car, I can muster only one thought: Alice who drank the potion in the house of the White Rabbit. Alice's words become my words. *I find my head pressing against the ceiling and have to stoop to save my neck from being broken.* And then, *That's quite enough,*

I hope I shan't grow any more. As it is, I can't get out at the door, I do wish I hadn't drunk quite so much!

Osama starts the car and Isa turns on the CD player, and Tupac's voice shoots out from the subwoofer: he fucked a fat motherfucker's bitch. I am staring at the western suburbs through the looking glass, and Osama is staring at me through the rear-view. 'I'll burn in hellfire for drinking,' I say to the boys. 'The Prophet—'

'Ouf,' Osama scoffs. 'This guy. Relax, bro. Forget about the Prophet, you think this is gonna matter when you do hajj and get your sins cleared?' Smoke makes its way through my nose and mouth as the car moves down Canterbury Road, the tar out in front starting to intertwine. 'Ay, it's hot in here, open the window,' I call out. Osama tightens his grip around the steering wheel, presses hard against the accelerator. 'Nah, cops'll smell the weed,' Isa replies, or maybe it was Mahmoud Mahmoud. We floor it down the woven road, the lights along the streets and from the narrow shops becoming beams slipping away from the rear window one by one. Isa turns up the music and Tupac screams that he's gonna hit a nigga up. Then I shout, 'Fucken siiiiiiick!' I feel a great smile swell across my face. 'You know what, you're a fucken good bloke, Osama, you're a good bloke. I never say it, but you're a good bloke, you're always looking after us and driving us around and shit, happy to share bitches and shit, let us smoke in your car and shit, you're a good bloke, man, *wallah* you're a good bloke. Hey, boys, isn't Osama a good bloke, he's a good bloke, ay, he's a good bloke. Osama, you know the Prophet said that intoxicants are forbidden.'

Osama jerks his head. 'This guy. Relax your ball sacks, bro, it's not gonna mean anything when we're older.' Then the car stops – I think. Osama's glare sharpens as his eyes lock on me from the rear-view mirror, red traffic light zapping from beyond his bloated cheeks. 'Forget about the Prophet, we're all going to Mecca one day,' he says.

The smile continues to grow, spreading so that I feel my lips crack open like a sardine tin. I say, 'You know, you're right. You're right, Osama, have I ever told you you're right? I really like it when you're right.' Then Isa Musa tries to open his flaps. 'This guy, when he's—' And I cut him off with, 'Shut the fuck up, Isa! All right, we get it, you're Palestinian, fucken rock thrower, fucken terrorist.'

The boys are silent, Tupac is cussing, the engine is revving and I'm babbling. 'None of you laugh, ay, always putting me on show, always put me in the back seat. If Osama made the same joke Isa would be sucking his dick right now.' Mahmoud Mahmoud chuckles. I go on. 'Mahmoud, bro, cuz, bro, you know what I love about ya? You never put me down, like, all right, you call me an ugly cunt or whatever, but you're not a dog, you know why? Because you dog me to my face. Ay, boys, you know what I reckon we should do? We should get some water, I'm thirsty. Are you guys thirsty? I'm thirsty, and I have to piss, you should pull over, I have to piss.'

That night I discovered that this state of relentless talking had always been brewing inside me, beneath the surface of my chest, and it was the first weapon I had obtained that could penetrate the skin of the Punchbowl Boys. I made no room for attacks against me, my loose and loud tongue drowning out their voices completely, and I could keep going like a porn star on ecstasy.

Smoke continues to pile up inside the car; I can no longer see anyone's face, just the red butts of joints. 'I'm hungry,' Mahmoud Mahmoud groans. My head spins as the car flies and the pockets of air begin to stretch and I feel like I am inside Lakemba Mosque, where emptiness fills the night. 'Hey, man, pull over, I'm getting dizzy,' I mumble, my stomach twisting.

'Ouf,' someone inside the car says, or maybe it shot out from over the yellow arches of McDonald's. 'I got all these girls,' Mahmoud Mahmoud shouts – I can feel him against me but his voice is exploding from the subwoofers. My eyes shut. I pop them open. Shut again. I pop them open. 'Boys!' I drop my head on Mahmoud Mahmoud's shoulder. 'Get off me!' he groans, pummelling my temple with his elbow; I don't think I felt it. My head bounces back the other way, I try to hold it in place. 'Argh!' I gasp, taking in as much air as possible, but suck up smoke instead. The fumes are seeping into my eyes, stinging. My head is against the small window as Osama turns hard, bashing my left temple against the glass, then my right temple falls back

The Lebs

on Mahmoud Mahmoud's shoulder. 'I'm hungry – get off meeh!' He elbows me in the head again, back to centre.

'Oh, Bani, I forgot to tell you,' says Isa Musa. 'I saw Mrs Haimi in Burwood the other day. Guess what? She's pregnant.'

'Miss Haimi's pregnant?' responds Osama. 'Fucken slut!' Then the boys snarl with laughter and Tupac roars with grief that he's gonna make sure all your kids don't grow.

I scream, 'Boys, what would Allah think?'

And Osama sneers, 'This guy. Don't worry, bro, it won't matter when you're older . . .'

I wake up on my parents' doorstep, where they leave me lying before taking off to McDonald's. Dad picks me up and lowers me into my bed. The apple in the window and the plaster designs of plants in the ceiling swirl until finally they come to life. I roll over and vomit across the tiles while my mother and five siblings sleep, or maybe they hear me but pretend to be asleep. My father mops up my bile, his feet swaying from side to side, and over and over he says in Arabic, 'Shame on you.'

———

The next morning I start again – wobbling to the bathroom. I avoid looking into the split mirror above the sink, afraid of what I will see. *'Allah saamehnee,'* I whisper. 'God forgive me.' I whisper because I do not want my father and mother and my siblings to hear my repentance, this is not for them; this is between Bani Adam and Allah. *I promise, Oh Allah, that I will never again drink alcohol or use drugs, that I will never again lose control over my body.* I wash my hands up to my wrists, starting with my right hand even though I am left-handed, three times, making sure that the water has reached between my fingers. *'Al-nadaafy min al-imaan,'* I say, repeating the phrase my father taught me when I was a boy. 'Cleanliness is equal to holiness.' Then I take water with my right hand, put it into my mouth and gurgle thoroughly and spit into the basin three times. I take water with my right hand again, splash it up my nose and blow it out twice. On the third time I use my left hand, which is only acceptable when necessary, to help blow the water out of my right nostril because my sinuses are completely congested. Then I wash my whole face three times, including my right ear to my left ear, and my forehead to the bottom of my extended chin. Suddenly, and without realising it at first, I am in the middle of *wudu*, the ritual of purification before we pray. I wash my right arm thoroughly from wrist to elbow three times and then I repeat with my left arm, before moving the palms of my wet hands lightly over my head, starting from the top of my forehead to the back of my head, and passing both hands over the back of my head to my neck, and then bringing them back to my forehead. With the same water, I rub the grooves and holes of my ringing ears with my index fingers, while also passing my thumbs behind my ears from the bottom upward. Finally, I wash my feet up to my ankles three times, starting with the right foot. I make sure that the water reaches between my toes and covers the rest of my feet, and as I do, remember the first time I washed my feet for *wudu* beside my father, ten years before. I stopped and asked him, 'Isn't it more rational to wash the bottom of our feet than the top?' I expected him to get annoyed with me, to tell me I was being blasphemous and then shrug my question off with a verse from the Qur'an in Arabic. Instead he smiled at me like he was proud, like I had stumbled upon a divine secret. 'Yes,' he said, 'if all we believe in is what we can see, and what we can touch, then it would be more rational to wipe the bottoms of our feet instead of the tops, but faith, Bani, has very little to do with what might seem rational.'

At the end of my *wudu*, while I stand in that small shining bathroom that my mother cleans every three hours, I recite out loud: *'Ash-hadu alla ilaha illAllahu, wa ash-hadu anna Muhammadan abduhu wa rasuluhu,'* – 'I bear witness that there is no god but Allah, and I bear witness that Muhammad is Allah's prophet and messenger.' With each drop of water that runs down my head, my arms, my feet, each drop that goes into my mouth and out through my lips, that is pushed up my nose and blown out of my nostrils, and that trickles through the creases in my ears, I am cleansing my soul, and making it up with God.

After the *wudu*, I go through my 8850 and delete phone numbers, starting with Osama the Indonesian and Isa

Musa the Black Palestinian and Mahmoud Mahmoud and Shaky the half-caste, and then every boy I have known at Punchbowl Boys.

Throughout the summer of 2003, I pretend that the Lebs who shaped me into a young man do not exist, but it is hard to avoid one in particular: Osama lives on the other end of my street in an old housing commission with his parents and nine siblings. The rest of Caitlin Street is home to Lebanese immigrants who first came to Lakemba in the seventies – that's why we call the suburb *Leb-kemba*. The Lebs in my street have knocked down all the post-WWII terraces and built McMansions with stone lions guarding their front doors. I walk past Abu Omar's house and Em Yusuf's house and Abu Hassan's house and Em Ibrahim's house towards Tripoli Bakery – a manoush shop on The Boulevard. The air is hot and dry and Osama's figure appears a hundred metres before me like bumfluff in the breeze. 'Bani fucken Adam, come here!' he shouts out, high voice slicing across Caitlin Street. I turn and start running the other way, heat piercing my skin as his words hit me in the back of the head. *He's hunting me; he wants to make me his bitch again!* I reach the corner of the street, right in front of the double-brick duplex Abu Jamal built for his twin boys, and just as I pivot onto Dunn Street my foot gets caught on a rock. I stack it face-first onto the nature strip beside a yellow Subaru WRX. I'm lying flat across the grass, my hands stinging, and I think: *You rock. You stupid* rock. *I'll murder you, rock. I'll injure a stone. Hospitalize a brick. I'm so mean I make medicine sick.* Then it occurs to me: *Hang on, I know these words.* I was a boy and my father was watching Muhammad Ali on the TV. The Greatest had his back against the ropes as a behemoth named George Foreman pummeled into his ribs. Then Ali threw a sneaky right and another right and a left and a right and a left and a right and, suddenly, Foreman was staring up at him from the canvas. Now I hear Muhammad Ali hovering above me, chanting, 'Bani, bomaye! Bani, bomaye! Bani, bomaye!'

I step into the cold box of the gym and I am hit with the smell of old sweat and worn leather. Shadow boxing inside the blue ring is a short, rock-hard man I later learn is named Leo. He sticks his head over the ropes and gazes down at me like I am a cockroach. 'What do you want?' he asks. He looks like a white bull, with deep sunken eyebrows, a hooked jaw and a flattened nose with flaring nostrils.

'I want to fight,' I respond. I try to sound adamant, like I know exactly what I am getting into, but I am terrified; I know I am talking to the fiercest person I have ever met, a champion carved out of concrete.

'You want to fight?' the boxer responds. 'Don't drink, don't smoke, don't do drugs, don't wank.' Then he spreads open the ropes and lets me into the ring and every day for the next two months he knocks me around. I stand before him, gloves shielding my face and he raises his focus mitts and screams, 'Come close, don't be a pussy, come close!' I step into his chest, my arms up, chin down. He throws a flat right hook with the mitt which breaks through my guard and lands against my jaw, my vision shattering before me like a busted television screen. Leo raises the focus mitt and he calls, 'Left,' and I snap out a left jab. He pulls the mitt back an inch so that I miss by a millisecond and he screams, 'Faster – don't be a bitch.' Then he says, 'Right cross.' I snap out a quick right jab, which lands dead-centre in the mitt, and he grunts, 'Harder – don't be a poof!' Day after day until I can see every punch he throws at me before he throws it and can 'left-right-duck-hook-uppercut' so fast and so hard that he doesn't see the blows that pull his mitts back towards his head; until suddenly I too am carved out of concrete.

My first amateur bout is held at South Sydney Juniors in Maroubra. Leo forces my tightly taped fist deep into a new leather boxing glove and he says, 'Breaking in a glove is like breaking in a vag: you have to pound it until it's covered in blood.' That sounds horrendous to me – when I think about losing my virginity and taking my wife's virginity, I see my wedding night: the two of us wrapped warmly together in white sheets, arms swathed tightly around one another, lips intertwined, bodies swaying gently in candlelight.

Leo is in my corner when I accidently snap my first opponent's nose in two with a clumsy left jab, the crack of cartilage ringing out across the stadium. After the fight, Leo unties the gloves and pulls them from me. He cuts the bandages, releasing my hands, which are covered in blood and trembling. Then he gives me a half-smile, which is the most he's ever given me, and he says, 'Now you know what it's like to pound a pussy.'

The day after the fight I run into Osama on the corner between Haldon Street and The Boulevard, right in front of the African hair salon where I once conked my black curly hair into White straight. Osama's cheeks bulge when his gaze locks onto me. My fists tighten, dry blood along my knuckles ripping open, and I step up into his chest. A drop of sweat runs down the centre of Osama's forehead – he knows there is something different about me, that if he speaks I'll punch a hole through his face. And then he just nods his head and walks on. It's over. I am free. Free at last. *Allahu Akbar,* I am free at last!

———

Beyond the meeting room at Bankstown Multicultural Arts is the office of Mr Guy Law and Bucky. Sometimes both Mr Guy Law and Bucky are inside; sometimes Mr Guy Law has gone overseas and it's just Bucky inside; sometimes Bucky is downstairs having a cigarette and it's just Mr Guy Law inside. Along both ends of the office are papers and posters and little Buddhas pinned to the walls. There is a row of office desks – each a different shape and a different bland colour – across each wall, and on the desks are fat grey computer monitors, even though flat-panel monitors have been out for almost five years now. Every desk has a different kind of office chair pressed up against it, some that are big and made of leather, and some that are thin and plastic like the chairs in schools. Today every chair is empty except for the one in the corner beneath the window that overlooks the Bankstown City Plaza. This is where Mr Guy Law is sitting. I stand in the centre of the office and tell him that I don't know what I'm going to do now that I've finished the HSC.

'University?' he asks while he peers through his Ghandi glasses and out his office window like a sniper.

'I didn't get the grades,' I answer. 'But maybe I can enrol in some kind of pathway next year.'

'Mmmm . . .' Mr Guy Law grumbles, gaze still out of the window. 'Gorgeous. Just gorgeous.'

'What?' I ask.

He swivels in his office chair and gives me his bright blue gape, sunlight from the window illuminating him as he glares upon me. 'Well, I can hook you up with some community arts work if you're interested. Just email me a head shot and biography of yourself.'

I accept this offer without hesitation, seeing it as the first real opportunity in my life to associate with a different race and class of people than Lebs: White writers and actors – artists – who are progressive and civilised like me! I sit at my computer and prepare my email to Mr Guy Law as soon as I arrive home. There are plenty of impressive photographs of me saved on my desktop that I can send to him – in most I was bare-chested and ripped into fifty-three-point-five kilograms of muscle, had my chin down and bandaged fists raised – but my first attempt at a bio reveals that I have few or no achievements worth listing. *Bani Adam has been published in 'Thug Life' and is an amateur boxer with the Belmore PCYC.* I email this to Mr Guy Law and twenty minutes later he sends me a revised version that reads: *Bani Adam is a Lebanese Muslim writer who recently graduated from Punchbowl Boys High School. He has been published in 'Thug Life' and he is a boxer.* I don't like being outed as a Punchbowl Boy, or as Lebanese and Muslim, because I am certain these details will damage my chances of getting work, but Mr Guy Law emails back assuring me that it will help him find something for me and that I'm not supposed to lie about who I am anyway. *But that's not who I was.*

I wait for eleven months, during which I continue to fight once a fortnight at South Sydney Juniors and read all seven novels of Ernest Hemingway – Hemingway seems like a good fit for me at the moment because he too was a boxer and a writer. I wonder if I could have taken Hemingway in a fight. I've seen bare-chested pictures of him where he looks broad and solid and has a stiff white beard like Zeus, but I'd be ten times faster than he was, and that beer gut of his just looked like a heavy-bag waiting to be fist-pumped.

I'm sitting on my bed reading *A Farewell to Arms,* which I borrowed yesterday from Lakemba library. Someone has underlined this quote: *War is not won by victory*. I read the line five times over when suddenly my phone starts ringing, breaking my fixation. On the other end of the call is a man who tells me his name is Joe. His voice is deep and casual like Mel Gibson's. Joe says he got my number from Mr Guy Law and that he is doing a show for the Bankstown Theatre Company, the organisation across the hall from Bankstown Multicultural Arts. He tells me that his show is based on the theme of violence and that he needs a Muslim fella for his research. 'So, you wanna do my creative development?' he says.

'What's a creative development?' I ask.

'How about we meet and I'll tell ya.'

This is how I come to be staring at a woman who looks and dresses and sounds like a man: it turns out that Joe is a chick named Jo. We catch each other in the doorway of the Bankstown Arts Service, yellow stairs that lead up to Bankstown Theatre Company and Bankstown Multicultural Arts erupting before us. Jo stands there with a newspaper rolled up in her left hand – maybe she's left-handed. By her side stands Addison, another woman who looks like a man, with short hair and a defined jaw, though her face is smoother and rounder than Jo's. I feel both women's energy pushing up against mine in a way that makes me uncomfortable, like they want to fight me.

Jo tells me she's bringing together a team of performance artists for three days of drama activities that will help her develop content for her show – that's what she means by 'creative development'. I nod while she continues to speak – something about Arabs and Muslims and men – but I'm only half-listening to what she says. The other half of me is playing over my phone conversation with her in my head, asking myself if I have given any indication that I thought she was a man. *Fuck, did I call her 'bro'?*

Finally, Jo unrolls the newspaper in her left hand and holds up a front-page article with six Lebs in the picture, standing beneath the headline, 'DIAL-A-GUN'. Their fingers are criss-crossed in mourning for the Black rapper who called himself a motherfucker and shouted 'Westside'. Hand signals and jacket collars frame their child-like smiles, and caps cast shadows over their faces, camouflaging their still-black eyes. The word 'Nike' scars their foreheads and 'Fila' scalds their shoulders and 'Adidas' their chests. The pull quote reads, 'Gang says it's easier than buying pizza.' Their eyebrows and eyelashes are those of the sand monkey and their dark-olive skin belongs to the desert snake. I see their flesh, and my flesh, from the outside, like I have become Lawrence of Arabia. 'A little people,' he called us. 'Barbaric and savage.' And the words drum in my head.

Jo waits patiently as I examine the headline. 'You'll be one of these guys,' she says. 'Any questions?'

'Yeah, how much do I get paid?' I ask.

She and Addison both smirk at me. 'Yeah, the money's shit,' Jo says in a casual voice. She sounds so familiar to me, as though she came from a life within a life that I had once lived. She is bobbing her head so that her short blonde hair swings back and forth, and all the while she keeps her eyes on me like a cat watching a pit bull. I am resisting the urge to stare down at her body and the body of her friend to uncover what kind of woman hides behind the baggy jumpers and cotton trousers and steel-capped boots.

'What's funny?' I ask.

Jo frowns at me as though I am the one who is being rude. 'Yeah, it's three hundred a day,' she mutters, again in that casual tone. Suddenly it hits me; *I know where I've heard that voice before*. She sounds like the Aboriginal boys I grew up with in Alexandria, even though she is neither a boy nor an Aboriginal, so far as I can tell. I might be wrong, though. So often I find that my instincts, which seem to come entirely from Punchbowl Boys, are wrong.

Jo gives me three dates for the development and each one of them starts over again like I'm staring at the western suburbs through my rear-view.

———————

The first development date is eleven months, two weeks and one day after I leave Punchbowl Boys High School. I return to the Bankstown Arts Service – yellow wooden stairs at the entrance creaking and cracking like popcorn with each step. To the left is Bankstown Multicultural Arts, where Mr Guy Law and Bucky work, and to the right is the Bankstown Theatre Company, which always has its front door closed and locked. Bucky tells me that the BTC is run by an Aussie man named Mr Daniels, who is like Mr Smithers from *The Simpsons*, and an Aussie woman named Ms Julia, who is like Gertrude Bell, Queen of the Desert. He says their work is to help Aussies like Mr Guy Law help Aussies like Jo help multiculturalism like me.

Even though I am working with the BTC, I sit and wait inside BMA's meeting room, where the carpet is still orange and swirled like bunny fur and the couches are still dusty. The old posters of Condoman and excerpts from Cormac McCarthy haven't been taken down to make space for new posters and so the room looks like the collaged walls of a five-year-old's bedroom. One of the newer posters is of a big-bellied naked yellow man sitting cross-legged. I'm pretty sure it's meant to be the Buddha. Another is a picture of a dozen Black girls in tight rainbow-coloured dresses with their hips accentuated and their smiles wide under a banner that says, 'Miss Africa Bankstown'. The posters are pinned off balance, some with tears and dog-eared corners; some have been there for so long they're starting to fade. The only image that looks as though it has received any love in recent weeks is the one beside the door to the main office. Laminated and mounted straight, it's a front-page article from the local newspaper *The Torch* with the headline, 'Arts

King Celebrates 20 Years'. Beneath the headline is a picture of the BMA director, Mr Guy Law. He isn't wearing his glasses and his nose pulls forward and his chin and forehead pull back so that his profile emerges from the left of the frame like a balding and withering shark. Twenty years is a long time.

I still visit Mr Guy Law's office every couple of weeks. He's hardly ever there but whenever he is he tells me about the changes he had made in his life as a 'White male' – that's what he calls himself. He tells me about the day he met his Vietnamese wife, at a gay rights march in the seventies. He tells me that he converted to Buddhism, and shows me his certificate of conversion. He tells me about his adoption of veganism and about how he learned to wash his bum with water instead of using toilet paper. He says, 'White people pretend to be the most civilised but we smear shit all over our arses.' He describes all the amazing places he visits, like Darwin, where he works with the Aboriginals, and India, where he works with the Untouchables, and Vietnam, where he works with the girls who are in danger of becoming prostitutes. I wonder if he tells them about how he works with the Lebs in Bankstown.

'Stop dreaming,' says Bucky as he takes a seat in front of me. He has a cup of coffee in his hand with brown liquid running down the side. *Typical self-hating sand monkey*, he calls me. Bucky speaks like a scholar but he sounds like a Leb, words coming out of his mouth as though he's been eating them. I know he's smart because he's Greek and gay like an ancient philosopher, and because I never have any idea what he's talking about. One time he said to me, 'I have no problem with incest, with a brother and sister sleeping with each other.'

'That's disgusting,' I said. 'There's a perfectly natural reason why brothers and sisters aren't supposed to root – they'll have retarded children.' Bucky was grinning even before I finished my response. He knew what I was going to say and immediately shot back, 'You're a social Darwinist, afraid of disability because it has no use to *Gwai Lo*.'

Gwai Lo? Originally, I thought that this was Bucky's impersonation of how Mr Guy Law's Vietnamese wife pronounced her husband's name. Seriously, what the hell was Bucky's problem with him? I was too superstitious to ask, fearing that Mr Guy Law's spirit would somehow appear before us if we bitched about him in his space of twenty years, which he had enshrined with Cormac McCarthy and Buddhism and African beauty queens and African condom men.

Bucky puts the coffee cup to his mouth and sculls as though it's a Solo. 'So, what do you want?' he asks.

Just before I answer I hear keys jingle, and there is Jo's shabby bleached head in the doorway. 'Ah, Bani-Bani-Bani,' she sings out. 'Come on.'

'I have to go,' I say to Bucky. 'I'm doing a creative development.' I give him a gentle smile, trying to reveal my excitement in this new stage of my life.

Bucky's thick eyebrows shoot up, as usual. 'You know you're an idiot, right?' He calls me that a lot. I never know what he's talking about.

———

The rehearsal studio at the back of the BTC is a big empty room with hardwood floors and white walls. Black curtains have been pulled back into the corners. At the far end of the studio is a row of windows that look down onto the alleyway of the Old Town Plaza. Standing in the centre of the studio are the women who look like men, Jo and Addison, and two people I've never met: a stringy, tanned girl whose bones protrude from her neck and a solid Aussie bloke. I drop my bag against one of the walls and slowly make my way towards the artists.

'Hi, Bani,' says the bloke in a deep voice. 'I'm Abu.' I am immediately drawn to his lower half. He is standing barefoot and bent over in three-quarter-length bohemian trousers, and he is scratching his left anklebone, which is accentuated like a golf ball. In my culture this would be considered rude, to touch yourself and feel yourself and rub yourself while greeting another human being.

Abu rises and points to the stringy, tanned woman as she turns to us. 'That's Jesse.' Before I have even considered her face, I am thrown by a musky scent coming off her, which is heavy and damp. Since I started training every night at the boxing gym, my nose pummelled by a barrage of sparring partners, my sense of smell has gradually been diminishing, and yet this woman's scent is so strong that it makes me feel like a coke sniffer.

Jesse smiles at me, showing her huge buckteeth as her face tightens, cheekbones poking out like spikes. She too is wearing baggy bohemian pants and stands barefoot. I try to look straight into her eyes but instead I find myself staring at the crease between her arm and her chest, where bristles of orange hair push out like sparklers. Back at Punchbowl Boys I remember Mr Flower talking about how the feminists wore steel-capped boots and didn't shave their body hair, but I have never met a woman who actually does that. Even men are expected to remove armpit hair and pubic hair in Islam.

I first discovered this in Year 9. We were on a bus heading for a sports carnival when fifteen or so of the boys suddenly flopped their dicks out at a bus full of schoolgirls driving alongside us. Our driver, an old Irish guy with black glasses like a sheriff, suddenly halted the bus, screaming and shouting that we were all rapists, and demanded that we get the fuck out. Then he left us standing on the curb along the Hume Highway somewhere between Bankstown and Liverpool. While our teacher Mr Watson screamed and shouted about our behaviour, I whispered to Shaky, 'Why are all your balls shaved, bro?' and Shaky replied, 'You have to do it every forty days, cuz, it's halal.' As punishment for flopping out their dicks, Watson made us all walk back to school, which took over an hour. And that's the story of how Punchbowl Boys was banned from sports carnivals for the rest of 1999 and why I started to shave my pubes.

It looks like Jesse is about to speak to me but then her concentration shifts to the door and she says, 'Arab X!'

He walks in like he owns the place, with the butt of a cigarette between two fingers of one hand and a can of Coke in the other. He's tall and skinny and wears a cap that says PLO. His face is covered in thick stubble and he's in a baggy Snoop Dogg T-shirt and Adidas tracksuit pants. Arab X is a Palestinian-Christian rapper from Bankstown whom I met briefly at BMA straight after high school. He doesn't ever tell anyone his real name. He calls it a slave name.

Jo invites the group to sit in a circle and in her laidback Aussie way says, 'Yeah, ah, so, thanks for coming, guys, welcome to Bankstown. So, yeah, we'll be looking at violence for the next few days.' The other woman that looks like a man, Addison, and the woman with the heavy scent and armpit hair, Jesse, and the Aussie bloke who was scratching himself, Abu, are all sitting with their legs crossed and their toes flexing, staring intently at Jo, smiling and nodding. But Arab X looks bored. He sits with his legs out, sipping from his Coke and staring at the soles of Jo's steel-capped boots.

'So, yeah,' Jo goes on, 'I'm really interested in exploring violence across cultures. We'll just sort of be fleshing out some ideas before our season next year, so I just want to say that it's great to be here in Bankstown, and I'd like to acknowledge BTC for giving us the space, and, yeah, it's gonna be a great couple days. So, yeah . . .' I find it difficult to adjust to the way she speaks, so uncertain and shy, so awkward, as though she's humble. I don't really know much about being humble – that's why the boys at Punchbowl always told me I thought I was better than them, I couldn't just accept things the way they were.

Jo turns to Addison, who says, 'Okay, guys, did you all bring a change of clothes?' She stands up and begins to loosen her belt. I stand up too but instead of changing I get stuck just watching her as she takes her pants off. They go down and I see the black fuzz beneath the thin fabric of her light-blue undies. I quickly shoot my head somewhere else, anywhere else. Jo and Abu and Jesse casually take their clothes off too, their small packages and flat chests glaring at me unashamedly. I'm not sure if I'm expected to take my clothes off in front of them. I look to Arab X; I trust that he will show me if this is acceptable etiquette for Arab artists but he just stands waiting in his black Adidas pants and Snoop Dogg T-shirt. He flares his sharp nostrils at me and says with a grin, 'I'm not changin', little brother.'

I consider not changing either, but I don't want to get my clothes sweaty. Unlike X I'm in respectable clothing: jeans that blend white to black from the centre and that spread perfectly over my shoes without scraping the ground, and a tight white shirt I bought for a hundred dollars from Tarocash on my birthday. I grab my bag and take it to the corner of the studio, behind the mass of pulled-back curtains. It's tight and dark and I have to keep pushing the folds of fabric out as I change into my Everlast trackies and singlet. I keep one eye out to make sure none of the other artists can see me – they're all changed and waiting – and then I fumble my way out of the curtains while slipping my Air Maxes back on.

Everyone stands in a circle facing Addison. She's wriggling her bare toes and smiling at us with glowing eyes. 'Okay,' she says smoothly, and then she takes off her dark-blue jumper and throws it a metre into the centre of the circle. Suddenly this woman's head with the short, spiky haircut shrinks to a walnut as her broad shoulders and muscular arms emerge like those of an orangutan. She's still smiling but now I don't see her coiled lips as tender; they make her look shifty, like she knows I'm surprised by – and maybe even a little jealous of – her burliness. Or maybe she thinks I'm attracted to it. I've never actually met a woman with a body like this to know exactly how I feel about it. The closest image that comes to mind is from a porno I once watched in Mr Smith's music class. A heavy-set girl in a red miniskirt with thighs like a buffalo repeatedly kicked a chained-up naked man in the nuts. It horrified me, and the other Punchbowl Boys, who gasped and cringed with every kick, but it also excited me, the idea that this woman had taken an interest in our anatomy.

Addison spreads her feet and starts to twinkle her toes against the varnished floor like a cat clawing for worms. Jo and Jesse and Abu spread their bare feet apart and start to twinkle their toes too. I wonder if they're going to make me take my shoes off when I notice that X hasn't removed his black Reeboks, which have holes in them.

Addison takes a deep breath and lifts her arms and head up into the air and everyone follows. Eight shades and thicknesses of brown hairy armpits glower at me. I keep looking to my left, to X, to check if he is participating in the activities. His arms are up in the air, two sweat patches on the armpits of his T-shirt. Next to him is Abu, whose head is tipped so far back that his Adam's apple protrudes from his throat like a dagger, convulsing as though it were on a hinge as he breathes.

'Okay,' Addison says again in her calm voice, 'let's just let ourselves dangle.' She crosses one leg over the other, twists and bends, her arse facing into the circle. She spreads her legs and folds over like a sheet of paper and then she stares at us upside-down with her tiny head hanging below her butt. She continues to talk at us from this position, saying, 'Just release through the head . . . let your weight drop.' I try to keep my eyes on her face, but the line between her arse and her box has been pulled so tight it now has an eye of its own. I feel so ashamed to stare, and yet I can't look away. Jo and Jesse and Abu have folded exactly the same way, their arses glaring into the circle, as flexible as pancakes, but X is as stiff as a cricket bat, bent over just enough for it to look like bad posture.

'Come on, Bani,' says Addison. I twist back to the head between the legs and find her reverse-frowning at me. There's no way I'm turning around and bending over so everyone can stare at my arse. I drop my head and shoulders forward, falling far enough to see through my legs and out the windows to the grey sky of Bankstown, but three inches short of touching my toes. I feel the strain of the stretch across my calves and the back of my thighs, up my spine and down into my neck. I listen for Addison's voice, which is saying, 'And just release . . . through the head . . . through the head,' and suddenly the voice of Punchbowl Boys soars over hers from the alleyway, and it's saying, *That's gay, bro, that's so fucken gay.*

I try to block out the past, and I bend forwards until my hands and my feet press hard against the floorboards and my big nose flatlines along the faint smell of old varnish. Addison calls this 'Downward-facing dog' and I hear the boys laughing from the windowsill and calling this 'Taking it like a bitch'. I feel my legs stretch as my hands and feet push deeper against the wood. I hear Addison and Jo and Jesse and Abu breathing, inhaling and exhaling as they release, and I hear X grunting in and grunting out as his tight muscles refuse to give. My hands pull in and my feet pull back and my crotch flattens across the floorboards, my spine curves and my head rises and my chest expands. Addison calls this 'The Sphinx' and I hear the boys laughing from the windowsill and calling it 'Bum sex'. I feel my chest expand as my hands push deeper and my feet pull further apart.

Addison stands upright, her thick arms dangling by her side, her body as loose as a rubber band, and then she twists, bends with her feet apart and stares at us upside-down between her legs once more. I hear the boys say, 'She wants it up the arse, bro,' but her reverse frown says, 'This is just stretching.' Downward-facing dog, rise like the Sphinx, hands up in the air, bend over, head between your legs, repeat and repeat, until finally we're all sweating and extended, our legs crossed and our palms and fingers pressing against each other like the Buddha. 'Just take your time,' Addison says, 'focusing on your breathing.' Deep breaths in fill my lungs and guts while X grunts like a muffler. Deep breaths out drop my chest into my stomach while the Boys of Punchbowl scream, *'Gronk! Gronk! Gronk!'* Addison finally smiles the right way up and her cheeks are slumped like a pothead's and then her shoulders retract, her head wobbles and she says, *'Namaste.'*

The hard soles of her feet push against the floorboards as Addison raises herself up and yells, 'Okay, guys, let's start moving around the space!'

Music plays while our feet drum across the wood beneath us. Strangled guitar chords and a man whining in a deep foreign language that might be German wail from the speakers of the BTC's boom box. I avoid Jo and Jesse and Addison and Abu and even Arab X by running close to the walls of the studio. I try to keep my heart rate steady and my body temperature cool and under control. Jo and Jesse come my way like marathon men, huffing and landing hard on the floor with each step. I sweep past them and get a whiff of their combined scent, which is like the inside of a laundry hamper. Abu moves around me on his toes and then I'm alongside X, who's walking slowly like a drug dealer, bored-faced.

The room starts to warm up and drops of sweat fall from our foreheads and my heart begins to thud. Then, just as I find myself sprinting from one end of the studio to the other, Addison says, 'All right, now, *freeze!*' I hit the brakes and nearly fall, taking three steps before finding my balance. The drumming of feet stops flat and everyone holds their final position. The huffs and puffs of steadying heart rates ease through the foreign music, where the chords keep stretching and the singer keeps whining in what I now think might be Russian. I keep my head fixed and look around with my eyes to see everyone suspended like Olympians painted on vases. Abu is balancing himself on one foot, and Jo rests on her thigh like she's doing lunges. I veer my eyes to the left and find X standing casually, his shoulders hunched and his hands in his tracksuit pants as though he's waiting for a bus. We stay frozen like this, waiting, breathing, until Addison calls out, 'Go!'

I start moving again, faster this time, running along the walls and then into the centre, straight at Jo before sidestepping her like a sparrow. I perfected the ability to sidestep, which I later transferred to boxing as a form of pivoting, while chasing the baby birds in Alexandria Park when I was five. They would fly low to the ground and snap from side to side and I would be behind them, a very young boy with minuscule wings. I slow down as I sweep towards Abu and smile, but his patched-up face is staunch as he flicks his straight brown hair out of his eyes and bounces past. Feet drum, sweat falls, heart rates build, chords unwind, and now I wonder if the man inside the boom box is singing in Spanish, when Addison calls, 'Freeze!' I tumble towards X, staggering as though there's a cliff before me. X freezes too, his long arms by his side and his thin legs stretched half a metre apart. He looks at me and tries to keep a straight face but then I see the corners of his dried-out lips curl and he smiles. He breathes loudly and I can smell this morning's cigarette from between his discoloured teeth. 'Go!' calls Addison and then X moves towards me, taking huge strides. 'You look familiar,' he says as we swoop past each other. I laugh and run, building my speed, letting the sweat fall from my head and down along my shaved armpits. I sprint at Jo and pivot left, run at Abu and pivot right. I hit the end of the wall and I turn and there's Addison standing at the other end of the room. Her bright blue eyes are on me like a high-class prostitute's, and she sprints at me as I sprint at her. She doubles in size as she tumbles towards me, her huge shoulders expanding and her hands cutting through the air like machetes. I charge at her full blast and for a split second it occurs to me that even though she looks like a man she's still a woman, and this is not a boxing match where I'm allowed to take her out cold – then all of a sudden she screams in my direction, 'Freeze!' We're in each other's faces, our chests rising and falling as we try to stay as still as possible. The guitar chords roil and the deep foreign voice moans, '*Yaaaa-aaaa-aaaa*' in what now sounds like an Aboriginal language. Addison's short, spiky hair shines with sweat and her hot, milky breath hits my face.

'Go!' she calls and we take off in different directions, she to the left and me to the right. Now Jesse is dashing towards me, her veined wrists throbbing as she swings them into the air. I'm about to dodge her when, not a second after releasing us, Addison again calls, 'Freeze!'

I pause right in front of Jesse's raised arm, clutching my breath tight. Her armpit hairs are moist like a wet nest. I hold my position and she holds hers as drops of sweat slide down her tanned lats. My heart batters and my blood burns and I need air so badly that I have no choice but to release my lips and inhale. A smell exudes from Jesse like steaming fish guts. It shoots into my nose and mouth but

refuses to go down and gets caught in my windpipe. I heave
and drop to my knees, sucking up as much air as possible.
Jesse's arm looms over me like Giambologna's *Rape of the
Sabine Women*. But I am not the man who has kidnapped
her, I am the third figure in the sculpture, the bearded man
below, who looks up in horror at the kidnapper and uses his
arm to shield himself from the bare arse in his face. 'Go!'
Jesse's feet and hands release and she takes off shamelessly.
She doesn't look at me, not even a glance.

———

After scoffing down a haloumi roll in Lebanese bread that my
mother prepared for me this morning, I spend the remainder
of my lunchbreak inside the bathroom of the Bankstown
Arts Service. I take off my drenched singlet and throw water
under my armpits and over my shoulders and I smear it
across my chest. All my body hair has been clipped or shaved
and so the water trickles down my bright olive skin like
ice melting in the sun. I repeat this cycle three times while
saying out loud, *'Al-nadaafy min al-imaan'* – 'Cleanliness
is equal to holiness.' I throw water over my face and head,
through my thick, curly hair, and repeat this three times
until I am drenched and watching the long curls dangle
over my forehead in the mirror. I dry myself with a towel
and then I spray my body with deodorant while I repeat
again and again, *'Al-nadaafy min al-imaan, al-nadaafy min
al-imaan.'* I take off my tracksuit pants and I soak my hands

in water and wipe down my thighs and legs and feet. I dry my legs with the towel, I slip my jeans back on, and then I pull the waistline forward and spray deodorant down into my crotch where it's snug because these are women's jeans, and down my legs where it's loose and free because the jeans are flared. I brush my teeth, scrubbing so hard that my gums bleed thick and dark red. I gargle water and I spit blood into the basin and then I brush again. While I scrub my mouth I stare down at the large plastic cup beside the toilet. Usually I see it with a few drops of water at the bottom but the past couple of times I've been in here it has been completely dry. I used to think that the Polish woman who cleans the building in the evenings used it for washing the toilet bowl but then I noticed it was only ever dry when Mr Guy Law was away, so it must have been his cup. I think he uses it to wash his bum like he learned in Asia. I've let the tap keep running so that no one outside can hear what I am doing. At the time I did not want the artists to know that I was different to them – that I kept in my backpack a fresh towel and a toothbrush and toothpaste and deodorant and wet wipes and nail clippers and tweezers and a small bottle of hand sanitiser. I knew from the way they dressed and the way they smelled and the way they walked around barefoot and the fact that they did not feel the need to wash after strenuous exercise that they would disagree with my definition of clean – or that they simply didn't care about being clean. I realised much later, however, that it wasn't dirt and sweat I was trying to wash off my body, it was the artists themselves, whose lack of shame when they bent over or scratched themselves or put their hairy armpits in my face suggested to me that they did not believe in sacred laws, which were all about respect. While I wanted to be an artist, I did not want to be godless.

I'm buttoning up my white Tarocash shirt with one hand as I walk back into the rehearsal studio. Addison is lying flat on the floor with her eyes closed and Jo is removing her CD from the boom box. The others have ducked out for water and coffee, and X is probably downstairs having a cigarette with Bucky, who always stands at the entry to the arts service smoking in the middle of the day. Jo has dried herself off but she's still dressed in the same clothes she warmed up in, a white singlet and navy tracksuit pants. 'Oh, that deodorant's strong,' she says in her tight, nasal way. I am suddenly abashed, wondering if there is something offensive about smelling sweet. By contrast, Jo hardly has a scent, except a faint haze that reminds me of the inside of an old boxing glove. It has never occurred to me that somebody would mind the smell of deodorant. Back at Punchbowl Boys it was the reverse – we minded the smell of sweat and carried aerosols in our backpacks, passing them around like cigars. We sprayed the deodorant in the morning before class, at recess after handball, at lunch after football or before we prayed, and then on the train home from school in case we ran into girls. One time I forgot to spray under my arms after a basketball game and in class Bassam Hussein stuck his nose in my armpit, took a whiff and shouted out, 'This guy smells like pussy!'

'That was good music you were playing before,' I say to Jo. 'What language is it?'

Jo's left eye scrunches up in confusion. 'It's English,' she says, and then she cringes like she's embarrassed for me. Her face is so masculine – bumpy, dry skin, the bones beneath tough and roughly edged. I shouldn't look at her for much longer; she might think I'm checking her out. I lower my gaze to her bare, pasty feet, which are surprisingly well groomed. Her toenails are shiny and evenly cut.

When all the artists have returned from their lunchbreak, Jo sits us in a circle. 'So, yeah,' she starts. 'Good warm-up this morning. So, you know, I've been talking with Addison, and we reckon we should tell a couple of drug stories.'

'Why?' I ask out loud.

Jo raises one of her fine eyebrows at me, thrown by the question. 'Because this is a development about violence,' she spits back with attitude. Her response sounds sarcastic, as though she is merely stating the obvious. I didn't mean to blurt out the question, I just don't think I'm ready to tell a drug story, at least not the most recent one, about getting drunk and my friends getting high and my father declaring his shame on me. I'm starting to doubt whether I can actually handle this development. I expect to be chal-lenged – that's why I want to be an artist, to undo what the

Boys of Punchbowl have taught me – but I thought that art was about challenging myself; it hadn't occurred to me that other people might challenge me too.

Jo goes first, 'sorta' and 'kinda' telling a story about a time she and her girlfriend were so high on ecstasy they thought they had warts growing on their faces and spent the night picking at them in the mirror. 'Yeah, and, um, the next morning we woke up covered in little wounds all over our faces.' I wonder if that's the reason her skin looks so bumpy. I try to think of a drug story I might tell if Jo forces me to; pushing back beyond my days at Punchbowl, I am reminded of my childhood in Alexandria. I see in my mind the heroin addicts and the prostitutes who came looking for my dad's brother, Ibrahim. One man with pale flesh and a moustache in the shape of a horseshoe pointed a shotgun at my grandmother and me. 'I built this gun myself,' he said, 'and I'm not leaving until Ibrahim gets here.'

Abu goes next. His hand is down his singlet, fiddling with the hairs on his chest, tugging on them like a bird grooming an elephant, as he speaks in his deep voice. His huge Adam's apple starts to jerk and I wonder if it's the reason he sounds like Richard Mercer from *Love Song Dedications*. For all I know, Abu *is* Richard Mercer from *Love Song Dedications*. Abu tells his story, about the time he got high on speed and had a foursome with his three best female friends. I can't help but think that that's not a drug story, it's a sex story.

Jo and Addison and Jesse have huge horse grins and they burst into laughter while Abu goes on, 'Then we stood in a straight line . . .' He continues to fondle the hairs on his chest as he talks. I'm guessing the women who look like men have heard this story before, which explains their pre-emptive laughter, but I also wonder if it's *them* in the story, that perhaps Aussies, unlike Lebs, are sexually ambiguous and genuinely able to have casual sex with their friends. Abu goes on, explaining how when you're on speed everything flashes by like a disco and you can fuck for hours, and how he and the three girls dimmed the lights and watched *Titanic* while they tried different positions from the *Kama Sutra*. I wish I could ask Abu some questions about his orgy – about how you agree on a foursome and how you ensure everyone involved is happy and comfortable and consenting; the Punchbowl Boys didn't even know how to get *one* girl to consent – but instead I stay silent and watch. I don't want to reveal my ignorance, my inability to understand the difference between sex and rape. What if the artists end up thinking *I'm* a rapist?

The laughter dies down as Addison and Jesse slide across the floorboards and take hands. Then Addison starts, lowering her voice to a whisper. 'So, we just like to go out at night and do dumb shit, you know, and one time we were stoned and it was, like, about 2am and we were sorta walking home, and, um, this group of guys just wanders up to us . . .' It suddenly dawns on me that Addison and Jesse are in a relationship. I'm mesmerised by their veiny hands clamped together, thickened by the fluorescent lights of the studio.

'And one of them unzipped his fly,' Jesse whispers, finishing Addison's sentence. Her right hand is locked in Addison's and she has raised her left hand out in front of her, bony and long, the tanned fingers spread open and swaying in and out like a claw. 'There are, things, just things, in this world,' she continues. Her voice is slow and breathy, and she is looking straight at me, her frog-eyes oozing and her sharp little nose jerking. I've been caught not listening. Or is this an accusation? Maybe the guys who attacked them were Lebs. Jesse keeps talking, gentle and wheezy and with her left fingers gesturing and jerking up beside her temple, as though what she is saying is so intense and complex that she needs her hand to keep her thoughts and words under control.

'You screamed,' says Addison, looking at Jesse and biting onto her bottom lip, exposing four large white teeth in what seems to be a smile.

'Yeah, but only to scare them,' Jesse shoots back. Her voice quickly turns coarse and masculine, even though she's small and thin, tanned skin glued to her bones.

'Yeah, okay, she scared them,' says Addison. Her hand is still in Jesse's, fingers clenched over her bony knuckles. 'Anyway, so I run into the middle of the road and stop this approaching car and inside is this guy and I asked him if he'd give us a lift home, and now . . . well, now we're friends.'

'That Andrew?' asks Jo.

'Yeah.'

'Whoa,' I mumble, so engrossed that I react without thinking. 'Lucky Andrew wasn't a ra—' And then I realise what I'm about to say, and I pause. Arab X sits up and looks at me with a sinister grin. Jo and Addison and Jesse and Abu all snap towards me too. They seem shocked, their lips hanging and their eyes bulging. I try to explain what I meant, 'um, um,' when Jo's eyes veer towards X. 'Got a story?'

X stands up and turns his PLO cap backwards. He bounces on his feet like he's shaping up for a boxing match and clapping his hands as he delivers some rhymes. 'Fight, fight, fight! Fight for your right!' he sings, 'Fight tha blue thugs and their war on drugs!' I try to listen but his loud, rhythmic voice is so familiar that my final days as a Punchbowl Boy hit me like I never left. I am the dumb Leb squashed in the back of a Celica while the Black rappers chant, 'Get high, get high, get high.' Arab X has finished ululating and I am overcome with thirst, like being back in the desert, dry and exhausted, heart pounding so hard that blood is going to explode through my fingertips. I feel the artists glaring, waiting for me to tell them about how weed and vodka lead to the funny and fortunate mishaps that occur when we go out at night and do dumb shit, but I don't have those memories to share. Drugs might lead to subject matter for artists, but they lead to hellfire for Muslims. 'I do not have any drug stories,' I say. 'Sorry.'

'Ah, Bani-Bani-Bani.'

———

At 5pm Jo dismisses us for the day. I stomp along the orange carpet and pink walls in the corridor of the Bankstown Arts Service, tumble down the yellow stairs and shoot across the red-tiled plaza towards the station. While the train tugs toward Belmore I concentrate on the memory of a sound – the skipping rope clicking against the concrete floor as it swings over the boxer's head. I keep that beat going round in my mind until finally I am walking across the Belmore PCYC hallway and can hear the real thing, rising from downstairs. The glove against the bag sounds like a hammer on fresh dough, the fist against the focus pad like thunder, the speedball against the dash like a *drumbaki*. It is as though a hundred-kilo dumbbell has been lifted off my chest as soon as I enter the underground gym. I am turned on by the smells of petroleum jelly and mentholated cream and fresh sweat and dried-up blood and tired leather, which immediately release the pressure in my nostrils and in my lungs and in my thoughts. Boxers make sense to me in a way that the artists do not. When a boxer uses drugs and has an orgy before a fight, they get knocked out like the total loser they are, but when the artist uses drugs and has an orgy before a creative development, they are celebrated as though they have won a world title. A boxer runs in a straight line, increasing their fitness with the destination right ahead of them, but the artist runs in circles, ending up where they started. A boxer fights a tangible opponent, a person they can see and hit, but the artist fights the air, figments of their imagination, ideas that are of no real threat to them. This is the reason I have to come to the boxing gym immediately after the first day of the creative development, because I crave discipline and order and I completely understand what it means to be a boxer.

Leo stands inside the blue boxing ring with two focus pads raised firmly in the air. His chin and eyebrows are down in his usual bull-frown, but his dim eyes are raised at the tall fighter in front of him. 'One, two,' he hisses, teeth clenched. Two small snaps ring out over the gym and bounce against the brick walls. Leo is grounded, always grounded, his feet digging deep into the blue canvas surface of the ring and his pads ricocheting the punches like his hands are bulletproof. The man in the ring with him is a twenty-two-year-old fighter named Mohammed Sakr, who is long and muscular and tanned yellow like an Arabian giraffe.

I begin my workout with skipping, which I do every night for twenty minutes. My wrists reel and my feet pounce no more than an inch above the ground, and the rope slips between the soles of my sneakers and the concrete floor and over my head like water moving straight through me. Skipping, after enough practice, is just like riding a bike. It does not require me to think, it just flows out of me while I gaze ahead. The other fighters and trainers are scattered throughout the old gym. Mr Li, who's Asian and only trains Asians, wears a body pad that makes him look pregnant and he uses his bare hands, held open like karate chops, to signal a series of punches to the stomach and ribs. In front of him is an up-and-coming prize fighter, a lightweight Vietnamese boy aged about seventeen, whose head is large in relation to his body and whose hair is long and straight and tied in a ponytail. I see this boy once or twice a week at the gym and I usually give him a flick of the head or a wink when we cross paths, but he never responds. His gawk is so sharp and so black and focused that it's hard to tell if he's even made eye contact with me. I watch as his bandaged fists whack Mr Li's body pad, three straight punches to the stomach that are fast and precise, that hold on to the impact and take their time returning to the kid's face for protection. They look like taekwondo strikes rather than boxing jabs, and I always suspect that Mr Li is a martial artist at heart, with a fixed understanding of fighting.

There is a massive Fob who is my age named Talasaga on the floor-to-ceiling ball. Sweat gleams across his skin like polish and he wears a short, spiky beard, which reminds me of Leon Spinks – a foul creature that beat Muhammad Ali once. When Talasaga first told me his name and his age and that he went to Belmore Boys High School, I recognised him as one of the local hard cunts the Punchbowl Boys kept on their radar. Rumours of Talasaga's strength and fighting abilities spread among the Year 11s and 12s on the lookout for a challenge. I'd only ever heard about the brawls that Punchbowl Boys like Antony the *khashby* and Samson the biggest Fob in our school had claimed to have had with Talasaga. They both said they won these fights but the scratches on their faces and their blackened eyes told a different story. Talasaga and I exist within the gym like two ghosts, never crossing paths, never training in front of the same mirror or on the same pads or alongside each other on the bags or while skipping, and we have never sparred with each other.

I start criss-crossing with the skipping rope, my arms moving in and out like scissors as the rope swings over my head, turning towards the mirrors in the far right of the room. This is where I usually go to shadow box but tonight there are primary-school boys – a group of little Lebos – working on punching bags as Mr Obeid rotates them for pad work. Mr Obeid is almost as short as the kids he trains but he is broad-shouldered with thick Popeye arms. His smile is warm and unthreatening, which makes him unique among the trainers at the gym. One of the boys Mr Obeid trains is his son and his pride, a thirteen-year-old five-foot kid named Jim with muscular arms like piles of potatoes. Jim moves and slips and hits like liquid as his father calls combinations and pounces around with the focus pads.

I learned to skip like I learned to walk: slowly and off-balance at first, constantly fumbling the rope between my feet until finally it became natural and rhythmic and instinctual. The rope flings past my eyes and over my head, the activities around me flickering like an old movie. Only after I finish do I realise that the skipping has taken me into a trance; I forget that I spent the day stretching my spine and the backs of my legs and thighs up to my butt like I was Indian and like I was gay, and running and pouncing around the rehearsal space with no target or objective to aim for, not for any reason at all, it seemed. I try to forget that today I listened to stories that celebrated the use of drugs and alcohol – the artist's pride, the boxer's downfall.

I move onto the speedball, which I've learned to hit by starting off really slowly and building up my speed. This is the great mistake that the cocky Lebos make when they walk up to the speedball – they try to smash it as fast as they can and it fumbles from them as soon as it has started to move. I build up so much momentum as the leather ball swivels back and forth that it starts to sound like a stampede and the whole gym rumbles and drums and my hands move so quickly that they blur in front of me until I can't sustain it any longer and the ball slips from my fists. Mr Li has been standing in his body pad like a walrus, watching my rotating hands the whole time, and when I catch his small, sharp, frozen eyes he winks at me and says, 'You good.' Then he turns back to his bigheaded Vietnamese fighter and says, 'Huh, huh, huh.' Two rips hit the centre belly target of his body pad and a sharp left hook hits the left rib target.

I use the speedball to build my pace and stamina and endurance and rhythm as a fighter, but Leo uses the speedball to teach me the art of knocking a man out – it's not how hard you hit him, it's *when* you hit him. 'Like two trains,' Leo says. 'What's gonna cause more damage, one train parked and another train going into it at a hundred miles per hour or two trains going into each other at a hundred miles per hour?' I watch the speedball as it slowly swings back and forth and I imagine it's a head I'm trying to catch as it comes towards me, and just as it's slapping back at me I've hit it and it pounds against the base and the gym thunders. I used to imagine the speedball as Osama, the brown, moon-eyed face of a smirking Indonesian who knew he was better than me. I used to imagine it as Shaky, the green-eyed face of a half-caste horny cunt with a swivel of dirty brown hair. But this time I hit the ball hard and recoil as it slams back at me. It is the face of an artist that smacks against the base, a person neither man nor woman, with short hair and harsh cheekbones and a strong jaw and a large Adam's apple and a thin smile. A great sense of dread dawns over me, like the air has been completely sucked from my lungs and my heart has plunged into the Dead Sea. Why has this vision presented itself? What does it mean? I suddenly see myself as a barbaric and savage animal, like the Sand People in *Star Wars*.

'Bani Adam!' a deep voice roars across the gym. Leo stands with his arms over the ropes, and the sunken glare of a bull smacked on his face. 'In the ring, now!'

———————

Gathered around the boxing ring at Belmore PCYC are the trainers and fighters and the young boys, their heads cocked over the ropes. Mr Li stands in the blue corner with his Vietnamese prize-fighter, whose thin, long eyes and slender eyebrows already pierce me. I don't know this fighter's name and so I start thinking of him as 'Vietnam'.

Leo stands with me in the red corner, rubbing my shoulders and huffing through his big nostrils. 'Waste that Nip,' he says into my ear like it's a secret but loud enough for Mr Li and Vietnam to hear him. Leo is a smartarse that way, always playing mind games to psyche out my opponent.

I lock my gaze onto the fighter in front of me and begin to dissect him. Vietnam's head is disproportionately large for his body, and even with precision head movement it will be hard for him to slip a succession of jabs. His long black hair is tied back, exposing his forehead, but it may come loose and get in his eyes – I feel no shame in hoping for my opponent's bad luck to help me out; a fight's a fight, winning is winning. His facial skin is golden and smooth against the low fluorescent lighting of the gym, shimmering with sweat from his exposed brow. The leather of my red gloves will slip off his skin and cut him like paper. His eyelids are

211

pudgy and swollen, his eyes tight and squinted up like two shards of black glass. A right cross will thicken the flesh around them and blind him. His nose is flat and wide and straight, which means it probably hasn't been busted before, busted like mine, which means he's either a novice or he's hard to hit, but this will be determined by two quick left jabs as soon as the bell rings. His jaw is small and round and looks as breakable as gyprock; his top lip protrudes because of his green mouthguard but his bottom lip is fat and hangs loose – his mouth will crack and his flesh will rip against a tight left hook. His shoulders are broad and level and his arms are solid but they have no shape, no bulging biceps or triceps, no throbbing veins. I can go pound for pound with this fighter, whose flesh looks rubbery like a dolphin's. His chest, pressed against a blue singlet, is broad and flat like a boogie board and his stomach is also flat, but it looks as rubbery as his arms, and perhaps it is soft. I keep my eyes on his eyes and I don't dare lower my gaze to his boots because he may interpret this as a sign of weakness and fear, but I can sense his feet, his knees and his thighs. They are thick and grounded, it will be difficult to knock him down, but perhaps those feet will cross and he will tip to the left and cover his left, and I will switch to the left, because I am secretly left-handed, secretly a southpaw, and I will land a left cross against his right jaw. He will blink and be staring up at me from the floor and I will stare down at him like Muhammad Ali staring down at George Foreman.

Mr Obeid clears his throat with an 'ah-hm' and then causally says to Vietnam and me, 'All right, boys, no low blows, no rabbit punches – I mean it, no punches to the back of the head, when I say "break" I want a clean break. In the event of a knockdown I'll give you till the count of ten to get up.' I give a little nudge of my chin to let Mr Obeid know I understand, but Vietnam doesn't flinch. I'm not sure if it's because he can't speak English or he's acting gangsta to intimidate me. 'Touch gloves,' says Mr Obeid. I've made it a rule that I only ever hold up my gloves but never come in for a touch. It gives me a sense of the other guy's character to see how he reacts; will he bump me, and if so, will he do it aggressively? Vietnam gently presses his black gloves against my red ones like he's kissing his sister and straightaway I know he isn't gangsta, he isn't trying to intimidate me, he isn't a hard cunt – he just doesn't understand the language.

Then we both walk back to our corner and turn to face each other. Mr Obeid calls, 'Fight!' I raise my guard and prepare to step towards the centre of the ring when all of a sudden Vietnam is right up in my face, firing a dozen straight jabs at my head and pushing forward like a steamroller. I'm already up against the ropes, dropping my chin and covering my jaw and trying to catch sight of his large head but the punches keep flying, so fast that all I see is a wall of black and red leather – my red gloves across my mouth and nose and his black gloves pounding against them.

Most of his shots hit my guard, which in boxing is usually a waste of effort, but these punches are heavy and precise and fast enough that my arms are straining and sinking, and finally a left jab lands against my forehead with a thud.

'Protect!' roars Leo, followed by a rumble of murmurs from below the ropes. I dip my chin as deep into my chest as possible, knowing full well that Vietnam might have knocked me down had that punch landed along my jawline. I tighten my cover around the right side of my face, biting down hard on my mouthguard, expecting Vietnam to follow through with a right jab, but instead he throws another left and it hits me in the cheek. My lips are flung open and saliva dribbles through my mouthguard and Leo's voice rings inside my head – 'Protect! Protect!' – while on the outside of the ring I hear the fighters gasping, 'Oah!' The blow is hard and shakes the inside of my skull and my vision pixelates for a split second before I snap back into the barrage of punches pounding my gloves and around my arms. 'Roll!' Leo shouts. 'Roll! Roll!' Just as Vietnam steps in closer and throws a wild right uppercut I pivot left, leaving my left foot stranded and swinging my body. 'And hook!' screams Leo. I throw a desperate right cross to scare Vietnam off but he is so fast and so cocky that he has turned as quickly as I have and again he is pressing forward and throwing as many straight jabs as possible. 'The hook was there, champ!' calls Leo, followed by some words in Vietnamese from Mr Li in the far right corner.

I pounce back and cover up again but still I can't get a lock on this kid who is trying to knock me out; all I see is the wall of his black gloves and my red gloves trying to protect me, and I've started to hold my breath in the fear that he might land a flush right cross just as I'm breathing in, and his gloves, which have been moistened with sweat, scratch my forehead and cheeks and nick my long-busted nose as they slide off my guard and off my face and fumble past me. Vietnam gets so close now that his forehead is up against mine and we are butting heads and I can hear him breathing deep and loud through his thick mouthguard and flattened nostrils as he begins to throw wild hooks towards my jaw and ribs. 'No chicken wings,' Leo calls, his voice starting to ease, 'No chicken—' I'm quickly reminded to lock my arms against my lats, instead of letting them hang out bent at the elbows, and so Vietnam just hammers into my guard, trying to break through. A sharp strain, like lightening striking my muscles, shoots down my wrists and I feel like they might fold in on themselves when suddenly Vietnam starts to throw a succession of wide round hooks that scrape the back of my head. I throw a hard left hook in return and it locks into his thin neck, and his elbows are open wide and he's so tired from all the punches, and I'm so overwhelmed by them, that there's nothing else either of us can do but lock our arms around each other and embrace. Both our chests are expanding and sinking against one another and Vietnam's chin is resting on my left shoulder and my chin is resting on his left shoulder and our ears, burning and throbbing red, are pressing against each other's, and our legs are spread apart with the tips of our boots just touching. I feel a great sense of relief as I try to catch as much air as possible, my lungs rising and falling, like I have sprinted off a mountaintop. Suddenly a great force pulls Vietnam and me away from each other and Mr Obeid is standing between us.

'Keep it clean, boys,' he says calmly, giving me a small wink and then stepping aside. I don't know if we are approaching the end of the round or if it's only been a few short seconds but Mr Obeid calls, 'Fight!' and straightaway Vietnam is on me again. His flush nose and sharp eyes zoom up and his black gloves slam into my face. Again I am moving back, trying to dance away as though I am skipping at first, but soon enough he is pinned on me and I am against the ropes and there's nothing I can do but veer up while he swings like a baboon. 'Cover!' screams Leo. 'Cover!' And Mr Li shouts something in Vietnamese, either telling his fighter to knock me out as though this were a street brawl or to ease off before he wears himself out. Vietnam's rapid punches drum against my bent arms and closed fists and at my head and against my ribs, and once or twice into my clenched stomach, and still he pushes forward, pushing I don't know where because I'm already cornered against the ropes. I begin to wonder if Mr Obeid is going to separate us once more but he doesn't appear and the punches keep flying and in my frustration I let out a loud warrior cry that goes, 'Aaarrrgghh!' I push forward with my arms and my shoulders and my whole body, embracing Vietnam's last two punches, which recoil and go limp as they flatten against the base of my head. Vietnam suddenly fumbles off me and I see him for what he is – inexperienced and arrogant and unaware of his strengths and his limitations. Mr Li is screaming in Vietnamese and Leo is roaring, 'Now! Now!' like a lion and the voice of the crowd below is like one enormous groan. Vietnam is regaining his balance and his arms are up against his chin and I can see he's about to press on towards me again, but just as he is putting his weight inward, I step with my right foot and right arm forward and my left foot back and I throw a left cross that slingshots from the left side of my chin across my body, through the space between his two black gloves and straight on to his nose, right as he's stepping into it. Vietnam falls back as I stagger and find my balance above him, and when I look down he is on his arse staring up at me.

I've gone back to my corner and Leo is giving me his bull-frown. He puts his arm around my neck and he presses his forehead against mine, and he says, 'I'm proud of you, but next time don't act like a faggot.' Then he lets go of me just as there is a nudge on my shoulder. I turn around and see Vietnam standing before me. His nose is inflamed, a cotton bud stuffed in each nostril. He holds out his black glove for a fist bump and says, in a nasal Vietnamese accent, 'Good shot, Lebanon.'

———————

The next morning I return to the Bankstown Arts Service for the second day in the development. The scratches on my face from last night's sparring session have disappeared but I have blown my nose twice between leaving the house and arriving at the BAS, and on both occasions a clinging clot of dried blood has revealed itself. Once again Addison bends over and talks to me upside-down between her legs. Then we are running to English voices and drums that sound Ghanaian as the artists build their sweat. We sprint and freeze, sprint and freeze, sprint and freeze. In the bathroom I blow my nose hard and another clot of dried blood, like a sundried tomato, splatters around the basin drain. This is my farewell to arms: 'Ah, Bani Adam,' I say, 'look how your blood coagulates beautifully.' I rinse up my nose until the blood has cleared entirely. Then I proceed to wash my face, my hair, behind my ears and between the crevices inside my ears. I take off my shirt and I wash under my armpits and over my shoulders and I splash water against my chest and then I dry myself off and I spray deodorant all over my body.

At lunchtime Bucky is standing outside the BAS with his eyes glowing and a cigarette to his mouth. As I step past him he snickers, 'Keep moving before someone sees you.'

I walk staring down at the footpath of red bricks in the Old Town Plaza, only sticking my head up momentarily to ensure I don't bump into anybody. The first time I look up towards the far end of the plaza I spot a pack of Lebs dressed in Adidas pants and Everlast singlets and Nike caps. The next time I look up there's an Aussie with straw hair and a bleached face who saunters past me in the direction of the Arab Bank. I cross through the centre of the plaza towards an elevated garden with a large bougainvillea. A woman in a black hijab has stopped under the branches that reach out like arms – she stands in the shade among the fallen petals, waiting for the sun to weave back into the clouds. I pass Muhammad's coffee shop and step into the station. There are hordes of black and brown and yellow and olive teen-agers slipping in and out of the ticket machines and I disappear among them like an ant. Behind the ticket machines are four Aussie cops talking down to two skinny Lebos, something about lighting a smoke on the platform. I step onto the right-hand side of Bankstown, onto the bus grounds where I can't make eye contact with one of the boys without being asked, 'What you looking at?' This is where a Vietnamese gang shot a straight-A student named Omar five years ago. He was a classmate of my brother, a good boy who wanted to be an engineer. While Omar sat waiting quietly for the bus, he was approached and asked if he had a staring problem. Then the bullets were fired, one in the shoulder, one in the left thigh and one in the right thigh. They said on the news that it wasn't the bullets that killed him; it was the heart attack that followed. My brother and I cried that night and my father kept on saying in Arabic, 'We are not more generous than Allah.' Every time I walk through this bus stop I am haunted by Omar's funeral – hundreds of boys from Punchbowl and Birrong watching as Omar's mother wept over his body. *'Bas Allah kaan-m-neeh,'* she wailed. 'But Allah this one was a good boy.'

I return to the plaza with a brown bag from Macca's in one hand and a large Fanta in the other. I insulted my mother this morning, turning down her offer to make my lunch again, another haloumi roll with homemade baba ganoush and tomatoes and cucumbers. 'I worry about your heart,' she said, and then, *'Akal al-baat ahsan men Macdanas.'* – 'The food of the house is better than McDonald's.' I remember my mother from as far back as when I was four, watching *Days of Our Lives* and then *The Young and the Restless* while she prepared *malfouf*, meat and rice wrapped in cabbage; and *warak eneb*, meat and rice wrapped in vine leaves; and *koosa*, meat and rice stuffed in zucchini. If only my mum understood how boring it is to eat the food of the house.

Jo and her artists, Addison and Jesse and Abu, are all sitting cross-legged under the bougainvillea in the Old Town Plaza garden, peeling back white paper wrapping and biting into Lebanese rolls. I stand before them, sipping my Fanta amid the petals. The artists don't say anything, just smile, bite into their falafels and follow the people who pass. Two

Indian women walk by in bright red saris, and behind them is a woman in a black burka carrying shopping bags. 'I love all the costumes,' says Jesse. Her tanned skin and big white teeth glow as the sunlight begins to squeeze back through the clouds.

Addison has stopped eating and is staring up at me. There's a draining silence between us as I sink onto the grass. I think she's fascinated by me but I don't know why and it's starting to make me feel uncomfortable. I've been meaning to ask her something and maybe now is a good time, since it might break the tension.

'So, what does *namaste* mean?'

She squints, as though she doesn't understand the question. 'It means "thank you".' Her response is blunt and hard – it almost sounds sarcastic.

'Oh, okay,' I mumble. 'So, then, why don't you just say *thank you?*'

Addison doesn't answer but her thin black eyebrows twitch at me. She drops her head into her falafel and takes a bite. Maybe I've offended her. *But why would my question be offensive? Maybe she's just hungry.*

'Mmm,' Abu groans, biting into his roll. His gigantic Adam's apple convulses as he swallows. He's left with tahini across his mouth, which he wipes off with his hand and then rubs his fingers through the grass. There's a bit of tahini left in his beard and he doesn't notice. 'I like Bankstown,' he grumbles in his deep voice.

I open my brown paper bag and am hit by the smell of sugar and wood. I slide out the Big Mac, hold it up in both hands. I bite. The special sauce is like a tablespoon of ancient honey. The meat and middle bread push back against the force of my jaw and some lettuce falls onto my thighs. Usually I wouldn't care but I wonder if the artists consider this littering. Lettuce is organic, right? They don't say anything, so maybe it's okay. I chew slowly and raise my head and there's Jo. 'Ah, Bani-Bani-Bani,' she says with a smug grin. 'How can you put that stuff into your body?'

'What are you talking about?' Suddenly the artists are all chewing in my direction. 'What?'

'Nothing,' Jo says, her grin expanding. 'There's just so much cheap amazing food around here.'

'What, *falafy?* My mum makes that crap.' I take another bite from the Big Mac but now it doesn't taste so good. The mustard and pickles are bitter on my tongue, like I'm in the park sculling vodka all over again, and it burns as I swallow. I am reminded of the first time I ate *falafy.* I was five and it was fresh off my mum's frying pan. I straightaway spat it out because it tasted like a lump of vegetable oil.

'I thought you were a boxer?' says Abu.

'I am,' I say with my mouth full. 'I don't drink.' Nobody responds. They put their faces back into their rolls and continue to munch. I suck up some Fanta and then go back to my Big Mac, eating now purely to satisfy my hunger. More lettuce and some sesame seeds fall onto my crossed thighs.

Jo turns to Addison as she swallows a mouthful of falafel and says, 'It would be good if we can get Bani to talk about this stuff in the show.' Her jaw is wide and heavy as she speaks and licks her teeth at the same time. *What stuff?* *My boxing? The fact that I don't drink? Or does she mean* *the fact that I'm eating McDonald's?* I feel like a pedigree pit bull, not because I fight or because I eat cheap meat, but because Jo is talking about me like I'm not even here. I want to ask her and the other artists what the problem is with McDonald's but their conversation has moved on so quickly that by the time I've swallowed I don't know what they're talking about anymore.

'We didn't plan it,' Abu is saying. 'She just told me she was pregnant and I was like, yeah, okay.'

'Is this your wife?' I ask.

'My *partner*,' he says adamantly. This was the first time that someone had made a distinction to me between having a partner and having a wife. I always assumed having a 'partner' meant you were gay but Abu was talking about a person he'd got pregnant so it must have been a woman.

'You don't have to get married?' I ask. I have never met someone who does not expect to get married and doesn't want to. In my culture, being with someone outside of marriage is a sin, but even if I were free never to get married, I wouldn't exercise that right. I can't wait to get married, to be a husband and to say I have a wife. I've already written my wedding speech for her, my future wife, who right now I can only imagine as fair-skinned and blue-eyed and softly spoken. *'My love,'* I will wail. *'Love threshes us to make us naked. Love lifts us to free us from our husks. Love grinds us to whiteness.'*

Abu drops his nose over his falafels and purple pickles, and takes a bite. Then he looks up at me while he chews. I feel the three women looking at me too, their teeth moving through the tahini like Mr Ed chewing out words. Abu's Adam's apple convulses. He swallows and says, 'We will have a ceremony that celebrates our love.'

Jo shakes her head and says, 'Ha, Bani-Bani-Bani,' as she and Jesse and Addison stand. I watch them make their way back toward the BAS; I never would have known just from watching Jesse and Addison that they are a couple. Maybe my questions about wives and marriage are offensive to them because they don't even feel safe to hold hands in places like Bankstown. But I'm not so different to them. I could probably give up my wedding. I just need *katab lik'taab* – the writing of the book, a girl's approval to be my wife and my approval to be her husband before Allah.

'I still don't know how you can eat that,' Abu says to me as the women drift away. His mouth is open, his tongue wriggling from side to side, trying to pick out the leftover chickpeas from his teeth. Finally he sticks his finger inside his lower jaw and picks at a piece between his canine and incisor that he can't seem to reach.

'So, who named you Abu?' I ask. I throw the last lump of Big Mac into my mouth.

'What do you mean?'

I'm trying to swallow as fast as possible so I can respond, but a smooth voice beats me to it. 'Abu's not Aussie, brother,' says Arab X. He appears from nowhere, emerging out of the Bankstown backdrop like it's his camouflage. In his hand is a can of Coke and some kind of sandwich wrapped in foil.

'I changed it when I was eighteen and three months,' says Abu.

'Why?' asks X. He flops onto the grass and pulls the sandwich up from the foil. The smell of bacon and egg fills the air around me like a rotting carcass suddenly dangling in the bougainvillea. Growing up, I simply accepted that I was not allowed to eat pig meat without ever questioning it. Then one day, and randomly, I asked Mr Abdullah why swine was *haram*. He looked at me with scorn, his entire face recoiling like he might spit. 'The pig is a foul, dirty beast,' he said, 'part rat, part cat and the rest is dog.' I cannot help what I breathe in but even the scent of Arab X's bacon sandwich is unbearable to me, like toxic waste. I feel my airways clog and tighten in their attempt to keep the smell of the sandwich out.

'I changed it because I hate the name Matthew Jeremiah the Fourth,' Abu explains.

'In Arabic "Abu" means "Father of",' I tell him. 'So my dad is "Abu Bani" and X's dad is "Abu X" and your dad is . . .'

A grin suddenly forms beneath X's stubble-ridden face and his bacon eyes tighten. 'And your dad is "Abu Abu".' X and I laugh, and for a moment it feels like we're Lebs again.

'Well, in Africa it means nobility,' Abu responds bluntly, as though he's insulted that we're discriminating against him. What do you call that – not offending someone because of their race but offending them because they have no race?

X cracks open his Coke can and the sound makes me think of people burning in fire. He takes a sip and then sings, *'Abu Salim, yoa-ya, zebu taweel, yoa-ya.'* The two of us Lebs continue laughing like a pair of oil merchants. And the Aussie frowns, because he doesn't get it, because it's not his language.

———

Beyond the yellow stairs the BMA doorway pulls at me like the Call to Prayer. I stick my head in, hoping to see Bucky, but instead there's Condoman and the Miss Africas staring back at me from the cluttered walls. The office door in the corner is half-open, so maybe Bucky's inside but I won't go that far in to find him. If he knows I'm searching for him he'll make a joke of it, he'll tell me I'm in love with him or that I'm supressing the gay inside me, or maybe he'll scoff because I'm a Leb who wants to be an artist. I'm afraid of getting close to Bucky because he might reveal a truth about me that I am not ready to know, and yet it is because he sees right through me that I am drawn to him.

I continue down the creaky corridor with the orange carpet and pink walls all the way to the rehearsal studio. In the centre of the room someone has lined up a row of video cameras, and from corner to corner the white walls of the studio have been covered with writing – Jo and Addison and Jesse have been busy. The three women are spread throughout the room, each facing a different wall with a black texta in their hand. I watch Addison's arm and shoulder muscles flex over her head as she moves a texta along the painted wall, and read the words to myself as she writes them. 'Aussies . . . are . . . the . . . biggest . . . sluts!'

I wander around the room reading the other comments the women have written. On Jo's side in thick letters it says, 'Lebz Rule' and 'Fuck Off Lebs' and 'Moey & Samantha 4Eva' and 'Call Samantha 4 Head' and 'ur mums so fat mike tyson wont chop her'. On Jesse's side it says, 'Ching Chong Chinas Go Back To China Bitch' and 'BLOODS 4 LIFE' and 'pac is still alive' and 'Dolphins Rape People Too'. I watch Jesse as she moves across the wall like a daddy longlegs and writes sideways in thin handwriting, 'watch ur back'.

When I turn to look at Addison's wall again I find her right up in my face with her blue eyes wide open and a soft kind of smile smeared from cheek to cheek. 'Bani, I never knew you were so trendy,' she says sweetly, and then she lowers her blue gaze down to my feet, down at the flares that have covered my shoes right to the tips. It occurs to me that she had just been looking at my back, where the patterns on my butt pockets are floral enough for her to realise that these are women's jeans.

'Oh, thanks,' I say.

'Ew, Bani,' she whimpers, biting her lip and letting her smooth cheeks sag like she feels sorry for me. 'There was a little hint of sarcasm in my voice.'

Does she mean what I think she means? How is it possible that a woman who acts so much like a man would make fun of me for wearing girls' jeans? I'm about to ask but just before I open my mouth I notice the words on the wall behind her head, staring at me in big black letters, piercing my heart. 'Muhammad is a camel—' and it is a great sin in Islam to tell you the rest.

I step past Addison and drift right up against the wall, examining each letter that makes up each word, and in my mind, the white masculine hand that had woven them just a moment ago. Jo wanders over and stands next to me. 'Bani, this is street art we have collected from the suburbs, it has nothing to do with what we think of you, good sir.' Her Aboriginal ocker has dissipated and all of a sudden she is speaking like she's Princess Diana. I wonder if that means she fakes her usual accent. She says this has nothing to do with what she thinks of me, but this actually has *everything* to do with what she thinks of me. She thinks I'm a fake too; that 'Muslim' is just a character I play. Is that what it means to be an artist, that all your beliefs are an act? The Prophet

Muhammad wasn't acting. When he first declared that there is no god but God, the merchants who got rich selling deities of stone and clay offered to pay him off, saying, 'If you want wealth we will give you wealth, if you want a beautiful woman, we will marry her to you.' Muhammad replied, 'If you put the sun in my right hand and the moon in my left hand, I will not renounce my message, which is from God.'

'Are we okay, good sir?' Jo asks me.

'Yeah, I'm okay,' I answer softly. I know now that I am not uncompromising like the Prophet Muhammad.

———————

When Abu and X return, all six of us sit in a circle in the centre of the rehearsal studio, surrounded by the graffiti quotes on the walls. I try to forget that the quote about Muhammad is up there too, but to me it sticks out and throbs like a cold sore. Jo stands and slips her hands into her pockets. She's put her casual voice back on, the one that makes her sound like a Black boy from Redfern, and she says, 'So, yeah, um, hope you enjoyed lunch. Here's what we've got planned for the afternoon . . .' She instructs each of us to take one of the cameras she's lined up and go out onto the plaza pretending to be a character from a movie or book or a story we've made up. She'd like us to film our character's interactions with the community. I want to know what's the point of this but it seems that every time I ask a question I reveal my ignorance and simply get a scoff or a wince or a sarcastic remark in return. I blame Punchbowl Boys – how uncivilised that place made me. If only I'd gone to a school in Newtown or in North Sydney, then I'd understand art. Maybe Jo wants video footage that explains how mundane interactions escalate into violence, which always seems to happen on the streets of Bankstown.

I wait for the others to collect their cameras and then I walk over and pick up the last one, a small black Sony. I pop open the side monitor and turn the camera on and then through the screen I see a wall with the words, 'Black Fucks'. Just as I hit record a man's deep voice screams out, 'Cunt!'

I snap back startled. Abu has taken off his singlet and is jumping up and down, eyes blazing as he looks around like some kind of dog on its hind legs with a camera flailing between its paws. His chest is broad and patched with thick, dark hair and I see the bones at the bottom of his ribcage contract as he tenses his flat, hairless stomach. He screams again, 'Cunt!' Momentarily I think he has got into a fight with one of the women but then I realise he has simply started his improvisation. I point the camera at his Adam's apple, waiting for it to move, but it just sits there poised like the head of a cobra peering through bushes. 'Cunt!' I watch carefully through the monitor at the long, brown hairs cluttered around his throat. The front of his jaw drops into my screen. 'Cunt!' And again, 'Cunt!' And again, 'Cunt!' Then he sprints from the studio and into the corridor, and I hear him screaming, 'Cunt! Cunt! Cunt!' as his voice disappears into the street. I wonder what character from which book or movie he's pretending to be.

I know who I'm going to impersonate – last year Ms Lion took me and the two other Punchbowl Boys who passed their half-yearly exams on an excursion to the Dendy Cinema in Newtown. We watched a film called *Bowling for Columbine*, which she told us was about guns in America. I was shocked when it turned out to be a documentary: *The movies are supposed to be for movies!* I thought. And: *How am I supposed to take a fat shit like Michael Moore seriously?* But all my pretentions change as soon as I'm out on the Bankstown Plaza with a camera in my hands – now *I* am the fat shit documentary filmmaker and this is *Brawling for Bankstown*. I lie across the red brick tiles of the plaza and film the first person who enters my shot – Jesse. She has placed her camera on the ground and is sprinting back and forth towards it, her toes halting in front of the lens. Suddenly she turns and I see her dark eyes lock on me from inside the lens of my own camera. She charges forward and becomes a blur. Her toes land right where my legs are crossed and she stops there and huffs down at me. I stare at her feet, which look like burned wood. Her toenails are crooked and yellow and there are long, fine hairs on her big toes. The sides of her feet are smeared with dust and charcoal but the tops are smooth and shiny, with a big lumpy vein running down the centre of each. Jesse holds her position like this for another ten seconds and then she moves again, running around in circles while Bankstown Plaza stops and watches. She throws some giant kicks into the air and finally knocks over her camera. I stand as she goes down to the ground, rolling her arms and legs until she finds herself face-flat on the bricks staring into her lens.

'Yeah, yeah, Bani Adam's in da house!'

I spin around to find X pointing his camera in my face before he skips past me and approaches two chubby Fobs in baggy T-shirts. 'Yo, yo, ma brothers!' he hollers, raising the camera up in their faces. I wonder if those Fobs already know X. He starts to talk at them and though I can't hear exactly what he's saying it all seems too casual for him to be a character from a book or a movie. Then again, isn't Arab X already playing a character, like Malcolm X? Maybe Professor X? I don't think anybody's doing this activity the way we were instructed; Jo told us to choose a character from a book or movie or to make one up but X is just being himself and the others are acting like junkies. I point the camera towards X, whose long frame is positioned in front of the two Fobs like a pine tree between two bears, and I make my way towards him.

X moves on and both the Fobs are grinning when they spot me approaching. That's what I love about Fobs in Bankstown – they don't take anything too seriously. 'Yo, brotha rappers, I'm Michael Moore,' I say putting on an American accent – pronouncing all my Rs like a pirate saying, *Argh!* 'Are you men aware that multinational corporations are exploiting you?'

On the garden in the centre of the plaza are three Leb chicks sitting cross-legged. They're in school uniform, in short-sleeve button-up shirts, two in tight navy-blue pants and the one in the middle in a navy-blue skirt flopped over her crotch. The chicks slant their heads at me as I advance with the camera. The last time I approached a girl this way was two years ago at the Easter Show, except I wasn't hiding behind a lens. 'Excuse me, ladies,' I say in my American accent, lowering the camera towards the girl in the skirt. Her top button is undone and her collar is up. Her lifeless hair falls from her head and her mascara-filled gaze bats at me from the side monitor. I straighten the camera so that it's perfectly aligned with her long thin nose and thin cleavage. 'Do you know what a corporation is?' The three girls look at each other and giggle like Betty and Wilma from *The Flintstones*.

'Why are you talking like that?' the middle one in the skirt asks. 'Are you from Campbelltown?' Her voice is cute and bubbly and nothing like the other Bankstown girls, who all say *Oh my god* like they are gurgling. I start to wonder if maybe I should break character and get the girl's number when all of a sudden Addison and Abu slouch past, swinging their cameras from side to side. Addison says, 'I just wonna fucken cigarette, mate, gimme a fucken cigarette,' and Abu – who is still topless and turning moist from the torso up – is saying back in a tight nasal voice, 'Get yer own cigarettes, cunt.' Arabs and Indians and Africans and Asians in the plaza watch them as Addison screams, 'What's everyone lookin' at?'

The three Leb chicks in the garden giggle again and I swing the camera back down at the middle one. Her enormous eyelashes flap and she says, 'Aussies, man.' Now she sounds like a typical Lebo.

'They're just acting,' I respond, like she's a dumb cunt.

She rears her plucked eyebrows and says again, 'Yeah, Aussies, man . . .'

I am the dumb cunt.

I wander the plaza searching for more interviewees and the whole time I feel the Leb chick in the skirt follow me with her eyes while she shares a cigarette with her friends. It's sad the way Lebs from Wiley Park Girls and Bankstown Girls and Auburn Girls trust Lebs from Punchbowl Boys and Birrong Boys and Belmore Boys. No Leb at Punchbowl ever wanted to marry a girl that put out in high school. Osama used to say it all the time: 'Leb chicks are dumb – they think we're gonna marry 'em but as if I'm gonna marry some Muslim who played with my cock.' Then Mahmoud Mahmoud asked, 'Would you use your wife's arse as a pillow and sleep on it, bro?'

'Every night,' Osama replied.

'Would you let your wife sleep on your arse?' I asked.

And Osama said, 'I'll fart on her head, bro.'

I steer clear of Lebo boys because they remind me of Osama and Mahmoud Mahmoud, and I steer clear of old Wogs because they can't speak English, and I steer clear of old Whitics because they don't trust Lebs. Instead I interview two Indian boys in button-up shirts and jeans and two Indian girls in tight, short dresses. 'Are you aware that multinational corporations are exploiting you?' Straightaway one of the boys, in a pink shirt and gelled black hair, looks dead into the eye of the camera and responds, 'Well, basically all this funding goes into generating a consumerist ideology so that half a billion dollars goes into brainwashing people.'

'Okay, so why aren't you kids in school?' I ask. They're clearly too smart to be the kind of students that truant.

'Sports carnival,' says one of the girls.

Next I interview a short, fat Aussie named Dillan who has Down syndrome. His beard is patchy and he tells me he's thirty but I think he's lying. A large group of Fobs standing against the railway fence listen in on our conversation, and they make their grins obvious to me as Dillan goes on about being a professional rapper. I ask, 'Are these guys your friends?' turning the camera towards them.

'Yeah,' replies Dillan.

'Which one?' I ask.

Dillan points at a Fob in a Bob Marley T-shirt and says, 'Him, the fat one.' Then all the other Fobs belly-laugh at their colossal friend, because only the disabled can get away with such remarks.

I return to the Bankstown Arts Service, where Jesse is lying in front of the entrance, arms above her head, armpit-hair flaming, camera tucked under her singlet pointing up at her chin from between her breasts. I think she's attempting to sneak footage of people walking past – maybe she's trying to make a point about how rich people don't care about poor people. I could have told her that no one here gives a shit about bums, but these people are poor, not rich, so I don't really know what she's actually trying to prove. I consider taking her arm and dragging her out of the way, but I'm scared to touch her. She might have a problem with a Leb putting his hand on her without permission. One time, the Punchbowl Boy nicknamed Eggplant got expelled for deliberately elbowing the boob of a student teacher who was doing her work placement in the Visual-Arts faculty. 'That's bullshit, Miss!' Mahmoud Mahmoud shouted at the head teacher of Art, Mrs Capsi. 'How can you get expelled for your elbow touching someone's tits?' Mrs Capsi exploded, screaming at our entire class, 'You don't touch women, do you understand? *You don't ever touch women!*'

I carefully step over Jesse's small frame, push open the glass door to the arts service and fall in. Then I keep my camera rolling as I walk up the stairs, watching through the side monitor. I take my time, pressing my feet hard against the yellow wood of each step and forcing them to creak, and I make loud huffs and grunts as I climb, as if I am the size and weight of Michael Moore.

As usual the BTC door is closed and the BMA door is open. I take slow steps through the meeting room, slanting the camera up from the lounge made of dust to the poster of Condoman on the wall. I zoom in on the speech bubble blasting from his mouth, 'Don't Be Shame, Be Game'. Then I move through the meeting room towards the office door. Beyond the laminated news headline 'Arts King Celebrates 20 Years' is the long, narrow office of Mr Guy Law and Bucky, decorated with little Buddhas and old computers. A bright white light shoots in from the window overlooking the plaza at the other end. This is where Bucky sits – his back arched and his big head fixed on a monitor. I walk slowly with the camera pointed towards him, the floor creaking like a seesaw with each step I take, but he doesn't turn. He doesn't even flinch. I film his flat hairy stomach and chest through the gaps between the buttons on his shirt. On my monitor the profile of his head keeps expanding until I'm so close that his thick black hair and smooth white skin fill the entire screen. Putting on my American accent, I say, 'Excuse me, sir, are you aware that multinational corporations are exploiting you?'

Bucky's glare remains on the computer screen and he keeps typing. His fingers move rapidly across the keyboard until finally he presses down heavily on the enter key. Suddenly he twists his large head and gawks into the lens of my camera. His eyes are like clumps of silver sand and the hairs between his eyebrows are thickening until he bears a classic Greek monobrow. With a bored tone of voice he says, 'Are you aware that the White people in your development are exploiting *you*?' Then he turns back to the computer and continues typing, and I am wandering out of his office like a total gronk.

The artists stand around waiting for Jo to assign the next activity, Arab X staring out the window, Abu scratching his chest, and Jesse and Addison stretching their hamstrings together, thighs pressed up against stomachs. I stand in the centre of the room, looking back and forth from each of them to the floorboards. The profanity about Prophet Muhammad gnaws at me from the desecrated rehearsal walls and I feel dirty and contaminated by its presence. I quickly pull my deodorant out from my backpack and I am about to spray my underarms when suddenly Jesse catches sight of me. She releases her hands from her stretch and holds them out in front of her like Harvey Milk before he was assassinated. 'No!' she screams.

'What, what?' I ask, my finger on the aerosol trigger.

'I can't stand the smell!'

'Oh, okay,' I respond. 'I'll just spray in the bathroom from now on.'

Her tanned forehead wrinkles up and suddenly there are four deep lines in her brow. With her lips punching out each word she says, *'Or. Just. Stink.'*

I can't just stink. I'd be a Muslim outcast. At the end of
Ramadan last year the head of the Alawite Mosque, Sheik
Salman, gave a long sermon in which he stated in Arabic,
'Before you come here make sure you've washed your private
parts and under your arms, and make sure you've sprayed
nice perfume, so that you don't put off the person praying
beside you.' But maybe Sheik Salman was just being another
dumb Leb. Maybe Jesse sees the truth – body odours and
human excrements are beautiful, and deodorants and perfumes and soaps and shampoos are shit.

Jo loads a new CD into the boom box and starts to bob
her head. 'So, um, I want you guys to wander around the
studio, and, yeah, um, let's call out the comments you find
on the walls.' My mouth goes dry and my vision blurs, my
fingers begin to quiver and I feel a crushing sensation all
the way down my spine, sucking me towards the floor. It's
as though my soul is being torn from my body, the thought
that these artists will be calling out, *The Prophet Muhammad
is a camel*—

I was in Year 7 when the Punchbowl Boys showed
me what I am supposed to do when someone insults our
prophet. Two men who looked like hippies from Woodstock
were standing by the front gates of Punchbowl Boys handing
a leaflet to each person that walked out after school. The
leaflet contained a picture of an anthropomorphised peace
symbol, which had crossed eyes and a frowning mouth and
skinny arms and legs. This cranky little Peace Man was

swinging an axe at a wooden cross and in a speech bubble he was saying, 'Muhammad you're next!' As soon as the hippies who had handed out the leaflet arrived at the train station the Lebs were locked on them like a pack of pit bulls, calculating a strike. I watched as a wave of Year 11s and 12s, led by a drug dealer named Hussein Bin Masri, who threw the first punch, swarmed the two men, tumbling into them and hurling king hits and fly kicks, knocking them over and stomping on their heads until they were unconscious. I was horrified by the incident, having never seen an extreme act of religious violence before, but I was also proud of the Lebs because I hated that leaflet, which desecrated the most sacred aspects of my life. Now I understand why the Lebs used to call me a traitor, because in Punchbowl they taught White people to be afraid to offend Muslims, while here in Bankstown, I am afraid to offend White people.

Jo stands back to observe the five of us meandering around the studio as her music smacks from the boom box. The beat inside the speakers is tribal, hands pounding against drums and birds squawking and lions roaring and snakes rattling and slithering like it is *Jumanji*. *Bom-bara-bom-bara-bom-bom-bom* and then Abu sings out, 'Aussies are the biggest sluts.' *Bom-bara-bom-bara-bom* and Jesse shouts, 'Lebz rule!' Addison, who's taking enormous strides, stops and looks towards the windows and yells, 'Call Samantha for head.' I wander from wall to wall looking for a comment. There are sentences in black texta that say, 'Fatala was here,' and 'Asians go back to where you came from,' and one in thin handwriting that says, 'Capitalism is so gay.' I open my mouth and let the air reach down into my guts and then I call out loud, 'Bloods for life.' Arab X's voice comes in over mine, tight and rugged, 'Asians go back to where you came from.' The comments spit back and forth across the room as we each walk from quote to quote and wall to wall. The drums start to get faster, *bom-bar-bom-bar-bom*, and the animals elevate their squawks and roars and slithers and the five of us hail over one another, 'Julie—' 'Slut—' 'Fatala—' 'Lebz—' 'Capitalism—' 'Asians—' 'Fobz—' 'Head—' 'Fuck—' 'Cunt—' 'Jessica—' 'Smalls—' 'Gay—' 'Slut!'

I pick up the scent of musky body odour. Jesse slips past. I'm hit by the smell of cigarette breath. X stomps past. I keep my eyes on the walls, scanning for something to say, and I call out, 'Tupac is alive.' I see the comment about the Prophet and straightaway I throw my head in the other direction. 'Watch your back,' I call, and over me Abu's heavy voice shoots out, 'Dolphins rape people too.' Then I hear X, 'Bloods for life,' and Addison, 'Tupac is alive,' and Jesse, 'Capitalism is so gay.' My heart thuds as I wait for one of them to insult the Prophet, but the words don't come. I wonder if everyone is intentionally avoiding it out of respect for me. 'Lebz rule' and 'Your mum's so fat Mike Tyson won't chop her' and then time and drums stop as the woman who looks like a man, with arms like an orangutan, screams out across the room, 'Muhammad is a camel—'

The words hit me harder than any punch I've ever tried to absorb in the boxing ring, sucking the air from my ribs and weakening me at the knees and feet, and I wander around the rehearsal studio confused and lost. I have read offensive comments about the Prophet Muhammad before, but this is the first time I have ever heard them spoken out loud, and it terrifies me because now I know that there are people who are genuinely unafraid of Allah, I know what that lack of fear sounds like, and the sound is now inside me. The artists continue to shoot their comments around the room, their voices crackling like radio static as I try to regain my focus, searching for something to call out in a desperate attempt to overcome my terror. Finally, Jo says, 'Okay stop,' and presses pause on the drums. Everyone's voice falls flat and some letters on the wall before me suddenly become clear and I shout, 'Aussies are the biggest sluts!'

We're breathing quietly and standing as penguins when suddenly I notice Addison, the Godless creature that just took a shot at my Prophet. Her eyes are fixed on me and they are turning grey, cracking like a rupture in the Sistine Chapel. Her thin eyebrows dip, her small fair head twitches, her pink lips tremble. I open my mouth a little – to ask *Are you okay?* – but before I can she throws her apish arms up at me and turns. Her bare feet stomp against the hardwood floor and her bleached back muscles clench. She ploughs through the studio door like she's the She-Hulk, and I watch as Jo and Jesse rush out the door after her.

'Ah . . . what just happened?' I look to Abu, who's sucking in both his lips, and he shrugs his broad shoulders at me. Without saying anything he slips to the floor, flattens out and closes his eyes, Adam's apple erected. 'What?' I say again, this time turning to Arab X.

'Nothin', little brother,' X says smoothly. 'Everyone's just takin' a break.' The rapper's gaze sinks on me and he steps in and spreads his long arm over my shoulder. He leans in so that his lips are up against my ear, drawing me away from Abu and towards the windows. Then he pulls me forward so that we take a few steps together and he whispers, 'Ay, bro, would you fuck a girl up the arse?' I'm so surprised by the question that I immediately pounce back to look into his eyes. They're wide open and black and bloodshot.

'No, man, no way,' I gasp.

X turns to look toward Abu, who's still lying there with his eyes closed and his Adam's apple slightly juddering. Again the rapper steps in close to me, washing me over with his cigarette breath as he whispers, 'Then don't worry about what faggots think.'

Jo and Jesse are the first to walk back into the studio and Addison steps in behind them. They're talking among themselves but it's the kind of talk that makes no sense unless you were part of their conversation in the corridor, just mumbles of, 'Know what I mean,' and, 'Yep, yep.' Then Addison slowly pulls away from the other two women and wanders towards me. Her eyes are moist and pink around the edges. She thuds against the floorboards with each step and the sound immediately takes me to her feet. She's slipped on her steel-capped boots, and something about that makes me nervous. Once she gets to me the corners of her lips curve upwardly and I'm completely surprised. 'Hey,' she says.

'Oh, hey.'

I get the feeling she's about to tell me something, but instead she just bobs her small head at me and stares. For a second it feels like she's delicately and innocently coming on to me, and staring deep into her damp, bright blue eyes, I wonder if I could just take her in my arms and give her a childlike hug and a gentle kiss on the forehead. I say, 'You know, I have plenty of movies we could watch together.'

'Like what?' she asks.

'*Fight Club.*'

'Seen it,' she responds bluntly. 'You should read the book, it's better.'

If only Addison and I were introduced to one another at a nude beach she would realise that I *have* read *Fight Club*. I would pull driftwood logs from the seashore, construct a sculpture out of them that casts a shadow in the shape of a human hand when the sun in the sky is just right, and then I would sit in the hand while she watches me, in a moment of perfection.

Addison gives me another head bob and looks towards Jo. Then she turns to me again and says, 'You know who you should read? Toni Morrison.'

'Okay,' I say.

'Yeah, but you won't understand her,' she says.

Why is she telling me to read Toni Morrison if I am too dumb to understand? I always thought Toni Morrison's whole thing was that you're not supposed to treat Africans and Arabs and Asians like buffoons. I'm suddenly reminded of a tale my father recounted to me as a boy. It was said – though my father made it clear that only Allah is all-knowing – that a merchant from Baghdad heard in a dream, 'Your fortune lies in Cairo. Go and seek it there.' On his arrival, however, the merchant encountered the police chief, who, having mistook him for a wanted thief, began to beat the merchant, demanding to know who he was and what he was doing in Cairo. Finally, the merchant told the police chief that he had heard in a dream of a great fortune wait-ing for him in Cairo. The police chief burst out in laughter and replied, 'I too have heard a voice in my sleep, not just once but on three occasions, which said, "Go to Baghdad, and in a cobbled street lined with palm trees you will find a house with a courtyard of grey marble and a fountain of white marble. Under the fountain a great sum of money lies buried." But would I go? Of course not. Yet, fool that you are, you have come all the way to Cairo on the strength of your idle dream.' It so happened that the merchant recognised the house the police chief described as his own, and he returned to Baghdad and dug under his white marble fountain to find the great treasures promised in his dream . . . If Toni Morrison is the great treasure, then I am the merchant, and Addison is the police chief, whose only purpose is to unite us.

'Yo, Bani-Bani-Bani,' calls Jo, surrounded by Jesse and Abu and X. She moseys past them, throwing her hands into her pockets and bobbing her head. 'So, yeah, look,' she says as she approaches, 'we're gonna let you go early today so we can plan for tomorrow.' She stops walking when she reaches Addison, and the two women who look like men stand before me as they did the first time we met.

'Why, what are we doing tomorrow?' I ask.

'Well, um, in the afternoon we're gonna give a demonstration of our work to the directors of the BTC.'

'Okay, and what do you want me to do?'

'Well, um, it's easy,' says Jo. 'You're gonna say, "Aussies are the biggest sluts," and the others are going to respond.'

I find Bucky out the front of the arts service smoking a cigarette. He's glaring over the plaza, completely bored, face like a slumped horse. 'Oh, hey,' I say. I become acutely aware of his cigarette-smoking style as he takes a drag. He cocks the orange butt between his index finger and his thumb with his other three fingers raised like he's holding a cotton bud. Bucky begins to say something to me as he breathes out smoke but I'm distracted by the people walking past, watching to see if the young Lebs or Asians or Fobs are looking at us in a funny way.

Most people walk past without even noticing us, but there is one man whose eyes deviate as he steps by with two friends. He's a skinny Indian guy, about the same age as Bucky, in a brown shirt and a brown tie – but he isn't staring at the way Bucky is standing or the way Bucky is smoking. His eyes veer to the ground and lock onto the denim flares that cover my sneakers. When I do finally concentrate on Bucky, on the movement of his fat lips, I realise that he stares at people more than they stare at him. He ignores the Indians and he ignores the two old Arab women dressed like ninjas but he stops to ogle the group of Lebs that step through us, the tallest among them darkly tanned and showboating a long, black mullet. Bucky watches the tall Lebo from behind, follows the loose singlet that dangles from his tight back. As a young Muslim male from Bankstown who had only ever known one openly gay man, I interpreted Bucky's gaze as a look of fear. I couldn't shake the thought that gays had to watch their backs because back at Punchbowl Boys, the Lebs and the Fobs often met up with homosexuals they found online to beat them up. One time they sent a gay man text messages pretending to be a guy named Trevor and arranged to meet him at Parry Park in Lakemba. A boy named Haroun took the role of Trevor while the others hid in the bushes. And, so they said the next day at school, just as the guy went down on his knees to give 'Trevor' a head job, Haroun whacked him across the face with a tree branch and then the other boys came out and joined the attack. The boys spoke about how they kicked 'the poof' in the dick until his testicles were crushed – jubilation in their eyes like it was September 11th all over again. I always thought that this was going to happen to Bucky one day, because he told me he met Lebs in the park for head jobs all the time.

'I'm going to Macca's, if you want to come,' Bucky says while he lets his cigarette dangle between his lips. I'm so shocked by the offer that I straightaway spit back, 'But you're gay!' I was raised in Newtown until I was ten, where there wasn't a Macca's in sight. My dad told me there used to be a McDonald's but it closed down because the people in the area had boycotted it. Next, Dad told me we were moving to Lakemba because Newtown was full of pooftas who would kidnap me and play with my bum. Then yesterday the homosexuals I was working with had criticised me for eating a Big Mac meal in Bankstown. All this has brought me to the conclusion that gay people are waging a war on Ronald McDonald.

Bucky breathes out a cloud of smoke that fills the warm air around me and he says, 'You're an idiot.' Then we move through the plaza and the train station, walking quietly until we reach the lights across the road from Subway. Bucky says, 'So, what's your favourite book?'

'*The Prophet*,' I say. 'Kahlil Gibran.'

'And what's your favourite chapter from *The Prophet*?' he asks.

'The chapter on love,' I answer. The lights change to red and we cross the street just as a group of Fobs exit the Subway and loiter on the footpath.

'And what's your favourite line from that chapter?' Bucky asks.

'"Love grinds you to whiteness,"' I say. I expect him to keep digging, but instead he falls silent as we walk through five Islanders, four of them laughing and one of them holding onto his dick and saying, 'Had the maddest wank last night, boys.' Bucky grins at me like we're both in on the same joke, but still he says nothing. His silence is starting to make me feel like he wasn't impressed with my answers.

'Well, what do you think?' I finally blurt out as we turn onto the street corner of the Bankstown library, a concrete building with black window shutters.

'What?' he says, and then, as though he knows exactly what, he adds, 'Oh yeah, whiteness grinds you to blindness.'

'No, that's not it,' I say.

'Sure, sure.'

At McDonald's Bucky orders a large Frozen Coke and a large coffee. While he walks towards an outside table with the iced caffeine in one hand and the boiled caffeine in the other, he tells me about his body fat index, how he has a specialised training regime at Fitness First, and how he diets regularly. I can't stop thinking how gay that all sounds. In boxing we don't talk about body fat index or training programs or going on diets, we just sweat and bleed and we don't smoke and we don't drink and the rest you keep to yourself.

Bucky and I sit outside like we're on a date, and we are finally far enough from the arts service for me to ask him a question I've been hanging onto for two years. 'So, what's your problem with Mr Guy Law?' From the first time I met Bucky, he has made resentful remarks about his employer, usually that Mr Guy Law was exploiting local migrants and refugees and Aboriginals. The only time I'd ever really heard this kind of rhetoric before was back in high school when we were studying the Black civil rights struggle. I remember a black-and-white video in which Malcolm X said, 'The White man is tricking you; he is trapping you!'

Bucky takes a deep gulp from his Frozen Coke but his face remains dull as he swallows, as though his teeth and tongue and throat are numb from the ice. Then his eyes veer to the left, to a group of young men sitting behind me. I can't see them but I can tell they're all Lebos from the sounds of their voices, all talking with their mouths full of Big Mac and McChicken about some girl's breasts, how she has huge tits but how it doesn't count because she's fat.

Then one of them shouts, 'What's fat, bro? Is Beyoncé fat, bro?' And another one of them, who only sounds slightly different, says, 'I'd let Beyoncé's fat arse swallow my whole head, bro!'

Bucky *hmm*s as his eyes veer back to me. 'What's my problem with Mr Guy Law?' he mumbles, repeating my question to himself. His lips have turned blue from the brown ice. 'All right, I'll tell you,' he whispers. 'Three years ago Mr Guy Law had this girl doing work experience in our office. He called her China Beauty, and one time, after I'd walked her downstairs and was returning to the office, I caught him sniffing her seat.' Then Bucky stops talking and picks up his coffee. He puts it to his lips and slurps. I watch him, waiting for him to continue but he doesn't, he just lowers the coffee and stares straight back at me with a thin line of milk and chocolate along his top lip.

'Yeah, and?'

'And what?' he says.

'Well, what does that mean?'

Bucky's eyes swerve to the left again as smoke starts to fill the air above my head because the Lebs behind me have lit cigarettes. I've counted three of them now. One is still going on about Beyoncé's arse and another one is talking about Angelina Jolie's tits and the third one, who sounds a bit like a girl, says, 'Beyoncé and Angelina Jolie both look like mutts.'

'What the hell do you *think* it means?' Bucky scoffs at me, and then, while he still has the large coffee in one hand, he picks the Frozen Coke up with the other and sips back and forth between the two drinks.

'Huh?' I say, and then I remember we were talking about Mr Guy Law and how he sniffed the Chinese girl's seat. I honestly have no idea what that means. I guess it's the same as a man sniffing a woman's panties, but even this baffled me when the Boys of Punchbowl broke into the staff locker room at Homebush Aquatic Centre and each took a whiff of the swim instructors' G-strings. It was the smell of Mrs Leila Haimi's wet hair in the early morning, when she had showered just before she came to school, that made me moan – her scent like warm milk.

'What do you think of the people in my development?' I ask Bucky.

'Look, sweetheart, I'm not interested in being the gay subplot in your hetero nonsense.'

'What's hetero nonsense?' I ask.

'Stop asking questions, I'm not your counsellor.' All of a sudden Bucky stands up and slides towards the group of Lebs sitting behind me. I turn around in shock and watch as Bucky locks onto the boy with a full head of black, curly hair and thinly plucked eyebrows. 'Got a light?'

The boy, who has the dark features of Lebanon and the golden skin of Syria, and who is sitting among two staunch Lebs with fair skin and hair razored at the sides, pulls out a zippo. He slowly flicks at the flint wheel with a smirk and sparks gel the warm night air around us until a small red flame hovers above his fingers. I watch as Bucky bends over towards the light with a cigarette in his mouth while he and the boy gape into each other's eyes. The Lebs around them were oblivious, distracted by tits and arses that could swallow men whole, but I was no longer seeing the western suburbs through my rear-view, I saw it ahead of me, and I dared not look back, for I might have turned into a pillar of salt.

———————

I return to the Bankstown Arts Service for the third and final day of the development. The artists take me through the yoga exercises and the running exercises and then I rush off to the bathroom to cleanse myself as though the entire routine has become my new *wudu*. No one has directly spoken to me all morning; they have simply given instructions for me to follow, unsettling smiles all around. After lunch, which I spend lying down in the rehearsal room and staring up at the ceiling, Jo gathers us in a circle and talks us through the plan for the afternoon's showing, which goes like this: 'Bani will do his boxing skipping, tricks and stuff, and the rest of you will, um, sit in a straight line and you will, um, each go from smiling as subtly as possible to laughing as hysterically as possible.' I want to ask why, why am I being asked to skip, and what is it supposed to mean that the artists will go from laughter to tears during the process, but I feel so close to the end of the development now that it's better to just shut up and do my job. 'Then Bani will say, "Aussies are the biggest sluts," and each of you will improvise a reaction of your own choosing on the spot.'

The skipping rope flicks so fast over my head that the brown leather becomes a blurred line. I pace myself, breathing slowly and pouncing from left foot to right foot no more than an inch off the hardwood floor. The rope makes a tick each time it hits the boards, as though it were a clock on speed. I gaze beyond the three chairs Jo has set up in front of us and fix myself on the door to the studio. Sitting in a straight line alongside me are the artists, Addison and Jesse and Abu and Arab X, and they too stare at the door with faces that Jo has instructed to be deadpan. The rope goes over and over my head, and then just as I feel the first penetration of sweat form on my forehead, the doorhandle turns and Jo appears. She's still dressed in her tracksuit pants and white singlet but she stands differently – her hands by her sides instead of in her pockets and her bony shoulders tense and firm. She wears a pair of blue sneakers but she walks slowly and heavily, as though she's in high heels. She steps away from the doorway, and behind her appear the managers of the theatre company, Ms Julia and Mr Daniels, whose faces flicker through my skipping rope like two lucent ghouls. They are both large and plainly dressed. Mr Daniels is an inch or so taller. His hair, drawn low over the tops of his ears, is grey, and grey also, with darker shadows, is his large, flaccid face. He is stout in build and stands erect, with fast eyes and compressed lips – a man who knows exactly where he is and where he is going. Ms Julia is slower, and she stands beside him and examines the setting. She's all puckers and creases, like a shrivelled pear, but her hair has not lost its ripe-nut colour. The managers take their seats with Jo and their heads move from my skipping to the row of artists sitting in a straight line. I keep my eyes on Mr Daniels in the middle chair as I start to puff two short breaths in through the nose and two short breaths out through the mouth, *theh-theh wheh-wheh theh-theh wheh-wheh.*

The artists alongside me begin to laugh, low at first so that their voices are just an amalgamation of *heh-hehs* and *huh-huhs* but as I build up speed and the rope goes *whoop-whoop-whoop-whoop* their laughter becomes hysterical, crackling over the air like a Chris Rock concert. I skip on, sweat dropping from my eyebrows and my heart thudding, two short breaths in, one short breath out, and now the artists laugh so hard that it becomes torture, as though they've been tied down and are being tickled to death. All the while Ms Julia and Mr Daniels and Jo look back and forth from my skipping rope to the laughing heads. My wrists and triceps strain, my thighs and calves burn inside my black tracksuit pants. I begin to criss-cross, the movement of the rope now going *whip-whoop whip-whoop* as I slide my arms in and out each second the leather goes over my head. The laughter is no longer believable;

Michael Mohammed Ahmad

it's just cheap mockery coming in so loud that it drowns out the sound of my skipping. It takes me back to the classrooms where the sand monkeys drummed on their tables and sang *'Abu Salim, yoa ya, zibo taweel,'* and 'Thug life, motherfuckers,' and threw paper balls at Mr Romero's head and called Ms Lion a slut and Mrs Haimi a traitor and they kicked Kadar Kareem's nose in and they sliced Rajab's head open. I hear it again and again, 'This guy, bro' and 'This guy, bro' and 'This guy, bro' until the words swing over me as quickly as the rope. I begin to double under, jumping so high and swinging so fast that the leather swoops over my head twice before I hit the ground each time I jump. The rope goes *woahoa-whoahoa-woahoa* and my feet pounding against the floorboards go *puh-puh-puh-puh*. My heart jackhammers into my ribs and my sweat flicks like fireworks until I've completely overcome the laughter. I keep going, faster and faster until finally I spring as high as I can and triple under, the rope vanishing and then a loud thud when my feet hit the ground.

I've got my eyes on Ms Julia and Mr Daniels and I'm breathing in and out like a whale and the sweat is running and my heart is pounding when the four artists silently rise to their feet and begin to wander around the stage like zombies, as Jo instructed.

After my next deep breath I say, 'Ay, everyone.' Addison and Jesse and Abu and X all snap towards me, like the un-dead picking up the scent of human flesh. Then I announce the line, again as Jo instructed. 'Aussies are the biggest sluts!'

The first thing I notice is Abu cringing. His Adam's apple jerks as his face contracts and he lets out a loud 'Eaaah!' He throws his hands in the air and kicks his legs like a loose gorilla. He makes his way to the corner of the room, between the wall where it says 'watch ur back' and the windowsill. Then he hunches over and rakes his hands through his long hair. I think he's intentionally pretending to be some kind of primate. His movements remind me of Blanka from *Street Fighter*. Next Jesse begins to walk towards me, but not like she usually walks, not like a light bodybuilder – she walks over like Catwoman, bouncing her thin hips and brushing one bony arm from side to side. Once she's in my face she tilts her head at me and says sensuously, 'What did you say?'

'What?' I ask.

'The line, say it again.'

I can feel Ms Julia and Mr Daniels peering at me, judging my every move and I'm not sure how this is all supposed to go, but I remember the one rule Jo has given me for this showing – to accept every offer the artists make. I deliver the line again, however this time it comes out softer, more reluctant, as though I'm asking it like a question. 'Ah . . . Aussies are the biggest sluts?'

Jesse's demeanour instantaneously changes from sexy to hideous, huge shrubs flaring from her armpits and her head straightening and her back stiffening and her lips sucking back into her mouth. She takes the wooden handle of my skipping rope from my hand and she holds it up in my face. 'How about I stick this up your arse?'

Her comment is real – it feels like she genuinely wants to hurt me, and so, without even thinking, I slip into a boxer's stance, drop my chin and twist my feet and hip so that I'm facing her side-on. I keep my arms loose and by my side but my fingers are slowly coming together. I watch her like a hound watching a pussycat; any shot she takes at me will bounce back at her head.

All of a sudden Addison pounces in front of Jesse and starts to scream in my face, 'Fuck me! Fuck me! Fuck me!' She gets in so close that her nose presses up against mine and I slip back. She advances on me, expanding her broad flat chest and clenching her white teeth. I sense her steel-capped boots grinding into the floor. Again she screams, 'Fuck me! Fuck me!' Her voice cracks like she's a squealing pig. Who is she telling to fuck her? Is she addressing the character I am supposed to be playing, the Shaky and the Osama and the Bilal Skaf, or is she addressing me, the real me?

I get up on my toes and start to spring, building some momentum, and then I shuffle away from Addison, bouncing around in circles like Muhammad Ali. Addison keeps coming at me, her small pale face convulsing and her thick arms spread open, and I keep skipping, dancing away from her in circles as I twitch my head, my arms loose by my sides. Addison screeches, 'Fuck me, cunt! Fuck me, cunt!' She takes a few strides back and then she runs up at me.

I feel the urge, the reflex, to clench my fists because I sense she is going to take a shot at me, but I remember you don't touch women, *you don't ever touch women*. I brace myself for a blow when suddenly two long, hairy arms wrap around her chest. 'Easy, easy,' Arab X shouts. His cheeks compress as he tries to hold back the woman who is as strong as any man I've ever known. Addison screams, 'Fuck me, Muslim! Fuck me, Muslim!' Her veins are seething from her fingers to her neck, and her neck bones are pulling and stretching upwards until finally she throws her arms out like two enormous wings and sets herself free. She charges at me again and I let out a loud warrior cry – 'Arrrgh!' – and then, just as my knuckles tighten, the woman who looks like a man freezes.

Addison turns and faces an audience I forgot was there, the director and the two managers of the theatre company. Abu, who casually wanders out of his corner, and Jesse, who is still holding on to my skipping rope, silently take an upright position beside Addison. Then the three turn and look to X, cueing for him to join them. They don't look to me in the same way but instinctively I turn from where I stand, my heart thumping and my fingers throbbing, and face Jo and Mr Daniels and Ms Julia, who are smiling towards the four artists. And the artists are smiling back when all five of us bow. But I am not.

The blue arse-cup gleams against the shiny residue of the toilet bowl as I cleanse myself in the bathroom. This time, however, when I raise my head and splash water over my face and feel my reflection move in the bathroom mirror, I keep my head skewed so that I don't have to look at myself. I can't look at myself – afraid of what I have become, an animal or a coward. And then, when I spray deodorant under my arms and neck and over my head and into the air in order to step through the mist, the scent of bubblegum makes me want to cry. The past three days I tried so hard to be an artist, to be White, to be one of them, but all they wanted me to be – and all they saw in me – was a dirty Arab.

I return to the rehearsal studio entrance to find the door half-closed, and from the corridor I can hear the artists talking. One of them, I think Jesse, but it easily could be Jo or Addison, is saying, 'Every time . . . he said it . . . it felt like . . .' She's speaking slowly and in fragments, as though she's overcoming some kind of trauma, and I know she's speaking about me, and the sentence they forced me to say, and how it impacted her as a woman and a lesbian and how it exposed me for what I am. I can picture Jesse's demeanour, her fingers elongated and her eyes closed, as though her thoughts are too complex and difficult to comprehend. And I can hear Jo and Abu and Addison, *mmm*ing and *mmm*ing and *mmm*ing as though they totally understand, as though they are one, while Arab X sits among them like a house negro.

I turn around and walk from the rehearsal studio, leaving my backpack, toiletries and skipping rope behind, and creep along the orange carpet, trying to lessen the creaks. The pink walls of fibro expand before me as I quicken my pace toward the stairs. BTC is on my left and its door is closed; BMA is on my right and its door is open. As soon as my foot hits the first yellow step I run down as fast as possible, promising myself not to look back – if anyone calls my name I don't hear it. I reach for the doorknob and tumble outside in one motion. The Bankstown air hits me like it's been charcoal-chickened. I bolt along the red bricks of the Old Town Plaza, past the garden and the bougainvillea, past Muhammad's coffee shop and onto the train station where cops guard the ticket booths and Lebs move in and out of the gate.

I wait for the train on the far end of the platform. There is no shelter here and the sunlight glows as it begins to recede. The people around me have become mannequins, defined by their clothing. The Arab man is a bland grey suit; the Pacific Islander woman is an Adidas T-shirt and wide, colourful skirt; the skinny Asian girl is a black pair of tights and a yellow singlet; the Pakistani mum is a hijab and thick mascara; and the Indian grandmother is a green sari and a red dot and a pair of Reeboks. Three Lebs around my age stand about a metre away from me and share a cigarette. They have my haircut, razored at the sides and gelled afros on top, heads like circumcised cocks. One of them is in a

Lonsdale T-shirt and the other two are in Everlast singlets the same as mine, except theirs aren't damp from sweat. There are also two Fobs leaning against the back wall of the shelter having a beer, both in long shorts and baggy T-shirts, both pudgy and looking shifty and smiley and stoned.

Across the train tracks is a billboard: a blonde girl with tanned skin and blue eyes is staring at me over a man's bare shoulder. Underneath her it says, *You could have an STI without knowing it.* Where have I seen this girl before? In what life had she been someone to me? And then a grainy voice says, 'Hello, Bani Adam.' Bucky is suddenly standing right before me with a dumb grin on his face like he's one of the Wog Boys. His lower lip is flopping out and there's a black mark on it, a blotch of ink from a pen.

'Oh, hey, bro,' I mumble. I try to sound relaxed but my voice comes out like a broken muffler.

'What's wrong?' Bucky asks seriously, then before I can respond he grins again and says, 'Did some slut just call you a misogynist?' He belly-laughs so loud that all the third world–looking people under the shelter twist in our direction. Tears emerge from between his squinting eyes as he looks me up and down. I don't react – just stand and watch like a hard cunt. Bucky wipes his moist eyelashes with his index finger, his laughter settling. Then, as he regains control over his voice, he says, 'So, you're looking very Lebo today.'

The words hit me like a sledgehammer. I clench my teeth on a sharp intake of breath and I scream, 'I'm not like them! I'm not like them!' Bucky stares at me as though the life has been sucked from his face, like he finally realises that none of this is funny to me, and now he's the one who looks distressed, eyes sinking and cheeks swelling. He grabs me with both arms, and he holds me up against him, and he whispers, 'Hey, you look beautiful – don't you know you're beautiful?'

I dig my head into Bucky's chest and I cry on him, grinding my face into the white fibres of his shirt and grumbling that I was confused and I'm sorry and I didn't know any better. All this time I wanted to be White, but Bucky loved me, from the moment he met me he loved me, because I was Leb, because I couldn't be anything but Leb. A hot gush of wind suddenly hits me as the roar of the train rises from the other end of the station like a sandstorm. I pull back and glare at Bucky, who is still holding onto me and whose eyes blaze like specks of tabouli, and I say to him, 'This is gay, bro, this is so fucken gay.'

Acknowledgements

SHUKRAAN IS HOW WE SAY 'THANK YOU' IN ARABIC. *Shukraan* to my doctoral supervisors, Professor Ivor Indyk, Professor Greg Noble and Professor Chris Andrews, for working with me on the original manuscript of this novel as part of my PhD thesis. *Shukraan* to my dearest friend, Peter Polites, whom I asked, 'What should I name the character based on you in this book?' And he said, 'Bucky.' *Shukraan* to my Black sister, Ellen van Neerven, and my Fob sister, Winnie Dunn, and my Wog sister, Tamar Chnorhokian, and all my brothers and sisters at Sweatshop: Omar Sakr, Stephen Pham, Shirley Le, Maryam Azam, Mariam Chehab, Mariam Hussein, Nitin Vengurlekar, Monikka Eliah, Jason Gray, Socorro Cifuentes, Amanda Yeo, Janette Chen, Sheree Joseph and Jessicca Mensah. *Shukraan* to Aunty Lina Kastoumis! *Shukraan* to the team at Hachette, Sophie Mayfield and Sophie Hamley and Alana Kelly and Claire de Medici and especially Robert Watkins.

And *shukraan, shukraan, shukraan* to my wife, Jane, and my son, Kahlil. I did not dedicate this book to you, because you are above it, but I dedicate myself to you.

MICHAEL MOHAMMED AHMAD IS THE FOUNDER AND DIRECTOR OF SWEATSHOP: WESTERN SYDNEY LITERACY MOVEMENT. In 2012, he received the Australia Council Kirk Robson Award for his work in community cultural development. Mohammed's essays and short stories have appeared in the *Sydney Review of Books*, *The Guardian*, *The Australian*, *Heat*, *Seizure*, *The Lifted Brow*, *Meanjin* and *Best Australian Essays*. His debut novel, *The Tribe*, received the 2015 *Sydney Morning Herald* Best Young Australian Novelists of the Year Award. He also adapted *The Tribe* for the stage with Urban Theatre Projects in 2015. Mohammed received his Doctorate of Creative Arts from Western Sydney University in 2017.

hachette
AUSTRALIA

If you would like to find out more about Hachette Australia,
our authors, upcoming events and new releases you can visit
our website or our social media channels:

hachette.com.au

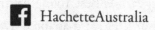 HachetteAustralia

 HachetteAus